WRATH OF THE TITANS
THE BATTLE FOR ARGOS

A novel by John Garavaglia

Based on the story by Ali Russell, Darren G. Davis and Scott Davis.

 Published by Markosia Enterprises, PO BOX 3477, Barnet, Hertfordshire, EN5 9HN.
FIRST PRINTING, December 2019.
Harry Markos, Director.

Paperback: ISBN 978-1-913359-12-6
eBook: ISBN 978-1-913359-13-3

Book design by: Ian Sharman
Cover by: Joe Phillips

www.markosia.com

First Edition

ALSO PUBLISHED BY
MARKOSIA & WRITTEN BY
JOHN GARAVAGLIA

DORIAN GRAY

DORIAN GRAY: BENEATH THE CANVAS

SINBAD: ROGUE OF MARS

INSANE JANE

ALSO PUBLISHED BY
MARKOSIA

THE THRONE ETERNAL

ZAK RAVEN: CODE ALPHA

SWANSONG

WORDS ON A WALL

STORIES FROM THE CHICKEN SHED HOUSE

THE DUCK POND INCIDENT

PROLOGUE

Violent eruptions shook the marshlands around the realm. But the kingdom of Phoenicia remained silent as a tomb. The markets in the heart of the city were quiet and barren from their usual vigorous activities. There weren't any sailors around the docks, and no slaves were being brought in from Aegypt or any of Greece's marble commodities. Phoenicia was in deep mourning for a death that had not occurred yet.

Inside the luxurious palace, Princess Andromeda emerged from the sanctified pool in which she had been given a final cleansing. It was supposed to be a day of tremendous joy, but instead she was forced to comply with the terrifying conditions of the Goddess Thetis' vengeful threat to the city.

Andromeda was still haunted by the very sight of the angry deity. A month earlier the princess was supposed to marry Perseus—the man who had freed the kingdom from Thetis' disfigured son Calibos' reign of terror. Calibos was this horrific parody of a man who was promised to Andromeda since birth, but as punishment for dishonouring Zeus he was transformed into a monstrous satyr-like being with one clawed hand, a hoof, and a long slithery tail.

Calibos' crimes were unforgivable. They were too many and too monstrous to be ignored. Thetis had spoiled and indulged him since birth. She bequeathed to him the Wells of the Moon near Phoenicia to rule. In return Calibos had turned that paradise into a wilderness. Without any remorse he hunted down and destroyed every living creature of beauty for sport and personal pleasure. He even dared to trap and kill Zeus' scared herd of flying horses that dwelt there. Calibos left only the stallion Pegasus alive and because of him mankind will not know the beauty nor have the services of the race of flying horses.

Now he looked like what he appeared on the inside. With this penalty he fled into exile into the marshlands where he had given himself the title of lord. His arrangement to Andromeda was annulled, and throughout his alienation he grew mad with rage and jealously. Then he cursed Phoenicia for anyone who would seek the hand of the princess will meet a fiery end.

For many nights a giant vulture that carried a small golden cage visited Andromeda. The creature's girth and size made it appear that it could swallow the cage easily. The sharp beak glowed orange in the moonlight, and it was stained with the blood of untold numbers of corpses it had been feasting on. At the back of its beak were tiny, dark red eyes and they glared something unholy.

It would shift its huge awkward, massively feet that was pointed with very sharp talons. The marble underneath the creature would slightly crumble, but the cage was firmly held strong.

Then Andromeda's soul would rise from her mourning body. The translucent apparition was no denser than the filmy curtains that veiled her bed. When the spiritual manifestation began to walk, it was as if it had no will of its own. Like it was a mindless automaton that did as it was commanded without ever questioning its authority. The second Andromeda would enter the cage and then seat herself on the golden chair within. She remembered how tightly she gripped the armrests and then a faint look of nervousness would cross her torpid face.

She could still feel the rushing wind that filled her chambers and the sound of the curtains fluttering. The vulture would hover carefully above the cage, and its claws grasped the perch very delicately.

From there on in, Andromeda no longer feared death. It was preferable to the use of her inner self. Death would have ended those dreams and finally set her free. She knew it would be a false freedom, but it was the only kind she could look forward to.

The vulture would carry her off to see Calibos and then he would present to her a riddle for her suitors to solve. To make the task more challenging, Calibos would change the riddle every day. If a man answered correctly, he would win Andromeda's hand. But if he should fail, he would be burned at the stake.

No one had ever given a correct answer.

Until one day a young man stepped forward. He was very handsome, but he was soaked in blood and grime. It looked like he had been involved in an awful battle. His hair was thick and curly, and was dark as the sea on a moonless night. For some reason Andromeda believed she had met this man before, but only in a dream. He introduced himself as Perseus, and claimed that he was the prince and heir to the Kingdom of Argos.

"Please," Andromeda whimpered, "don't make me ask you the riddle. You seem a like kindly man. I would not see you perish like all the others. I beg you, for your own safety, abandon any thoughts you may have about me."

Perseus answered with all the confidence she lacked. "Do not fear for me, Princess. I know well the conditions. Ask your riddle."

"I would rather—" She stopped in midsentence and sighed deeply.

"Then this is the riddle, bold stranger. In my mind's eye I see three circles joined in priceless, graceful harmony. Two full as the moon, one hollow as a crown. Two from the sea, five fathoms down. One from the earth deep under the ground.

"The whole a mark of high renown. Tell me, what can it possibly be?"

Andromeda opened her eyes and stared with forlorn hopelessness at the handsome stranger.

"Have courage, Princess." He tapped one cheek with a finger and appeared almost to be mocking the question. "Now, what can it be? Three circles joined, two moons and a crown?"

"*Tell* me," she pleaded.

Perseus did not turn his gaze from the princess. "The answer is…a ring. A ring formed of two joined pearls on a circle of gold!"

He threw open a flap of his cloak and held something aloft.

It was a hand—cut cleanly at the wrist and dark with dried blood.

Light flashed from the index finger.

"The ring of the Lord of the Marsh—the pearl ring of Calibos, here on the claw hand of Calibos himself."

He threw the grisly trophy on the floor. It slid across the smooth marble to stop abruptly at the foot of the statue of Thetis.

"The ring. A present from his mother the goddess Thetis. Is that not truly the right answer to the question?"

Andromeda did not reply. Her head was in her hands and she was sobbing uncontrollably.

"Tell me, is it?" Perseus pressed her.

Finally, the princess regained control of her emotions. "Yes, yes!" She gasped over her weeping.

"We fought in the swamp," Perseus explained to her. "Battled on his own ground. I spared his life on one condition: that he would renounce his curse, which he did. There will be no more bonfires in the city square, and no more nightmares. No more young men need to volunteer their lives."

The citizens cheered and applauded jubilantly, knowing that the horror of Calibos has finally ended. No longer they would witness ghastly public burnings in the town square, or hear the wails and sobs of mothers grieving over their slain sons. When Perseus faced the townspeople, they began to chant his name in both appreciation and respect.

"You are freed." He said to the people. "Phoenicia is free." He turned back to the princess, who was staring at him with a mixture of wonder and delight. "And you are free, Andromeda. Only I am not, for I am captured by your beauty and bound by your love." His eyes dropped.

"I know that I have won you, by the terms of the curse and by the binding your mother the queen placed upon it. But I have won only a title." He looked into her face, and smiled awkwardly.

"I ask—not demand—that you give me a chance to win also your heart."

She gazed into his eyes with hope. "I will gladly give that which you could take, Perseus. You have already won more than I thought I had left to give."

Shortly later Perseus and Andromeda were both scheduled to be married. They found happiness in each other's arms while Andromeda's mother, Queen Cassiopeia, conducted the ceremony before the statue of Thetis. Everything was going according to plan until Cassiopeia's pride in her daughter's beauty angered the goddess.

The entire temple quivered as though from an earthquake. Then it was accompanied by a cry of anger and outrage that came from no human throat. Everyone turned up to see the great statue cracked and a great darkness came over the city.

Suddenly the head of Thetis tumbled from the idol's neck. Splinters of marble spewed in all directions as the massive carving continued to bounce down to the floor of the temple. Perseus grabbed Andromeda who was frozen with fright and they tumbled away to safety.

The marble head rolled slowly to a rest, and the stone eyes flashed open. Then it was followed by an otherworldly voice that echoed through the room.

"Hear me, vain and foolish mortal woman! You *dare* to compare your daughter's beauty to mine, to one of the immortals? *In my own sanctuary!* You will regret your boast…and all will sorrow for the delight they feel over the cruel misfortune of my mortal son Calibos."

"Forgive me, Thetis!" Cried Cassiopeia. "I did not mean—"

"In thirty days," the head continued relentlessly, "on the eve of the longest day of the year, your daughter Andromeda must be taken to the old sacrificial rock, where the first Canaanites paid homage to the gods of the sea who were so generous to them and their ungrateful offspring. There she must be bound and chained to the stone, a sacrifice to appease the anger of the sea goddess and to atone for your blasphemy—a sacrifice fit for the Kraken."

Perseus held Andromeda close, but there was no one to comfort the distraught Cassiopeia. Perseus knew all too well that the Kraken was the last of the powerful Titans. It was the last of those otherworldly creatures that fought alongside Chronos against Zeus.

Since the dawn of time everyone knew the horrid legend of the Kraken. It was a colossal elemental beast. It doesn't think. It doesn't feel. And the gods feared it.

"And if we refuse?" Asked Perseus, who was not intimidated by the voice from the gigantic stone head.

"Proud child, you are the cause of much of this." Thetis answered. "She must be delivered to the Kraken at the setting of the sun on the day indicated, or else the Kraken will be free to destroy Phoenicia and everyone within the city. For the insult that has been done to me, for the cruel injury you inflicted on my son, I demand the life of Andromeda."

"If I am the cause," Perseus replied firmly, approaching the stone head, "then I should make the restitution. Let the Kraken have me instead."

"It is too late. I have spoken. Andromeda is to be the sacrifice. In thirty days."

Then the headless statue split in two. Panic had spread throughout the city. Since that fateful day Perseus and several others had taken off to seek counsel from the three Stygian Witches. Legends say that they were all knowing and may have conceived a way to destroy the Kraken once and for all. Even if Perseus would find them and showed him a way to defeat the Kraken, he wouldn't live to use their advice. It has been said that the witches have a finely-honed craving for human flesh. Once when Calibos' plague infested the city, the queen sent ambassadors to consult the blind oracles. But not a single one of them had returned.

Now the thirty days were up, and Perseus had not returned.

Half a dozen handmaidens commenced to dress the princess when she stepped out of the pool. They all looked at Andromeda and wondered how pale she was. How she was paler than normal.

Andromeda knew she must not show fear. The people backed her and she couldn't afford to let them down. She bravely stood under the terrible strain and maintained such dignity and calm. She knew she would never be able to enjoy or use in the service of her people. Characteristics deemed to uselessness by the unpredictable whim of an outraged goddess.

There was nothing to do but to finish it.

A solemn crowd had gathered in the square outside the palace. Today there was no division between soldier and priest, merchant and citizen. All were joined together in common despair.

Their feelings were amplified by the slow and steady beat of the drummers flanking the palace entrance. There was very little conversation. All of them knew that Andromeda was to sacrifice herself to save the city. Dozens of women had volunteered to take the princess' place—futile gestures, for Thetis' demand had been specific. But it made Cassiopeia feel better.

A little.

She dropped the veil and by herself the farewell coronet of flowers on her daughter's head. Both mother and daughter stared into each other's eyes. They shared the same lineage, the same blood, and each knew her place and obligations.

No tears clouded Andromeda's eyes. For now, at least, she held back the fear. If Perseus had not come, it meant he had failed. If he had failed, then he must be dead. And if he was dead, she had no desire to live.

The procession left the palace. There was none of the usual cheering when the royal party approached, only a murmur of sympathy from the crowd. Soldiers were not needed to make a path, and the crowd parted silently.

Onlookers leaned silently from windows and trees to watch the trek pass, and threw garlands of olive and laurel leaves in its path. But only the soft lament of the drums broke the quiet.

Even the city gates seemed unnaturally muffled when they were swung open. Soldiers and priests alike led the column out of the city turning south along a well-worn wagon track. The cliffs that sheltered the southern part of Phoenicia's harbour rose high and straight from the water.

The march had filled the peninsula, which overhung out into the cove. Four priests flanked Andromeda, who was followed by her mother and her attendants. It was close to sunset. They would have just enough time to honour Thetis' command.

Soldiers who had straggled along in the wake now had spread out along the edge of the drop. The sacrificial rock waited below. The cove was a pleasant place on most days, but haunted only by the forgotten memories of less civilized times.

The black-cladded priests had assembled their massive calling horns. They were usually used to bring the people to prayer, or to announce festive occasions. Today they would sound a requiem.

Cassiopeia and the rest of the people stood back while the priests gently helped the princess down the steep path. They were determined that she would not suffer so much as scratch during the descent.

One priest had tears in his eyes.

An older companion chastised him sternly. "Do not weep and shame us before the princess, who does honour to us all."

Until now it seemed that calm would prevail, but for all her resolve and inner strength. Andromeda was no more than a young woman, and she was terribly frightened. As the first manacle locked tight around her right wrist her nerves finally gave out. She started struggling and screaming just like any other mortal.

More shocking still to the bystanders was the sudden, piercing shriek that came from higher up, from the queen. It was the first time in twenty years of rule that anyone had heard her lose control.

"Quickly," said the high priest through clenched teeth, trying not to look at Andromeda's pleading face. "Secure her and let us be away from this place." He could feel his own will cracking under those pitiful sobs.

At last it was done.

All four manacles were locked, and Andromeda was fastened to the cold rock. The priests hurried to climb the path, unable to keep from brushes at the dirt they felt, but they did not show. None of them would ever forget the last screams of the princess no matter how long they served the city of Phoenicia.

The sun had set into the still waters over the horizon. Horrified and yet unable to move away, the accumulated crowd waited with their priests and queen, to see the fate of their doomed princess.

Finally, a child pointed and a hum of fear rose from the crowd. The sea was beginning to boil and foaming with a force that hinted at something enormous below.

There was a great roar of displaced water as that immensity erupted from the very dark depths. Screams and shrieks of terror came from the crowd, which pulled back on the edge of the cliffs then the waters subsided. For a time, nothing was visible in the waves except for a great towering fin that moved steadily toward the little cove.

Andromeda was barely conscious and her screams had faded into a steady whimpering. She kept her eyes averted from the cove and tried to tell herself it would soon be over.

A massive wave hit the rocks, as a great tentacle flicked into the air and wrapped itself around a rock the size of the palace. Its mate surfaced soon after and sought a grip on the other side of the entrance to the inlet. Then the rest of its gargantuan body pulled itself above the water.

The head was covered with scales and spiny growths; a huge beak overlapped the mouth. The gigantic tail sprang up from the water and sent waves smashing against the rocks. Its eyes were the size of ships that glared down into the cove, and they were shining with a restrained fury.

The last of the Titans gawked at the people by the cliff. As it turned its attention down toward a certain rock and the small life that still throbbed there, its head buzzed with a peculiar humming. Suddenly out the sky, there came a small flying thing that was presumably made of metal shot across the frozen landscape of its face.

Andromeda recognized the creature as Bubo—the bronze owl—and he was trying to distract the Kraken. The creature swatted a tentacle at Bubo like he was an irritating fly. The wind of the immense limb's passing was enough to send the owl spinning. It tried to regain control, but it the rocks.

There was a noisy, sharp clang.

The owl did not shatter, but neither did it rise again into the sky.

The Kraken stared at Andromeda once again. Much as the Titan might have wished her single death to linger, the day was almost gone and it was under order to finish the simple work by dark.

If the one life was not present in the precise location, the Kraken had been promised an entire city to destroy. But the life was there, and in its frustration at having so little work to do, the monster was anxious to finish it quickly and return to its lair beneath the sea. There it would brood in silence, and ravish a very rewarding day.

A giant tentacle began to descend into the water. Andromeda turned her face to the rock and waited for the end.

Wings sounded into the sky again and again the Kraken paused. Diving down out of a sunset sky came a cloud. On its back rode a scratched and bruised figure of muscle and determination. It wore no armour, carried neither a sword nor a shield. Instead, it held tightly to a wad of red cloth.

There rose no clearer from the masses. Already this evening they had witnessed two manifestations of the gods. A third left them struck dumb.

They watched in awestruck silence as Perseus and his flying white horse Pegasus swept low overhead, but a tingle of excitement, of hope, was beginning to rise in some.

The Kraken slid slightly backward in the water. It was uncertain what to make of this second and much larger aerial intruder, but it was ready to swat it from the sky as quickly as it had the first.

Perseus dug his thighs hard into the stallion's flanks using his legs to steer Pegasus toward the head of the Kraken, now looming below like the crest of a mountain. With his hands Perseus began to unwrap the tangled bundle he carried. The rising wind made it difficult to handle.

Andromeda had noticed the arrival of her betrothed. She was too emotionally drained to do more than stare.

Perseus had it all planned so well, but as so often happens, not everything goes according to plan. He had decided in advance how to approach the Kraken, and on what kind of angle of descent he should have tried and figure out when the opportune time to reveal the severed head of the Gorgon Medusa. All Perseus had overlooked were the damned knots he had tied in his cloak. Now he was trying to unwrap them in such a panic.

Too close, too near! He shuddered.

He dug hard at Pegasus' side with his right leg. The stallion swirled, almost too late. Then a tentacle slashed right at them. It connected with the horse's hindquarters, but the blow was enough to send them both tumbling to the sea.

Pegasus desperately tried to right himself, but there wasn't enough space between him and the water. The winged stallion rolled twice as its rider was thrown into the sea. Perseus was still clutching the red bundle, but he fell head over heels. The impact of striking the water broke his grip. Pegasus plunged into the bay nearby.

Perseus flailed at the water and fought his way back to the surface. He was still sore all over from the concussion; he floated there as he fought to catch his breath.

Hindered by its own weight the Kraken turned slowly. It was hunting for the man who had fallen from the flying horse. Perseus dove and swam for the nearest rock. There was no sign of the precious package Perseus was so damned adamant about.

It had slipped away from him when he had landed in the water. Now it was rising from the sea next to him. It was rising in the gleaming metal talons of a hesitantly clicking and whirling Bubo.

By one of those ironic coincidences that fate seemed so fond of, the rock that was near Perseus was the one that projected farthest into the water. So, in addition to finding himself again on dry land, Perseus also discovered he was momentarily reunited with his one true love.

He staggered out of the raging waters in front of her and their eyes met for an instant. That was enough to sustain him throughout eternity. He whirled to face the Kraken, which had located him once again.

At that precise moment, Bubo dropped the still-bound cloak into Perseus' hands. The mechanical owl rose and soared close by the Kraken's eyes. It was enough to distract it for a few precious seconds. Without having to worry now about mounting his seat on the Pegasus or fighting the wind, Perseus finally unknotted the cloak.

He reached into the bundle, and he warned Andromeda to keep her eyes averted, and grasped a handful of cold, rubbery coils. Pulling it clear out of the cloth, he held out the face of the Gorgon Medusa to the Kraken.

Just by simply staring at any living being, Medusa could turn anyone who gazed into her eyes into solid stone.

The eyes of the Gorgon opened.

The snakes Perseus gripped grew agitated. He held fast, ignoring their cold caress as they wriggled between his fingers.

Instead of hair, the severed head of Medusa was nothing but a nest of writhing, tailless snakes. The Gorgon's teeth were not squared off, but pointed, like the canines of a wolf. Reptilian scales covered her entire face. The eyes were a violent emerald green and shockingly bright and piercing.

Those burning green eyes locked onto the Kraken's.

The Kraken, the last of the Titans, was frozen in its place in the water and was mesmerized by the still evil power of Medusa. Those huge inhuman eyes began to cloud over. Slowly the giant tentacles slumped and the dragon fins stiffened. While those on the cliffs locked on in amazement, the Titan turned to stone.

That massive body was thousands of years old. It could not survive any altercation of shaper or consistency. Once petrified, the Titan began to crumble. Huge chunks avalanched from its sides.

As it exfoliated it became unbalanced. With one final rumble, the shell of the last Titan tumbled slowly backward into the open sea.

Andromeda risked opening her eyes, but she was still careful to keep them away from her love and the abomination that had saved them.

"Is it over, Perseus?" She asked. "Are we truly safe at last?"

"Almost," he replied grimly. Drawing back his arm, he heaved the loathsome and ghastly façade of the Gorgon as far as he could.

It landed in the cove, and there was such an eruption of foam and steam where it landed. One would have thought that Hades himself had risen to take lasting possession of it.

Eventually the hissing died down, the blood red waters had been dispersed, and the cove was once again nothing more than a peaceful place for children and fishermen to pass the time.

The manacles were impossible for the imprisoned to reach, but simple enough for a free person to unlatch. Even if that such person was just as determined and eager as Perseus. In moments the princess stood safe and free in his arms while a vast sigh of relief and wander rose from the collected magnitude.

There came at last, an awful moment as the sea resumed its boiling. But there was only the one Kraken. What sprang from the water as though propelled by a catapult was not a threat, but the revived Pegasus.

It climbed rapidly, seeming to have to find its wings all over again, like a butterfly emerging from a cocoon. Pegasus whinnied forlornly for his friend and Perseus responded with a shout. There was very little room on its chosen rock to stand and the stallion moved to another. It stood there, trying to keep its footing.

As Andromeda embraced her betrothed, she had a feeling that their story will be forever written in the stars above them. She imagined an outline of a bold young man, and just right next to that constellation would be the silhouette of a young woman. Then another star would emerge, only this one was a winged horse and it was accompanied with a form that was in the shape of an older woman, but still radiant lady. Then mankind would look on them and remember until the end of time.

But Andromeda knew this was only the beginning.

FIVE YEARS LATER

CHAPTER ONE

The sun had begun to rise on the darkened Greek countryside. The giant burning star's piercing rays chased the shadows away as if it extended a gigantic hand on the earth, and all of the obscurities scurried away like frightened mice. The only silhouettes were left standing were the thousands of soldiers standing outside of their camp, greeting the new day. Once the warriors were clearly visible, hundreds of tents, herds of warhorses, and carts started to appear all around them.

They all have been waiting for a long time for this day. The looks of worry and determination ran across each and every one of their faces. Many were sharping their swords on the gigantic grindstone, while others were praying to the gods for safety and victory in the upcoming battle.

No one was praying as much as their king and general in his private quarters.

Perseus knelt before an idol of his father Zeus—the King of the Gods—in the tightly sealed tent. There wasn't a single trace of light in the whole place. However, being the creature of habit Perseus was he could walk around the cramped area blindfolded. He was a well-built young man blessed with good looks. Even with a few days of scruff on his face, while dark circles had formed under his eyes for the total lack of sleep. He couldn't afford such a luxury for there was a war to win, and he had been called to prove his worth yet again.

"Father," he addressed the statue of Zeus, "I ask for your strength and perseverance on this day. May your light guide me to victory."

Perseus suddenly heard his tent door-flap being raised. A very thin man entered and a worried expression was carved onto his face. Then it spread much wider when he heard his king letting out such an impatient sigh.

"Arsenios," Perseus said, without looking over his shoulder, "you are late."

Arsenios approached Perseus and knelt before him. "My Lord, forgive me—"

"Are the men ready?" Perseus interrupted him.

"Waiting for your command, but wondering why they were roused so early."

"They shall soon have their answer." Perseus replied, gesturing for his attendant to rise. "And what of Polydectes?"

Arsenios stared at Perseus in puzzlement, like a child who was unprepared for a test. Arsenios' face was narrow and angular, although partly obscured by his brown hair, which had grown long, and the scratchy beard he was now sporting.

"I was not aware he would be accompanying us—"

"He is not," said Perseus, heading for the exit. "But his ships will be."

"His ships?"

"Let us wake him."

Arsenios bowed to his king and followed him outside. Once Perseus set foot on the dew-covered grass he looked up heavenward and let out a world-weary sigh, as he readied himself for what was to come.

Polydectes, the benevolent ruler of the island Seriphus, took up residence in a very lavish tent that was adorned with various urns, sculptures, and beautifully bright woven rugs that really held the room together. Polydectes laid on the floor sound asleep as he clutched an animal-skin blanket that covered most of his huge belly.

Faint traces of light peered through the door-flap and shone on the many golden rings on his fat stubby fingers, and then it made its way up to the bracelets on his wrists. When the light reached up to his face, he lazily turned his head aside.

His eyes suddenly fluttered opened when he felt the sharp end of a sword that was pressing against his thick stubby neck.

Polydectes woke up startled as his loud snores turned into breathless hiccups. He scuttled to the other side of the tent without taking his eyes off the blade. He slowly gazed up to the face of his assailant to discover it was none other than Perseus standing over him.

Angered by this outrage, Polydectes waved the blade away.

"Curse you, Perseus!" He huffed, getting himself off the ground. "I don't know who I should distrust more—you or the Corinthians!"

"I need your ships." Perseus retorted, with no essence of an apology in his voice.

Polydectes looked at him in a very strange manner. *First, he scares the living daylights out of me. And now he has the gall to ask me for a favour?*

"My ships?" Polydectes finally spoke. "In the middle of the night? Go back to sleep, you may use them at first light."

He climbed back into bed and pulled the blanket over him. Then he rolled over to his side, facing away Perseus with hope that the young king would take the hint.

"Sleep has no place in war. And first light is far too near."

"If you are hoping to catch the Corinthians at rest, you are foolish. Alexion and his men are always ready for battle."

"On the contrary, the more awake the better."

Polydectes sat up quickly, and a look of confusion ran across his face. "Then why do you need my ships? March your army around the inlet. Unless you are planning to flee."

"When have you known me to do such?" Perseus replied, not sounding amused.

"You are still young, Perseus. Now, get some rest. No ship of mine leaves without my command."

Perseus could not believe what he was hearing. He wasn't asking for a favour, but issuing a command. His patience—like the hair on Polydectes' head—was wearing very thin, and heaved out a sigh of frustration that resembled a very low and rough growl. He was on the verge on pulling the sluggish fat man's covers off his bed so he could send him rolling down to the ground.

Before Perseus could speak and act out his revenge fantasy someone spoke.

"Then it shall be mine, Father."

Perseus and Polydectes look over to the shadows to discover a young man with green eyes. The interloper bowed down to Perseus.

"Nonsense, Hesiod." Polydectes said to his son. "What do you know of commanding ships and armies?"

"What better teacher to have than King Perseus?" Hesiod replied, with enough courage to look his idol in the eye. "He has yet to lose a battle."

"You are too kind, Hesiod." Perseus said humbly.

"Perseus' time will come." Polydectes warned his son, before turning his attention to Perseus. "You cannot win forever."

Perseus gave him a smirk. "Because you have not?"

Polydectes scowled at the Son of Zeus, and then nestled back into his blanket. He waved a hand toward Hesiod to send him on his way.

"Do what you will, Hesiod." Polydectes said in frustration and defeat. "But should one ship be missing from my fleet…"

Hesiod looked to Perseus with such eager and anticipation, as he waited for his first order as a soldier in his king's army.

"Ready your oarsmen." Ordered Perseus. "We leave as soon as my men are on board."

Hesiod didn't make any haste on running out of his father's tent to gather the men for the battle. For a split second, Perseus saw a smile on the young man's face before he took off to perform his duty. When he was about to leave, Polydectes stopped him.

"Let me remind you, young king, that your men follow only because you are the Son of Zeus."

"My men follow me because I lead them to victory." Perseus sternly clarified, as he walked out of the tent where his attendant Arsenios followed him across camp.

"Were you not too harsh with Polydectes?" Asked Arsenios. "He is a man of much anger."

"I have not time for his arrogance and laziness."

"You are making a very powerful enemy, My Lord."

Perseus stopped his trek to turn to face Arsenios. The meek attendant felt something bad was going to happen for questioning his king's methods. He closed his eyes briefly, waiting for the forthcoming blow. But a grinning Perseus greeted him with a pat on the shoulder.

"You worry far too much, Arsenios." Said Perseus.

Smiling, Arsenios replied, "Only because you worry far too little."

The sound of running feet filled the camp. Both Perseus and Arsenios turned to see Hesiod running up to them in great stride. The young soldier stopped in front of them and took a breath.

"The oarsmen are boarding now, my Lord."

"Good." Said Perseus, admiring Hesiod's work ethic.

How could it be possible he was spawned from Polydectes' loins? Perseus questioned himself. *He and his father are nothing alike. Perhaps arrogance and laziness skips a generation in their bloodline.*

"Tell my men to remove their armour—"

"'REMOVE?!'" Arsenios said in alarm.

"But to keep their sword and shield with them." Perseus continued, ignoring his attendant's sudden outburst.

Hesiod nodded in response and turned to go, but then looked back.

"May I say that it is a great honour to fight beside you on this day, King Perseus?"

"Hold your honours until after the battle; you may feel differently."

They both shared a smile, and then Hesiod ran to the ships. It was the fastest pace Perseus had ever seen in any man. The boy's speed may even make the gods' messenger, Hermes, tremble if the God of Swiftness would find himself in a footrace with Hesiod.

"My Lord, fighting without armour?" Said Arsenios, this time getting Perseus' attention. "It will be a massacre."

"The men may keep it, if they wish to drown." Perseus casually replied before he made his way toward the ships.

CHAPTER TWO

The night passed heavily, and it was nearly time for the changing of the guards. Two sentries manned their posts on a cliff in front of the Corinthian army camp. Pollo could barely keep his eyes open. He had all the rotten luck on drawing guard duty. He would have loved to be at the party in General Alexion's tent. His leader spared no expense on providing the best ale and the sweetest wine in all of Corinth. And to add more salt in his wounds, Alexion also gathered several of the loveliest concubines in the entire realm. But the night watch wasn't as bad as he thought. At least he had his friend Titus pulling the detail with him. It was better than standing next to one of those old grizzled veterans who had no sense of humour whatsoever.

Pollo turned his gaze over to Titus, who was slumped against the rock's wall. Pollo leaned further to examine his partner and discovered he was in a very deep slumber. A mischievous grin ran across Pollo's youthful face. He unsheathed his sword and held the blade on its broadside. Then he slowly crept over to Titus and with a very gentle swing he swatted his friend's right flank.

Titus awoke with a start. He snapped into attention and quickly drew his sword. His shield was up and he raised it to his face.

"Who goes there?" Titus said, his sword was shaking in fright and he was moving wildly. "Answer me or I will run you through!"

Then he heard the stifling laughter from behind his back. He knew that laugh all too well. Titus gave out a frustrated sigh for he had learned he had fallen victim to another one of Pollo's ill-played pranks.

"Behold Titus the Brave," Pollo snickered, "the mightiest warrior in all of Corinth." He joyously applauded the spectacle before him. "This never gets old."

Titus lowered his shield and then stared at the sword in his friend's hand. Then he finally figured out why his lower back was stinging so much.

"Put down that sword!" Titus said to Pollo, feeling humiliated yet again. "Every time I see you, you're waving it around or pointing it at somebody."

"Be at ease, friend Titus. It was all in good fun, like the others before it."

Titus scowled at him. "Is everything a joke to you, Pollo?"

"Only when it is funny."

"Do you always give yourself into folly all the time? If Alexion found out if you have been shirking your duties, he would put you in chains or even worse."

Pollo humorously frowned. "Why do you have to be so serious all the time, Titus? Would it kill you to have a little fun every now and then?"

"Not if it would cost me my life or my brothers."

Pollo rolled his eyes. "What you need is help, my friend."

Titus gave him a questionable look. "Help?"

"Yes," Pollo replied, "help. Now if you just kindly bend over and hold on to that rock there, I think I can get the stick out."

Titus snorted in anger, and then he noticed Pollo's signature smile had been replaced with a look of horror. Titus crossed his arms and shot him a dirty look.

"What is it now, Pollo?" He asked impatiently. He didn't have time to put up with anymore of his friend's foolishness.

"Ships," said Pollo. His response was soft and hardly audible. It was as if he was submerged in water and he was running out of air. "Ships coming toward us."

Titus narrowed his eyes. "Nice try, Pollo, but I am not falling for one of your tricks again."

"I am not jesting, Titus." He hastily replied. "There *are* ships coming straight at us! I believe they are from Argos." He pointed straight at the horizon, but Titus refused to budge.

"If you're done on making a complete ass of yourself, I'll be getting my things ready when the new shift comes—"

"Titus," Pollo grabbed his friend's head to make him face the water, "**LOOK!**"

In the distance they could see several ships crossing the inlet. Titus was in complete and udder shock.

"By the gods!" Exclaimed Titus, as he stared at Pollo. "Alert the men."

Pollo didn't have time to reply. He moved so fast he nearly tumbled several times before he scrambled downward the cliff, and headed for the camp to warn Alexion.

Thick and claying, smoke swirled through Alexion's tent. Traces of human sweat and the sharp scent of spilled ale, as the heavy air muted laughter and dulled the flash of bright eyes. Women swirled, smoky tendrils caressed them, as they danced free from one soldier's embrace and into that of another. Hungers of all manner would be sated there, thirsts quenched, hearts inflamed—all in a celebration of life and preparation for the upcoming battle.

Alexion sat cloaked in shadow in a darkened corner. He'd drunk enough ale to soften his grim expression—but had not softened it enough to tempt women to join him. He watched the others abandon all pretence of civilization, not descending into the savagery they would attribute to barbarianism, but regressed into childhood while coveting adult pleasures.

Those who did not lay claim to the veneer of civilization felt no need to justify letting it slip away. Plunder was for the strong, and taking then ensured pleasure and the future. The strong earned the right to these things through courage and cunning, speed and daring and skill. His men knew this and respected it. While there was still the craven who might scheme, a strong arm and a sharp mind would see through their subterfuge and out an end to their plotting.

"Excellency, Excellency!" Exclaimed a voice that caught Alexion's full attention. Pollo the sentry entered the tent unannounced with a panicked expression on his face. The young lookout raced over to his master's throne and quickly kneeled before him—averting his eyes. "Forgive me, Your Grace, but I have vital information I must disclose."

"Well, out with it then." Alexion huffed.

"We have discovered several ships approaching land, Excellency." Pollo explained. "They are Argos ships."

Alexion rose from his place, nearly spilling two half-naked women to the floor. "Fetch me my armour."

The morning sun sparkled on the water, bathing the ships in light. They were anchored near the beaches of Corinth, while smaller boats slowly made their way to shore. Aboard the boats are groups of men, holding their shields to create an impenetrable phalanx.

Armoured men in closed ranks were stepping from the forest. Their swords were unsheathed in perfect unison, and their shields bore the Corinthian crest.

The Corinthians began a measured march toward the Argos army. Several drummers paced behind them, hammering out a rhythm to which the soldiers marched. Alexion's heart pounded double time to that beat, and began his search for Perseus.

Then trumpets blasted and horsemen broke from the wood lines, and raced across the fields. They weren't the lightly armed scouts, but the heavily armoured cavalry. The warriors had long swords with sharp points, equally suited to slashing and stabbing. They all would have towered over Perseus if they were on foot, but in the saddle, they became juggernauts of destruction.

The Corinth army stood waiting on the water's edge with their weapons ready. Their commander, Alexion, sat atop of his horse behind his many foot soldiers. He eyed the boats suspiciously.

Finally, the boats dropped anchor, and began resting in the shallow waters. Corinthian soldiers waited for the Argos army to leap out of the boats, but no one moved.

After what it seemed like forever, Alexion nodded to a group of soldiers. They gingerly approached the boats.

But there still wasn't any movement.

"What games are you playing, Perseus?" Alexion loudly wondered.

He nodded again, signalling the soldiers to act. The Corinthian warriors quickly grabbed the shields of one boat only to find the vessels empty.

Then the Argos army emerged from the waters with swords drawn.

Hundreds of wet soldiers stormed the beach, and grabbed their shields from the boats and began stabbing at every confused Corinthian in sight. Amongst them were Perseus and Arsenios. They fought well, while delivering fatal blows nearly every time.

Alexion tried desperately to control his men, but the front lines were being brutally massacred.

Hesiod watched the battle from the ship's bow on the inlet. He was in complete awe of Perseus and his soldiers.

He turned to his oarsmen. "Faster! We must come to King Perseus' aid!"

Then Hesiod turned back to the battle with excitement on his face. Pure joy bubbled though him. He imagined himself fighting dozens of enemy Corinthian troops.

Then the thought sobered him. He couldn't help but notice the looks on some of his comrades' faces. A few of them looked ashamed—as well they should—and resentful. They'd given in to panic while a younger man had not. Even at that young age, Hesiod recognized that they would eventually forget their shame, and instead revel in the forthcoming victory when Brave and Noble Perseus will vanquish Alexion's forces.

The others—the warriors—their reactions had been easy to read as well. Some refused to believe. Some of them had been in combat, but had never killed an enemy. Others, knowing just have difficult that was, couldn't believe so young a man had done it alone.

Perseus and his men kept on pushing the front lines of the Corinthian army back. He cut through the forest and scaled the rock face leading toward the battlefield. Then he heard the jingle of tack and crack of leather. Over the hill, came many riders who were armoured in leather and light mail. Steel helmets protected their heads and hid their faces. Just as Alexion had sent in another company, another ship dropped anchor and more Argos soldiers came ashore with Hesiod leading the way.

The young soldier plunged headlong into the furious battle, being extremely aware of everything going around him. Sounds sorted themselves into the hush din of metal-on-metal impact, or the wet crack of sword cleaving bone. The hiss of air from punctured lungs differed from the wet gush of entrails flowing from a slashed belly.

Men shouted.

Some gave orders.

And others begged for mercy.

Words came in hard, guttural tongues and even in the language of the ancients. Light flashed from blades, blood splashed red and filled the air with a tang that erased the scent of smoke.

Hesiod caught the first glimmer of the knowledge that would keep him alive. Combat appeared to be chaotic, but, in fact, had an order and flow. Currents ran through it as strength channelled against weakness.

Lines surged and collapsed, while voids opened and were filled. So, they could move with the energies to survive. To hesitate or defy them was to be drowned in a river of blood.

Arrows sped through the air—launched by Corinthian archers. Hesiod grabbed the arm of an enemy soldier and spun him around, using him as a shield. Three arrows thudded into his chest, but Hesiod slipped from beneath the dead man's falling body. Then he slashed another Corinthian across the stomach.

Hesiod ran toward where he'd thought he had seen Perseus, but all he could see was more arrow-stuck bodies everywhere around him.

Some were Corinthians, while most were his own comrades from the ship.

The massacre would spare no one.

Hesiod couldn't find his king. He cut through the fray, slashing and stabbing anyone who blocked his path.

He was too quick to be hit.

He was also too short to be followed.

And he sure as hell was too easily lost in the smoke to be hunted.

Less than fifty paces from his own position, Hesiod saw a dozen of his comrades engaged with one of Alexion's enforcers. He was a towering figure and his powerful sword arm spun like a windmill with a vicious blade at one end. Bellowing, the brute scooped up one of the Argos troops and snapped his neck with one flex of his giant fist. Then he threw the corpse over his shoulder and it hit a passing Corinthian rider. The impact was hard enough that the horse rolled over the man who was riding it.

Even over the dull, ongoing roar of battle, Hesiod could hear the crunch of bone; both of soldiers—Argos and Corinthian—were dead. The horse panicked and struggled to rise in a mist of sun-baked dust.

Hesiod started for the horse, but another of Alexion's soldiers leapt in his way. In front of the young warrior was a massive, scarred battle axe in the man's meaty hands. He swung back, hefting the bloody axe, swinging it up and over. Hesiod stepped in to meet him, swinging his sword down and across. The axman took the hit just beneath his chest plate and he grunted in what seemed to be a surprise as his belly opened beneath the hammered blade. Blood spilled from the wound, as he fell to his knees and Hesiod swept past him and then took the struggling horse's reins in one hand. He sacrificed a few precious seconds to calm the animal before mounting and returning to the battle.

The sight of his men suddenly being outnumbered shocked Alexion.

The sun was high in the sky now, and Perseus and his men were still fighting. Fallen Corinthian and Argos soldiers lie side-by-side on the ground, butchered.

Perseus demonstrated his skills and rank of general, while Arsenios fought beside him. A group of Corinthians surrounded him, but Perseus methodically defeated each and every one, as he ignored a fresh wound he just sustained.

Then he looked up to see Alexion fleeing toward a pass in the cliff.

"Should we go after him, my Lord?" Asked Arsenios, after he cut down another Corinthian enemy.

"No, he is baiting us." Answered Perseus, as he watched a few Argos soldiers running toward the pass. "He wants us to follow. Alexion would never leave his men."

"Why would he—"

Suddenly an ungodly roar silenced the din of battle. All the soldiers—both Corinthian and Argos alike—turned to see a hideous beast with the body of a lion and it had three heads that resembled dragons.

There were loud quaky sounds and it seemed as though the earth was moving—like something was taking giant footsteps.

Arsenios' eyes had widened in fear. The sound got louder. The vibrations felt stronger. Whatever it was it was coming closer.

And then they all saw it.

It was entering the valley.

Arsenios stared in horror. *Oh, no,* he thought.

The monster swung its mighty head. Arsenios gasped. Its three boxy heads were bigger than Arsenios' whole body. And its body was bigger than a house.

It let out another furious roar, and then proceeded to crush and tear apart any man that crossed its path. It blocked the entrance to the pass with menacing fury. The Corinthians smiled to the Argos soldiers.

"What in the gods' name—" Arsenios yelped.

"A khamaira." Perseus quickly identified the creature.

Arsenios looked at him with such scrutiny. "You know of these?"

"Native to the southern regions." Perseus advanced toward the beast and grabbed two other soldiers, as they headed for the pass. Then he waved over to Arsenios. "Come!"

"And you also know of slaying it?" Arsenios nervously added, as he begrudgingly followed his king.

Hesiod had developed a much firmer belief in the power of his sword and in his own skills than the willingness of the gods to stoop on down to assist his fellow Argos warriors. He worshipped them for having created him, but knew better than to rely on them in time of need.

He drew strength from the combat, his consciousness was retreating into the numb single-mindedness necessary in order to fight—and win. Hesiod had ceased to hear the repeated crash of sword on shield. He was no longer aware of the blooming ache between his shoulder blades. His armour was heavy, but he could scarcely feel its weight upon his shoulders. He was only half conscious of the screams and groans of the battle. He could barely hear the snapping of their bones and the pounding of their falling bodies when they hit the ground.

He tirelessly cut down the Corinthian fighters, planting his sword through muscle and bone, and then pulled his weapon back out to kill anew. Blood streaked his helm and breastplate while his vision was stained with red and his nostrils burned from the sickly-sweet smell of death. He fought on, pivoting and dancing to face each armoured warrior as they came at him from all directions. He brought his foot up from the horse's right side to deliver a swift blow to the face of an opposing Corinthian.

Then Hesiod saw Perseus and Arsenios out in a distance and made his way over. Though he was new to the battlefield and this was his first taste of warfare, he has had much training. His moves proved to be unsure, but skilled. However, he did not yet fight with the ease of a seasoned soldier.

Then he glanced around. He and the rest of the men were armed with any kind of weapon that could fight a monster like that. They only had swords and shields. And no blade was enough to stop a khamaira.

Also, none of these men had any experience with monsters. They only dealt with humans, and left that kind of fighting to the likes of their leader Perseus.

Hesiod rode across the battlefield with his sword drawn. His mount forged a path between the locked armies of Argos and the oppressing army. The bodies of the dead flew beneath his horse's galloping hooves. Their leather armour was slicked with blood.

Ahead, he saw a Corinthian soldier pulling his sword from an Argos warrior's crumpling form. He stepped out to meet Hesiod as he rode. A feral grin crossed his blood-spattered face as he realized the boy was actually the prince of Seriphus. Hesiod raised his sword, as his rage spilled out in a wordless cry, and struck him down. Hesiod did not look back to make sure he was dead.

At first it seemed to Hesiod the shadows had sprung to life. Formless, they drove against him, seeking to tear him from his battalion. He swung his sword blindly as he tried to break away from the press of Corinthian warriors.

The sky had begun to unravel in scarlet threads. The sun, rising against black pines, filled the grove with a baleful light. Then Hesiod started to fight against the fear that chilled his heart and drained him of his strength.

Then he searched the field for where the fighting was the most violent. Just north of his position there was a rise in the land with a few small stands of scrubby trees near the top. The maliciousness of the combat there drew him onward. Men were shrieking in sadistic wrath as they beat their shields and brandished their spears. He urged his horse north; sure he would find Perseus there.

Perseus moved toward the khamaira, and began to study its every move. Blood was dripping from its mouth, as a result of crushing many soldiers in its massive jaws. Perseus turned to the two soldiers and Arsenios.

"On my word we—"

Arsenios was silenced by another roar of the monster. One of the soldiers, Atticus, stared up in horror and his breathing became erratic.

He shivered with fear. His large bronze helmet rattled on his head. He stumbled backwards and bumped into Arsenios.

Atticus was scared. After all, he was only a soldier in the Argos army for a little over seven months. What he wanted to do more than anything was not to die on his first mission. He had so many things he had yet to experience. He didn't even have the pleasure of feeling a woman's warmth. He thought by enlisting in the army would get him so many women he wouldn't know what to do with. This wasn't worth risking his life.

"I cannot!" He panicked. "My Lord, I cannot! Fight men, I will, but not this…"

Fear overcame the young solider and he fled back down the pass screaming. Perseus glared at the coward, until suddenly Hesiod was in his face.

"I shall take his place, My Lord." Hesiod said boldly, as he dismounted his steed.

Before Perseus could argue, the khamaira charged towards them. The men took turns battling the heads. With the three heads distracted, Perseus finally managed to climb up on it. He raised his sword and plunged it into the beast's neck.

But he was too late.

In its final moments, one of the khamaira's heads struck at Hesiod. The boy wasn't quick enough, and the beast's powerful jaws closed around him, emitting a horrifying crunch.

Perseus stabbed the monster again, and the body writhed in pain, as the creature fell to the ground.

Perseus' other solider watched the amazing feat in awe. His jaw dropped and his eyes widened in excitement.

"Tis incredible, slaying such a beast!" The young Argos soldier said, with adrenaline coursing through his veins. "I have heard of stories of your battles before, but seeing with my own eyes—you truly are blessed by Zeus."

He was expecting Perseus to say something profound to him, but all he saw was his hero kneeling beside Hesiod, who was mortally wounded. Suddenly, the young warrior felt terrible. He totally forgot about the wellbeing of his fellow comrade. He removed his helmet in respect and knelt before them.

"I am sorry to have failed you, my Lord." Hesiod said weakly.

"You fought well today and have failed no one." Perseus replied.

Hesiod reached out for Perseus' hand. Perseus gripped it tightly.

"King Perseus, I go, praising your name to the gods."

Then he felt the boy's hand go limp, and Hesiod, Prince of Seriphus, drew his final breath.

"My Lord! My Lord!" Cried an Argos soldier, emerging in the pass. "I have Alexion!"

Perseus didn't care about Alexion. How could he enjoy a victory if it had cost him a boy's life in the process? All he could see was Hesiod's angelic face with the illusion of him slumbering peacefully.

CHAPTER THREE

The sounds of merriment and celebration filled throughout the camp. Soldiers were laughing and drinking with the weight of battle had been lifted off their shoulders. The only person without a smile was Perseus, who was still caked in mud and blood. He aimlessly walked through the rows of tents, while soldiers nodded and praised them. But he didn't acknowledge them. It seemed he had left the world and he was stricken deaf and blind.

However, he did manage to hear something coming from a nearby campfire. On what he heard he didn't like one bit.

"So, there I was, hot on Alexion's trail until this ugly beast with three heads showed up right in front of me."

The voice was very familiar to Perseus. It was something he would never forget. Only this time it wasn't overwhelmed with fear, but laced with conceit and wrapped around with lies.

"What did you do, Atticus?" Asked a soldier in anticipation.

"I knew my king needed me, so I gathered all the courage I had and faced the monster head on. I was able to get a few cuts in before Mighty Perseus finished him off."

"Hear, hear!" Said another soldier lifting up his chalice of wine.

Perseus turned his head to find the soldier who had abandoned him and Hesiod to the khamiara. The whelp was drinking with his friends and bragging about fabricated deeds.

"What in the name of Zeus?" Perseus spat in anger.

Silence had befallen to the group and trembled to see King Perseus approaching them. They all bowed respectfully, but Perseus lifted Atticus to his feet with his hand around the soldier's collar.

Atticus was shivering in terror. He had never seen his king so livid before in his entire service to the Argos army. Perseus leered at him with hatred, and Atticus felt it pierce through his soul.

"The strong shall always protect the weak, and the cowardly are kept safe by better men." Perseus scolded the young soldier, as he lowered him to the ground.

Just when Atticus thought he was safe, Perseus ripped the fabrics off his uniform.

"You are not worthy on wearing those colours." Then he picked up the boy's helmet and threw it across the camp. "You are not even fit to be a soldier in Argos or any kingdom at all."

"My Lord," Atticus stammered and his eyes became watery. "I beg you not to act in anger. Forgive my actions this day—"

"Your cowardice got a man killed today. The penalty for desertion during wartime is punishable by death. Since I am not a cruel king, I hereby release you from this army. Speak to me again, and I shall kill you myself."

Perseus stormed out of Atticus' presence, leaving the outcast stunned, and alienated from the rest of the soldiers and comrades.

Anger had clouded Perseus' mind. He couldn't find a way to explain to Polydectes the death of his only son. He knew he had better to come up with something quick because he was near the lazy man's tent.

When Perseus finally approached the tent, he saw that Arsenios was waiting for him. The expression on his face was quite grim.

"My Lord, King Polydectes has been waiting for you," Arsenios began, with dread in his voice. "I have been listening to him speculate, dare I say plan, your demise."

"Such is the conversation of many kings."

Arsenios held the tent flap back for Perseus to enter, and quietly followed. The young king found Polydectes pacing around the room. His robes were flowing behind him.

Perseus took a breath to steady himself. "Polydectes, I deeply regret the loss of—"

"I am told that Queen Andromeda shall bear you a child in a matter of days." Polydectes interrupted. "Hopefully your own son will not be so foolish as to follow you into battle."

The undisguised malice in Polydectes' voice was more than Perseus' fraying nerves could take.

Taken back by the Seriphian ruler's barbs, Perseus softly replied, "I can only pray that he fights well and dies honourably, as Hesiod did today—"

"There is no honour in death." Polydectes quickly snapped. "Do not attempt to console me with lies, Perseus."

Silence filled the tent for several moments. Perseus could not find the nerve to speak. It was the time for Polydectes to vent. If it were Perseus' own son, he would feel the same way.

"After your victory today, I am sure the great Argos will no longer need the assistance of Seriphus or its army, so we will set sail—"

"Polydectes, do not speak in such manner—"

"I may speak as I choose!" Polydectes shouted with outrageous fury. His rage was so immense it would shake the top of Mount Olympus. "Because of you, my son is dead this day!"

"No!" Perseus contested. "Because of *you*, your son is dead!"

Polydectes stalked over to Perseus and stopped until he was only several inches away from his former ally's face. "I know you get your strength from the gods, but how can you stand in my presence and accuse me of such?"

"I accuse you of nothing you are not guilty of. Yes, Hesiod fought as a soldier of Argos today, but only because his king lacked the courage to command the Seriphus army—"

"Do not insult my army—"

"Not your army, but its leadership!"

That outburst silenced Polydectes. Perseus could feel his blood boiling and a huge vein was being formed on his forehead. It felt like he was going to grow another head like a hydra. He felt enticed on touching it with his finger and trace the outlines of bulge as if it were a topographical map. But he refrained from doing so because he feared it would rupture. He took his time to calm himself before he would say anything. He knew at this point of the conversation he should coast.

"Perhaps if his *father* had been there, Hesiod would have been better looked after."

"I suggest you hold your tongue." Polydectes advised Perseus. "You are making enemies quicker than you realize."

"I speak how I feel and no less."

"And with such simplicity you make light of a father's grief. Hopefully no ill fortune shall befall the child of King Perseus. And that you may be spared from the pain you have caused me today."

Perseus' eyes narrowed, and glowered at the fat king. "I caution you to choose your words with more care."

"Mighty and Noble Perseus…" Polydectes mocked.

Perseus shook his head and stormed out of the tent, with Arsenios in tow. Polydectes settled back into his bed, with numerous thoughts churning and he began to weep.

Perseus lay on his cot, his eyes were fixated on some point in his tent's ceiling. He did not feel like sleeping, despite his fatigue. His arms ached from battle, and a dozen bruises and cuts nagged him with their small pains.

He could never remember the last time he ever had a decent good night's sleep. He frowned, and his eyes were flickering beneath their closed lids. He was cold and overwhelming drowsy, but he knew that it was vitally important for him to stay awake.

Whenever he did manage to dream it would be only of his wife Andromeda. He could see her sitting at her vanity, putting on her jewellery. In the reflection, she would see him and she would turn and come back into the centre of the room. His blue eyes were dark with worry, and she would feel a long familiar rush of love. She had married a warrior but knew Perseus as much more than that. He did not rule lightly. Everything he had done and everything he would do was the result of great deliberation. He had seen the results of battles that had not been thought out and had lost too many warriors to unnecessary violence.

Perseus woke up from his reverie to hear the sound of Arsenios entering his tent, but he doesn't bother on looking over.

"What news do you have, Arsenios?"

"How does my Lord know—?"

"You would not otherwise be awake at this hour. Come, tell me."

Arsenios approached Perseus, as he sits up on his bed. "It concerns Polydectes."

Perseus and Arsenios watched every ship in Polydectes fleet sailed off to the horizon at the rising sun. Perseus clenched his jaw and mulled over the dissolved allegiance and the many soldiers in Argos' ranks.

Looking over to Arsenios, he said, "Say nothing of what transpired last night."

"The men will wonder."

"Corinth is ours," Perseus swiftly countered. "We no longer need the service of our Seriphian brothers."

"Yes, my Lord." Arsenios nodded.

A whinny of a horse distracted the both of them. They turn to see a lone horseman in the distance, riding towards the camp.

Perseus examined the stranger with much suspicion. "Arsenios, take some men and ride out to greet our new guest."

Before Arsenios could speak, Perseus was already on his way through the camp. He strolled through the many rows of tents and horses, inspecting his army. Then he turned to see Arsenios and the horseman approach.

Arsenios cleared his throat. "My Lord, this loyal servant would not betray his master's orders to reveal the purpose of his trip. He was told to speak with no one but the King. Will you grant him council?"

Perseus pushed Arsenios aside and walked up to the horseman, who slowly backed up several feet. Then the stranger kneeled before him.

"My Lord."

"What business have you here?" Perseus asked the horseman.

"I bring word…from the Queen." The horseman answered, and then he handed him a gold ring.

Perseus studied the ring carefully, and quickly recognized it belonged to his wife Andromeda.

"Speak."

The Horseman replied, "Lady Andromeda and *your son* anxiously await your return."

A smile crossed Perseus' face. Arsenios took notice of this action and concluded that this was the first time he ever saw his lord and master smile in this whole war. Then he saw Perseus' smile turn into a state of worry.

"And she is well?" Perseus nervously asked the horseman.

"Both the Queen and our Prince." The horseman said proudly.

Perseus gave out a sigh of relief. He glanced over to Arsenios, who in return nodded in respect.

CHAPTER FOUR

Filled with such splendid news, Perseus mounted his horse while a worried Arsenios handed him up a sword and helmet.

"My Lord, I beg you to wait for the army." Advised Arsenios. "The road is dangerous for so few."

He glanced over to a small group of mounted soldiers, waiting to escort the young king. Perseus smiled down to Arsenios.

"I fear where I would be without your concern, dear Arsenios."

"Let me accompany you." Entreated Arsenios. "That I may see you arrive in Argos safely."

"And who would command the army?" Perseus asked. "You are my most devoted friend. I trust you. The men trust you."

Arsenios was touched. That was the highest honour he had ever received. He took it with pride and it humbled his heart.

"I shall pray to the gods for your journey and that Zeus may watch over you."

Perseus smiled to his friend. "Save your prayers for those who need them, Arsenios."

Then he spurred his horse and took off to the countryside with the mounted soldiers riding after him.

On the top of Mount Olympus, there rested a bleach-white palace on the side of a cliff, completely isolated from the civilization of the mortal world. Palaces and temples were constructed of pure white imagination began to materialize beyond the clouds. "Great marble" those who sometimes roughly tried to ascend the sacred mountain called it. Soaring structures rested firmly on foundations of deep belief and enveloped in the subconscious of all men, these networks were built partly on Earth, but mostly in the mind where nothing is what it seemed.

The beautiful structure gleamed in the sunlight. On the balcony the Greek gods lounged on various beds with silk pillows, and bathed in the sun.

Right by Zeus' majestic throne there stood a strange construct. It was a model of an amphitheatre. This is where Zeus would observe the playacting that men called their lives. With a single touch or a mere gesture, the gods would alter the play. It amused Zeus to form his stage in the image of man's own.

Behind the shinning metaphor were dark marbled walls filled with row on row figures set in small niches. These mortals whom the gods presently attended to were represented by such figures. Most men were not represented, their life-streams being of no importance to the future of the world. Occasionally, a figure would be added, sometimes another would be removed. Empty alcoves awaited others that there destined to play important roles in the course of human history.

Thetis—the Goddess of Nature, and spouse to the Sea God Poseidon—and Aphrodite—the Goddess of Love—were gossiping in the right side of the terrace. Ares—the God of War—wasn't enjoying the fine weather. He was cladded in his finest battle attire and waited impatiently for a new battle to commence. He hated to sit around and do nothing all day. It just wasn't in his nature. He was a being of action, not leisure. Meanwhile, Hera—the Queen of the Gods—lazed on a pillow, while her husband Zeus leaned over the balcony staring out at something. He wasn't fixated on any part of the world. He was lost in thought.

Then Hermes, who was small and frail, emerged from the palace. "Your Highness!"

Zeus turned around to see Hermes rush toward him. The other gods watched in slight irritation.

"Perseus was victorious yet again!" Hermes yelled excitedly. "This time at Corinth!"

"My Perseus…and Corinth?" Zeus said ecstatically. "It must have been a difficult battle. Alexion is a very gifted warrior."

Then you looked over to the rest of the gods who didn't even acknowledge the news. They were too busy dozing in the sun and enjoying an assortment of fruit and wine. Zeus even took notice of Ares still sulking about the tedium of this dreary little party. He of all people should have been fascinated by such news. Perhaps he was cheering on the side of the Corinthians. Should have figured. Ares was always such a sore loser.

"Have you not ears?!" Zeus bellowed at the top of his lungs. The gods looked over at him with fear. "Did you hear what Hermes has said?!"

"Your golden child sacked another city in your name…how impressive." Hera said sarcastically, taking a sip from her golden goblet.

"May the reign of Perseus live on forever." Toasted Thetis.

She held her resentment for Perseus deep within her entire being. Thetis managed to perform a rather convincing smile. She will never forgive him and Zeus for her son Calibos' untimely demise. And how Queen Cassiopeia's transgression against her went unpunished. Thetis wanted so much to smite Perseus, but Zeus had forbidden her from doing so. She didn't want to cross Zeus—her king.

Zeus couldn't hear the Goddess of Nature's feign good cheer. He was still being distraught by his wife's cold reception, and of course her snide remark toward his son.

"What ill will have you against Perseus?" He asked her.

"None." She replied. "How could we? I would only like to see him succeed without his father's intervention."

"I know not what you speak of."

"You fool no one but yourself." Confronted Aphrodite. "We are aware of your assistance to Perseus."

"We only wish you would bestow such honours on our children as you do on your own." Hera stated.

"That they may have an opportunity to become glorified heroes." Thetis chimed in on their argument.

Zeus replied, "I was not aware of your displeasure. What would you have me do?"

"What do you say we make a wager, Husband?" Asked Hera. "Allow Perseus to fight his own battles. Let us see how magnificent he truly is."

"And he will show you!" Zeus assured the rest of the Olympians. "Perseus is an excellent warrior, even on his own."

Hera got off her pillow and sauntered over to Zeus. She seductively put her arm around him.

"So, you will agree then?" She asked him again. "Come not to Perseus' aid, and should he prove his worth, we shall no longer question your interference."

Thetis shot Hera a nervous look.

"I accept your challenge only because I have faith in my son." Zeus said proudly, as he remembered the quest Perseus had set on years ago when he went through the trials to defeat the gigantic Kraken. "Your thinly-veiled seductions tempt me not."

Zeus turned his back on Hera and proceeded back inside the palace, being followed by Hermes. Hera tried to hide her hurt feelings, but it was no use. She stormed out of the party and went to her chambers. She couldn't wait to see how well Perseus does without his father out there to hold his hand. Then Zeus would be the one with hurt feelings. All she had to do was wait and see.

King Perseus rode in triumph through the streets of Argos. Many of the citizens were expecting him to arrive ahead of his mighty army, which they all have heard fought its way across Greece, but all they saw was their noble ruler. Flowers were showered down on Perseus as the mobs yelled and cheered. The progress of his horse through the applauding streets was very slow.

This wouldn't have taken so long if I had taken Pegasus, heaved the young king.

He wore the white silk robes and a bold red colour cloak. He carried a golden sword at his waist. The blade was a gift from his father Zeus, which was created by the great Hephaestus—the God of Fire and Forge. Perseus was weeping with exhaustion, and scarcely heard the cries of "Perseus!" which greeted his appearance. For seven months he had fought in many atrocious battles, lost some very good men, and alliance ties were severed.

The people knew him as "The Son of Zeus," and those words seemed to describe him perfectly with their suggestion of dangerous journeys and audacious conquests in legendary lands. He became a legend in his lifetime. He was loved by good and feared by evil.

Andromeda, Queen of Argos, rested in a gold-plated bed amongst luxurious blankets in her royal chambers. It was indeed a room fit for royalty. An array of painted urns and marble statues decorated the huge room. Long billowing curtains led to a balcony that overlooked the beautiful city of Argos in the warm summer night.

Filmy curtains of near transparent silk that were all brought in from distant lands encased the bed. Men and animals had perished so that a queen might be spared the inconvenience of mosquito and fly bites while she slept.

Andromeda had her soft blonde hair pulled back, revealing her youthful beauty. The young queen was very statuesque with the sort of blue eyes that a man could truly lose himself in. She radiated confidence and grace whenever she moved. She looked down in admiration on her new born son, Perses, who was suckling on her breast.

The young queen heard very faint footsteps in the hallway, and they grew louder on each pace. The gentle rattling of the doorknob started Andromeda and she cradled her baby tightly. But she was relieved that the unannounced visitor was Perseus.

Even though he was a very valiant warrior and also a man of honourable fame, he had spent most of his time away from home. He was like so many of the soldiers he commanded during his campaigns, and similar to all the other nobles in these ancient times. Perseus was always on leave fighting in the great wars and petty quarrels that were always afoot in Greece. But during the brief intervals of peace he would return to take his ease in his luxurious palace. During those times it was his chief delight to be with his beautiful wife Andromeda—and now he was also in the presence of his new born son.

Perseus was accompanied with an attendant who was trailing just behind him. Andromeda's face was besieged with happiness.

"I was beginning to wonder if you were ever coming home." She said smiling, and then she frowned. "Or if you had taken a new wife in Corinth."

"Do not speak of such things." Perseus soothed his wife. "The battle proved to be more difficult. The Corinthians had a khamiara—"

"That is no excuse." Andromeda said, sounding very strict. Then she gave him a grin. "I've been fighting my own monster."

Feeling his wife's gaze on him, Perseus looked up and smiled. The corners of his eyes were crinkling. Perseus looked down to her arms to see her holding their son. He couldn't stop smiling. Their eyes seemed to connect, and Perses gurgled happily. He climbed into bed with Andromeda, and kissed her forehead.

"I bear you a son, and that is all I get in return?"

"What more would my lady ask of me?"

Andromeda gave him a lecherous grin. This enticed Perseus to lean in closer, and then he remembered about the attendant who was still in the room with them.

"Leave us." He ordered the servant.

The attendant nodded in response and vacated the royal chambers. Now alone, Perseus kissed Andromeda passionately, and then he regarded his son.

Perseus cocked his head, as a playful smile was tugging at his lips. "Mighty Perses." He said approvingly to his son. "Already engaging in battle."

"Please! Do not ruin this moment with talk of war." Andromeda pleaded. "Each day I pray to the gods that the time of battles and conquest draws to an end."

"As long as there is land left to claim and men to fight, there shall always be battles and conquest." Perseus replied, putting his arm around her. "Now, come to me."

They all nestled together into the bed. They were all one happy family. His heart filled with joy and appreciative to everything he has been blessed to him. Perseus looked up to the heavens and smiled at his father.

The next day was very awkward for Perseus. He traded his sword and armour in exchange for silk robes and a golden crown. He had been in the battlefield so long he had forgotten what it was like to be an actual king. He walked down the shiny marble floors through the great hall in the palace of Argos with Perses in his arms. He followed Andromeda who was being guided by the arm by her uncle Phineus.

"After the races, we shall gather here for a feast that would feed all of Argos and then some…it pleases me that you were able to come, Uncle." She said to the rosy-cheeked man as he smiled and patted her hand. "Then, with enough wine to satisfy Dionysus, and an altar for Zeus, who I want to pay homage for giving me so fine a son."

She turned to see Perseus staring absentmindedly out a passing window. He seemed lost in thought, and she felt there some place he would rather be in besides this palace.

"My love?" She addressed Perseus, who in return didn't provide any answer. "Perseus?" She called again, only this time with more zest.

Perseus finally sprung back to reality, and squeezed out a smile. "Yes, it all sounds lovely."

"In three days' time, we are to present our first born to the people of Argos, and yet their king is somewhere else."

"Forgive me." Apologized Perseus, as he felt both embarrassed and ashamed.

"Wherever you are, my love, leave, and come back to me." Andromeda said, caressing his face.

"Quite a home you have for yourself now, Perseus." Said Phineus, surveying the palace. "Much different than what you were accustomed to."

"Uncle! Please." Andromeda said, as she felt mortified of her uncle's snide remark. She hoped Perseus didn't hear it.

"Let Phineus speak, Andromeda." Perseus retorted. "It is clear he has something to say."

"No, no. You are family now." Phineus eased his nephew. "I was simply commending your glorious transformation—solider to king—very impressive."

They heard a commotion coming from the south door. Perseus' face brightened immediately to see Arsenios being escorted in by the palace guards. He roughly handed Perses over to Andromeda, and began to make his way to his comrade. Andromeda didn't even bother to hide her annoyance, as her uncle looks on in amusement while Perseus and Arsenios embraced.

"My Lord." Arsenios said, silently thanking the gods for escorting him home safely.

"It is good to see you, my friend." Perseus reciprocated the pleasantries. "How are the men?"

Arsenios replied exhaustingly, "Tired…hot…"

Perseus turned to several nearby servants, who were waiting for the king's next order. "Bring my men food and drink at once." The servants then retreated to the pantry to provide sustenance for the ailing soldiers.

"We are making camp on the northern border." Arsenios informed his lord. "Everyone waits for your command."

Andromeda sashayed over with Perses over her shoulder. Arsenios respectively bowed toward her and the new prince.

"My Queen," he humbly greeted her, "I congratulate you and my Lord on the birth of your son."

"And I thank you, Arsenios." Smiled Andromeda. "It is good to have you back. Although my husband has already made that evident."

"And Corinth?" Asked Phineus. "Who did you leave in charge?"

"Charon." Arsenios answered.

"Excellent." Perseus said with gaiety. "And what of Alexion?"

"He waits for you in chains."

"Perseus." Whispered Andromeda, as both Perseus and Arsenios turned their attention to her. "Uncle Phineus has just arrived. Can talk of armies not wait?"

Perseus' face was marked with regret. "Andromeda, these men are tired and weary, and have not seen their families in seven months' time. With all due respect to Phineus, I will not ask them to delay their return home any longer."

"Yes, Andromeda," Phineus agreed. "Let them go."

"Of course." She said in defeat. "I know too well how a wife misses her husband. Forgive me."

"There is nothing to forgive." Perseus kissed her on the cheek, and turned to face Arsenios. "Ready Pegasus. We leave at once."

When Perseus was about to head to the door, Andromeda stepped forward. "You will be back before the announcement?"

"I swear it." Perseus promised her, and then he took his leave.

Andromeda looked down to her infant son and gave a frustrated sigh. Then she heard her uncle approaching.

"If only he cared for his family the way he cares for Argos." He said to her.

"That is not fair, Uncle. Corinth was an important battle—"

"Save your excuses, Andromeda." Snapped Phineus. "It matters not to me."

CHAPTER FIVE

Perseus had reached the northern border at sunset. He walked amongst his men, shaking their hands and embracing some of them as well. He was clearly more at ease in this environment than he was at the palace. Word of his arrival spread throughout camp. In a matter of moments, a crowd gathered around to get chance to see Mighty Perseus.

"Long live King Perseus!" Yelled one soldier, and then the rest of the throng joined in with the cheers. Perseus smiled to see such loyalty in his ranks.

Another soldier boldly advanced to Perseus. "My Lord! Where are we heading now?"

"We will follow you to Hades and back should you ask." Said the warrior next to him.

"Hopefully that shall not be necessary." Perseus replied, listening to his men's laughter. "Comrades, I command each of you on our success at Corinth. Many say it takes a great general to lead an army, but what they forget is that it takes a great army to win a battle. Because we fought as one, we were victorious and showed another enemy the strength that Argos possesses." All the men nod to each other in agreement. They hung onto his every word and they froze in anticipation. "And as your King and General, I now order you to return home! Lay with your wives, play with your children, and prepare for the harvest."

The soldiers erupted into various cheerful shouts and applause. Perseus made his way through the crowds, with numerous men patting him on the back, smiled and nodded to him. Perseus was truly adored by his troops, even if he was younger than half of them.

He pulled Arsenios close and whispered, "Take me to Alexion."

Alexion was held prisoner in a tent at the other side of the army camp. He sat chained up to a large wooden stake. Pride and confidence had faded from the great general's face. He barely looked up when his captor, Perseus, entered the tent.

Come to gloat, god's son? Thought Alexion.

"Certainly, the people of Argos will welcome such a prisoner to your jail."

"I do not intend to bring you to Argos." Confessed Perseus. "You may return home. Only, give your word you will never again raise a sword against Argos."

"Such a modest punishment," Alexion replied, sounding disappointed. "And what if I go back on my word?"

"Then you would not be the man that you are said to be."

Alexion nodded in agreement. "You are just, Perseus. If Corinth had to fall, I am glad that she did to Argos."

"You fought well."

"Not as well as you." Perseus said in respect.

"You are but a boy yet to carry the weight of a kingdom on your shoulders with ease."

"Such is my fate." Perseus admitted. Then he turned to the jailer. "Bring him some food."

The guard nodded and left the tent to forage some food. He had hoped the rest of the soldiers didn't already devour the entire pig that was roasting on the spit.

"Perseus, I cannot accept your offer." Alexion declined, as Perseus quickly identified the sin of pride in his captive's voice. "I am a general; battle is all I know."

"If you refuse, I have no choice but to keep you prisoner. I implore you to reconsider."

The soldier returned to the tent with a plate filled with food. Hot, steamy pork filled the nostrils of Alexion. He briefly licked his lips and closed his eyes to envision the taste of that delectable roast.

"Every man is destined to fall." He said to Perseus. It was a grim reminder to every general and civilians alike. "He cannot choose when or how but must simply accept this."

"You bring your fall upon yourself." Perseus answered promptly. "I offer you the chance to go free. There are many pleasures in life away from the battlefield."

"And would you enjoy these pleasures, Perseus?" The young king looked to the ground, knowing the he would not. "You and I are much alike. We live in a world where we dire for glory and conquest. Take that away, and there is no joy to be had. We are simply ghosts waiting for Hades to call."

Perseus gazed upon the plate of food before Alexion. Then he gathered his thoughts for a moment. He produced a shiny knife from his robe and laid it down on the plate.

"For your supper." He said, locking eyes with the disgraced Corinthian general. They both knew what it was for, and Perseus took his leave of him.

"Perseus…" Alexion said smiling and nodding in appreciation to his better.

He stared at the knife as if it were an old friend. He saw Perseus' reflection on the flat surface. He kept watching it as soon as the Son of Zeus vacated the tent.

The sun was rising in the northern border, and Perseus thought it was going to be a beautiful day for his steed Pegasus to take flight. He mounted on top of the beautiful white horse, as Pegasus' wings were neatly folded at his side. Instead of a rough leathery saddle, Perseus used a rich blue blanket on the graceful creature's back. Pegasus' bridle was exquisite with several gold adornments sparkling in the light like miniature suns.

Arsenios and a few other palace guards sat atop their horses. They were all prepared to leave. The soldier who guarded Alexion rushed to Perseus. He was in a state of alarm.

"My Lord! My Lord!" He cried. He paused for a moment to catch his breath. "Alexion of Corinth is dead!" This news struck Perseus like one of Zeus' thunderbolts. "He killed himself with his dinner knife. Forgive me, my Lord, I was careless to leave him with such."

"It is alright." Perseus consoled his subordinate. "Have you the knife?"

The soldier looked down, feeling ashamed. "No, my Lord. I searched everywhere."

"Tis' no matter. Take care of him, and send word at once to Corinth—the people should mourn their great general."

The solider hurried away, while Arsenios handed Perseus the knife Alexion was given. Perseus took it without a word, and the men set off to Argos.

CHAPTER SIX

Hundreds of torches lit the night sky that set the city of Argos aglow. Sounds of commotion reached Perseus and his entire group.

"Have they started the celebration early?" Perseus asked Arsenios.

Arsenios shook his head in wonder. Perseus took a second to inspect the disturbance.

"The gates are closed." Perseus noticed.

Then he signalled his men to ride their horses through the now opened gates. The sight that greeted them was utmost disconcerting.

The palace guards threw open the citizens' homes in a search frenzy. Torches lined the street, while people lingered about, and whispered indistinctly. Perseus quickly dismounted Pegasus and confronted the group of guards. They quickly recognized their king and bowed down before him.

"I am sure you have good reason to break into your citizens' homes." He said firmly.

"My Lord..." Began one of the guards, but Perseus was on the warpath.

"Explain to me your orders and who gave them to you."

"Queen Andromeda—"

Before Perseus could react, his attention was drawn to a guard who had exited an Argos residence and kicked at nearby bucket in furious anger.

"He cannot have simply vanished into thin air!" He roared, with his hands balled up into fists. He ceased his tantrum to discover Perseus just several feet away from and quickly bowed.

"Whom do you speak of?" Perseus asked the angry soldier.

The guard looked over to his brothers-at-arms, wondering what to say to their king. None of them responded to his silent plea. They all began to cower when Arsenios lifted the guard up to his feet.

"Your King asked you a question. Have you not the respect to answer him?"

"Forgive me, my Lord." The guard said to Perseus. "I despise that you must hear this from one as lowly as myself—"

"Speak already!" Perseus shouted at him with such impatience and anger.

The guard took a moment to find the right way to break it to Perseus. "Prince Perses..." he finally spoke, "...is missing."

Arsenios shoved the guard against the wall, and then he brought his knife to the snivelling man's throat. "You have but a moment to explain yourself before I slice your throat for blasphemy."

The scared guard looked over to Perseus, hoping his lord would show mercy. "My Lord, please!"

"It is alright, Arsenios." Perseus said to his major-domo. "Let him speak."

Arsenios released the guard, but he was still angry. He wouldn't tolerate such incompetence, especially to something outrageous as this episode. His dagger was looking for a new sheath.

The guard held his throat and felt a small drip of blood emerging from a tiny cut. He looked at his king with great fear. "Queen Andromeda called for us not long after sunset…she could not find your son. It seems that the nurse that was tending to him has disappeared as well."

One guard cautiously knelt before Perseus. "He speaks the truth, my Lord. We have been searching since that moment! We closed the gates and are in the process of inspecting each residence. We shall not rest until we find him!"

Perseus staggered back in disbelief. He felt very faint and thought he was going to pass out. Arsenios caught him, and grabbed him tightly. Perseus couldn't breathe. It was as if some foul demon was siphoning the life out of him and there wasn't a damned thing he could do about it.

He finally managed to speak, "Arsenios, you must handle this. Do no let anyone leave Argos until Perses is recovered. I must speak with Andromeda."

"Of course, my Lord." He promised, as he slowly let go of Perseus when the king regained his strength and ran to Pegasus. "Perses will be with you by sunrise."

Perseus nodded to his most trusted friend and raced through the city streets. Countless townspeople looked at their passing ruler in fear and sympathy, but they were nothing more than a blur to Perseus. At one point, Pegasus galloped so quickly that his hooves came off the ground, giving the people a glimpse of this real power.

Perseus stopped abruptly at the front door of the palace. He rolled off the majestic creature and the guards escorted him inside.

He stormed into the master bedroom—a picture of a man in turmoil—to discover Andromeda sitting on her bed crying hysterically. She tried to hide her red face with her hands but it was to no avail.

She was a mess.

Her eyes were bloodshot and her long blonde hair was dishevelled. She was hardly distinguishable.

Perseus rushed to her side and held her close. She could feel his hands trembling. She had never seen him act this way in their entire marriage—even before then.

"How could this have happened?" He asked her. He was still in shock of this ghastly revelation.

Andromeda continued to cry, and shook her head. "I was resting, with Perses beside me and the nurse was keeping watch. When I awoke, both of them were gone." She wheezed, trying to draw another breath and paled visibly. "I have prayed to every god for mercy and that they may return Perses."

Perseus looked away from her. He had never been so angry in his whole life. He hadn't felt such pain since his mother passed away years ago. He was on the verge to summon Arsenios and lay waste to the land and the surrounding kingdoms to find his son.

Andromeda stared at her husband furiously. She gripped the bed sheets very tightly, as if she was actually choking the kidnapper. She could feel several of her nails breaking on performing this action. But the real person she was truly angry with was the man who shared her bed.

"Had you been here, you could have protected us—"

"Do not act out in spite, Andromeda." He hollered at her. This surprised Andromeda. This was the first time Perseus ever raised his voice toward her. It startled her, and she grabbed a pillow in defence. "I cannot play nursemaid and king—"

"Then how about a father?" She yelled back at him.

Her voice was cold and dead, and Perseus was startled by the change in her. She didn't sound at all like the passionate and dynamic woman he married. This outburst hurt Perseus more than any sword or arrow. She clenched her fists so tightly that Perseus could hear the nails digging into her palms.

Her voice was ringing with pent-up rage. "Instead you left yet again—"

"You knew where I was."

"Yes, where you always are! With your army!" Andromeda had never screamed at her husband before. It was the scream of a broken soul.

"Expanding your empire!" Perseus disputed. "Ensuring that our son shall become a king and never a slave."

"How noble of you." Andromeda sarcastically replied. Her anger was undiminished.

Perseus sensed her shutting down emotionally as an ominous chill came over her.

They both looked away from each other. Both of their tempers were raging. They had enough munitions to yell at each other for the whole night and the morning, too. But they both knew that it wasn't going to help in the search for Perses.

"Andromeda," Perseus said, with a much calmer tone, "you married a soldier. You cannot expect me to abandon what I have known all my life."

She hesitated, and for a moment, Perseus thought he was getting through to her. When she spoke again, he could sense that there were traces of uncertainly and vulnerability in her voice.

"You have a new life, Perseus." Andromeda was speaking with a broken heart. "Can you not see how the gods have blessed you?"

Perseus stared hard at Andromeda as time stood still. The person or persons who had transpired this transgression in the sanctity of their own home tarnished her beauty. Such a cruel deed such as this will never go unpunished. He began to march out of the bedroom.

"Where do you go now?" Andromeda asked him, feeling scared and abandoned.

He looked back at her. "To join the search for my son." He said harshly.

"You must stay." She persisted. "I cannot bear the burden of my grief alone."

"I will not stand idly, while others look for Perses."

"No!" Andromeda screamed. Her severity caused Perseus to turn fully around to face her. "I have grown tired of waiting for you to come home, Perseus. If you leave again, I shall have lost a son and a husband this night."

"Your grief makes you foolish, and you know not what you say."

"I know exactly what I say because I have had much time alone to consider it." She was aggravated from Perseus' pig-headedness and bravado. He was about to cross the line where he would lose her forever. "I have passed too many days in unhappiness."

Perseus' feelings of annoyance had been replaced by sadness. His wife needed him now more than ever, but when another minute went by the further away the kidnapper flees with Perses.

In his short young life, Perseus had no regrets. Until he decided to leave Andromeda in the bedroom alone and crying, while he organized a search party for his son.

CHAPTER SEVEN

Perseus couldn't sleep that night. All he could think about was the safety and wellbeing of his son. The moment Perses was stolen, Perseus first dreamed of fire raining down from the heavens. He had every palace guard and the city's sentries searching everywhere in Argos. From the lavish residences of the kingdom's elite to the darken alleys of the seamy slums.

Perseus, who was now displaying an icy demeanour, kept watch on top of his royal balcony. He looked over the city with a stone face. He wanted to cry, to rage, to rant and roar…but everything inside him just felt numb. There was no trace of emotion or any faults. The torches that lit Argos were dying out, and he prayed to Zeus that the sun might be much more helpful. Then he sensed Arsenios' presence.

"You did not find him." Fumed Perseus.

"No, my Lord." Arsenios remorsefully replied. "We searched everywhere."

"You must be tired." Retorted Perseus, now sounding more composed. "Get some rest."

"And you, my Lord?" Arsenios asked, studying Perseus' current state of mind. War had worn the young king down, but it seemed the theft of his new born son had aged him even more. "Should you not rest as well?"

Perseus blinked his eyes several times to keep them from drying out. They were red and glassy, and his hair was unkempt.

"Rest does not come to those with heavy thoughts." He said, brushing past Arsenios as he made his way to the stables.

He had to prepare Pegasus for departure. Once Perseus got to the stables, he threw an extra blue blanket over the horse and affixed the golden bridle. He paused for a moment while his emotions caught up with him, and then he leaned against Pegasus. Arsenios appeared with a saddle in his hands.

"My Lord, I am accompanying you on your journey."

"You know not where I am going." Perseus quietly dismissed him.

"Do you believe it was King Polydectes?"

"My heart hopes an ally would not act in such a manner." Responded Perseus, as the sound of heartache emerged from the back of his throat. "Nevertheless, I have my suspicions, but I must be sure before I act."

"And I will act with you. I have been charged with protecting you."

"I release you of your charge."

Once Arsenios heard Perseus' latest order his eyes widened in surprise. "Then I shall come as your friend."

Perseus smiled to Arsenios. “I could not ask for a better one. That is why you must stay with Andromeda.”

“She is displeased with you.”

“Are not most women displeased with their husbands?”

Arsenios looked like he was going to say something profound. But all he could muster was the sound of laughter, in which Perseus joined in with him. Then he climbed on top of Pegasus, and kicked his sides.

“She has suffered a great loss and will be angry at my departure.” Perseus spoke with a heavy heart. “You must watch over her and protect her from others and herself.”

“Yes, my Lord.” Arsenios heard and obeyed.

“Everything I hold dear, I entrust to you in my absence.”

“How long will my Lord be gone?”

Before he urged Pegasus out of the stable, Perseus answered, “Until I find my son.”

Perseus gave a gentle tap at the stallion’s sides and sent the horse galloping down the trail. He pressed his mighty steed on through the deserted streets and rode with the wind at his back while breathing in the warm, humid air. It smelled rich, familiar, with all the odours he associated with home. He enjoyed riding Pegasus and the freedom of the outdoors, but at the same time he steeled himself for the confrontation with his child’s kidnappers.

He had no idea who they were, but he would find out soon enough. He urged his mount on, and they dashed through the streets of Argos to the countryside. Hoofs drummed through the city as the folk yelled and scattered had only a fleeting glimpse of a mailed figure on a white stallion. A wide scarlet cloak flowing out on the wind followed it. For up the street came the shout and clatter of pursuit, but Perseus did not look back.

They didn’t even slow down their pace when they arrived at the gate, while the guards proceeded on opening it. Perseus urged Pegasus forward and the white stallion thrashed through the underbrush with his hoofs thundering against the turf and continued to race through onto the other side.

Perseus looked up to the heavens and began to pray. “Father, I ask for your strength and perseverance. May your light guide me.”

A cloaked figure stood at the back of a horse drawn wagon in the darkest part of the woods. His identity was hidden from head to toe. The only thing that was visible was a blue ornate ring on his finger. Out of the corner of his eye he saw a young woman approaching into a huge clearing.

Young and beautiful she carried a bundle in her arms. She frantically looked over her shoulder on each step she took. She literally jumped when she heard a strange voice.

"Were you followed?"

"No." She yapped, meeting the masked stranger. "That I am sure of. Yet I feel the eyes of the gods looking down on me in anger."

She opened her rag-covered cloak and she stood glittering in luminous azure robes made from fine silks. There was not a trace of dirt or grime on her compared to her co-conspirator. So, she stood out even further. The woman practically shone in the clearing and she was lovely. Her olive-skinned flesh was smooth and ageless. Her brown eyes were captivating, but they were filled with fear.

"They will not harm you." The man assured her.

"No," she shook her head. "I have done a great evil this night…for you."

"You knew the consequences of your actions, and yet, you are here." He reprimanded his young accomplice. "Do not hide behind the pretence of guilt, for you feel none."

The woman looked down to the bundle, pulling back a small portion of the blanket to reveal a babe's smooth little face.

"I did not…until I looked upon his face."

"And how many babes were slaughtered when Argos invaded your city?"

"Yes, but ne'er were my hands soiled with their blood. Ne'er me thinks were King Perseus'." She culpably declared.

"Your compassion has made you soft." The man remarked in such disapproval. "Go, and say nothing of your actions."

The woman tentatively handed over the pilfered child to the cloaked figure, who roughly grabbed him. The baby began to cry, as his naïve abductor did so as well. She slowly walked away, as her employer returned to his wagon.

Unbeknownst to her, a hideous wolf creature exited the wagon. The cloaked figured stood up to the monster with no fear. The huge wolf heeled and stood in attention.

The man leaned forward and whispered into its ear, "See to it that she is not troubled for too long."

The creature nodded and leaped out of the wagon. Four more followed it, as they raced through the woods. Then the man climbed into the wagon and signalled his driver to make haste.

The woman wandered through the woods with tears streaming down her cheeks. Suddenly, she heard something coming from behind her. She whipped around to see no one.

"Hello?" She said nervously.

Then something ran past the side of her.

It was a flash of both shape and odour. Something big and powerful was moving too fast to properly register. When she tried to describe the silhouette, what came out was more monster than a human being. It was the first time—the only time—that her memory failed her.

She turned to the opposite direction to see nothing there as well. She began to think all the guilt she had acuminated had finally gotten to her. She knew what she had done was wrong and nothing she could so would ever be redeemed for such an indiscretion. She must go back to Argos and confess her crimes to her King and Queen.

As she was about to head back, the sound of horrible screaming filled the forest. It sounded like a pack of wolves howling along to the souls of the damned in Hades.

"Is someone out there?" She asked again, her breathing now being painfully irregular. She scanned all around her to find nothing but trees and bushes. The ungodly sound was coming from everywhere. "Please, you're frightening me." She turned back to find her way.

And *it* was there.

She slammed into it and rebounded.

With an awful realization she knew it was circling her.

Not hunting—taunting her.

Playing with her.

The thing moved with hideous speeds and she felt lines of fire igniting along her cheek. Hot blood poured from the gashes and ran into her mouth and down the side of her throat.

The woman whirled and ran straight through the dense brush. Her legs were as heavy as iron weights but she willed her foot to move. Hope flared like a spark in the darkness of her mind and she raced toward the path she was headed. In the woods behind her she could hear the thing as it smashed through the brush in pursuit. She lifted one heavy foot over the other, but when she tried to lift the other one she simply could not. With a cry of pain and defeat she collapsed.

Then she heard the scratching of clawed feet scurrying on the dirt. The thing loomed up all huge and terrible over her and she became petrified with terror.

Then something pierced through her ears.

It wasn't the sound of wolves howling...but it was a baby crying.

The baby she stole from Queen Andromeda.

The woman's heart sank and she began to weep when the horrible crying grew louder and louder until it was the sound of a thousand crying children. She covered her ears, as the sound became more deafening but it was no use. She was plagued by the infernal castigation of listening to all those poor babies crying for their mothers that they will never see again. It was beginning to be too much for her, and then she dropped to her knees and held her head in pain.

"Stop!" She tearfully pleaded. "Stop! Please!"

The more she begged, the more the crying grew louder. She knew she deserved this, and it was a fitting punishment for such a heinous deed. She closed her eyes and saw the young Prince Perses looking at her with those heavenly blue eyes of his.

They were such trusting eyes.

And now she will never see them again—also Perseus and Andromeda would never hold their son again.

She closed her eyes to force her wits to focus on the matter at hand. She wasn't out here to gape at the mysterious wilderness or to succumb to the terrible guilt. As she came back to her senses she felt a pang in her heart. With great trepidation she turned away, moving carefully past the brush. She paused, looking first the way she'd come and then turned to pick out her path among the thick yews. The trees had long since won back the path, cracking paving stones with their indefatigable roots and spreading back wood until they wasted hard against the trees. These trees were ancient, she knew, some of them planted by her forefathers and the trunks were still reaching up from the black soil to the roof of heaven. First, she looked at one direction and then over to another until she saw the path; a shadowy tunnel formed by the overstretched arms of the trees.

She nodded to herself. That had to be the right way even through it had been so long since she'd walked these woods that it seemed entirely new and foreign. The way a child would see the forest and the way an adult remembers it are so different.

She moved forward, bending her slender body nearly in half in order to enter the tunnel of branches, within a few steps the roof of the tunnel rose in a gentle slope and she could straighten to her full height.

The corridor of yews paid out into a clearing and she stepped again to make sure she was going the right way. She squinted her eyes to make out something in the horizon—

Crash!

Something smashed through the dried bracken behind her. The woman spun and leaped to one side, her heart was racing now and it was pounding on the walls of her chest. Something moved through the brush…invisible in the woods.

"What in the name of the gods?"

Suddenly the thing burst from the bushes and drove right toward her.

She screamed in fear and raised her arm in defence. The creature flew out in front of her as she stepped back, and a laugh escaped her chest.

It was a fawn.

It was small, beautiful and fragile and indifferent to the young woman with the horrified expression on her face. It tippy-toed down the corridor of yews.

"Stupid deer." She muttered under her breath.

With a rueful smile she shook her head. She was aware that she was losing her mind, but she welcomed the increasing buffer that gave her against sickening reality. She turned and found her path. But ten steps deeper into the forest and then she lingered for a moment, looking back. As silence reclaimed the shadowy landscape the day seemed bigger, brighter, less familiar. Silence was like a dreadful presence; she could feel it watching her.

"Who's out there?" She called, but without wanting to she pitched her voice as a whisper.

Silence answered her, but she still felt as if she was being watched, as if familiar eyes were on her.

She cleared her throat and raised her voice. "Reveal yourself!" She yelled.

Nothing.

She looked up, and even though the dense ceiling of tree branches she could see a paleness like frost. Something moved behind the trees.

"What is the meaning of this?"

She tried to track it through the woods but it was already gone.

A sound made her turn and she caught another flash of it. There and gone.

Suddenly there was a blur of dark movement that slammed into her with impossible speed. As it whipped past her it made a strange ripping sound.

The impact knocked her halfway around and she stared numbly in the wrong direction, her eyes were bulging and blinking. The world dwindled down to an envelope of darkness that seemed to wrap itself around her.

She heard a soft sound, the crunch as someone stepped on wet leaves, but when she looked at the foot it was wrong.

It was so very wrong.

The creature's feet were shoeless and misshapen.

Not a human foot at all.

Not an animal either.

She raised her hand and saw the eyes of the person that was stalking her. They were large and as yellow as a harvest moon. The eyes glared at her and she felt her hammering heart suddenly go still in her chest.

Understanding struck her harder than the blow that had stalled her. She screamed, and then she ran.

Her stomach was a furnace that slashed loosely and she clamped her hands over her abdomen as she blundered through the brush. Her mind refused to accept the reality of what had been dire to her—to accept it was to allow it and she could not.

She ran. Staggering, stumbling, leaving a widening trail of red behind her. Even through the sound of her own desperate breaths and the slap of her feet on the leaves she could hear the thing following.

Not running.

Stalking.

"Hera, help me…" She breathed, but her voice was ragged and wet.

She risked a single backward glance. Just once.

And it was not there.

Sunlight had outlined the corridor of trees with a ghostly aura and nothing behind her moved except the tree branches she herself had disturbed.

The werewolves grew closer to the woman, while she caught glimpses of them surrounding her. She circled around the clearing in much vain, but no matter how hard she tried she couldn't see them.

She gasped and swayed on the spot. Her brain was telling her to run, but her legs would not move. The wolves turned and looked at her.

The ones she thought of as the animals circled her as she closed in, moving so silently through the greensward that may as well have been ghosts. The tall one—the alpha male—was waiting for her. It drew her in like a moth lured inescapably toward the flame.

She did not even sense the movement beside her. A shape passed across her face and her cheek was opened, and blood gushed onto the grass at her feet. She gasped and looked around, watching a wolf backing silently away with hunger in its eyes.

Another shape came in, and another, and every time she spun around, there was a fresh cut on her face, a gash on her stomach, and a chunk of flesh ripped from her arm.

She tried to scream, but found she could not. The breath was struck in her, the scream, hidden inside where sweet reality had long since fled.

I'm going to die, she thought. The green grass around her was speckled red and growing redder by the second. *I'm going to die here and…*

Then one of the gigantic wolves leapt out of the woods in a single bound and tackled her.

She heard the sound of her own death. She saw the flash of claws as they tore at her. She heard her clothing rip, heard the separate sounds of parting flesh and tendon, and there came the scrape of claw on bone. She heard all of this from a great distance, detached from the pain that must be coursing through her nerves. She heard, but did not feel. The tethers that held her to the broken flesh were stretching and stretching.

The wolf leaned over her and she saw those dreadful yellow eyes. She saw herself reflected there.

When it suddenly stopped tearing at her and ran away into the darkest depths in the woods. She watched as if she were only a spectator watching a gruesome play. It was not real, and this was not quite like her.

The pack of ravenous wolves stood powerful over her.

She tried to say something—perhaps a plea, or maybe a prayer—but then the claws struck her with such terrible force that the monsters' sharp nails raked across her chest and tearing her garments in a red flash. Her body shuddered as shock and convulsions burst through her nerve endings and she fell to the ground dying.

"No..." She cowered, "...no."

The pain was so vast, so monstrous, that the woman was thrust into a world of red-hot insanity. The alpha male shook its head, worrying at her, gnawing on her until finally it reared back and ripped flesh and muscle from her shoulder. Blood sprayed the wolf's face and blinded her. It splashed into her mouth and she tasted it—hot and salty, smelling of copper and fear.

But no ears other than her own heard her protest. The darkness that crept toward her from all sides was all black and infinite. The creature swallowed the meat and prepared for the final bite. The killing bite would end all of this pain and madness. The last thing she heard was the long and terrible howl of the beasts, sounds that rose from the forest into the cloudy sky. The whole forest shook with her blood-curdling scream.

CHAPTER EIGHT

Andromeda threw open the giant doors in the great hall, disrupting Phineus while he was having his breakfast. Arsenios dutifully stood at the end of the table. Andromeda frantically looked around the room in a crazed manner. She was both a physical and mental mess.

"Have you seen Perseus, Uncle?" She asked Phineus, her voice crackling. "I cannot find him anywhere."

"Nay, not since last night, after his return from the army camp." He answered, wiping his mouth with his napkin. "Are you telling me he has gone off *again*?" He sighed and sipped wine from a goblet encrusted with glitter and jewels.

Andromeda ignored her uncle's reply, and focused on Arsenios. "Arsenios, where is my husband?"

"My Queen, I know not—"

"Please!" Squawked Andromeda. "Do not try to protect him. I must know."

Arsenios lowered his eyes in shame. "He left…this morning."

Andromeda leaned on the table for support. This news hit her as hard as a punch in the stomach. Her hands started shaking and her lips were quivering. Phineus took no notice to her niece's sudden breakdown. He nonchalantly continued to eat his breakfast.

"Fine time for him to go gallivanting." The old man said sardonically, and then took a bite of warm crispy bacon.

"To find Perses, my Lady." Clarified Arsenios. "But I know not of his destination, nor how long he will be away."

"*Finally* he cares about his family." Phineus seethed. "A little late, is he not? And to leave without giving word to his Queen."

"No, Phineus." Said Andromeda. "My words were harsh. And I fear I wounded him as greatly as he had wounded me." Then she looked at Arsenios with a fretted face. "Did he go alone?"

"Pegasus is his only companion."

Andromeda pulled out a chair and took a spot at the table. "How many palace guards have we?"

Phineus raised an eyebrow. "What?"

"A hundred and twenty, my Lady." Arsenios answered.

"And what of the army?"

"Dispersing as we speak."

Andromeda drew a breath. "Who is your best soldier among them?"

"Tellus, without question." Arsenios replied.

Phineus nearly choked on his food. "A hundred palace guards?"

"And they shall set out to find Perseus." Andromeda commanded.

"Have you gone mad, woman?" Gulped Phineus. "You are leaving the palace, and therefore the city, defenceless. If Argos is attacked, she will fall."

"The grief of losing a child is unbearable, but I will not stand to lose a husband." Andromeda retorted, feeling the hole in her heart growing larger. "If any ill-will should befall Perseus, the state of Argos concerns me not."

"I worry for the people of Argos." Acknowledged Phineus, feeling the sting of Andromeda's words. "Subject to such hasty decisions made by their queen."

"Shall I ready the army, my Lady?" Asked Arsenios. "They cannot be far gone."

"No, Perseus wanted them to return home." She replied. "Let them be. Only send for Tellus."

As Arsenios took his leave to perform his queen's orders, he couldn't help to overhear her conversation with Phineus.

"I am here for you, Andromeda, unlike your husband. If you need assistance with your other…duties, you need only ask."

She achieved a small smile. "Thank you, Uncle."

Perseus and Pegasus galloped across the countryside. It twisted and turned through many forests that were more ancient than any of the races of men—both savage and civilized—who had lived there. Vast oaks with trunks as stout as stone towers; gullies that dropped away into spider-infested darkness, paths that led into the hearts of bottomless bogs.

They treaded a slow pace, but it didn't affect their will. Finally, the winged horse slowed down and started to trot. He simply could not advance any further at such a pace.

"No, Pegasus." Said Perseus, softly kicking the horse's sides. "We must get to the Granae before sundown."

Pegasus snorted in defiance. They had been on this trek all morning long and he needed to rest. Every time Pegasus tried to stop his master kept on urging him.

"I know you are tired," Perseus sympathized, "you can rest when we get there."

After trying to impulse him again, Pegasus reared and sent Perseus to the ground. He landed hard and turned to face Pegasus with an irate scowl. But it soon faded when slowly got up.

"Alright, you win." He groaned. "We shall walk."

Pegasus whinnied in approval and allowed Perseus to climb back aboard. Perseus took the bridle and let his four-legged companion have his way. They kept a very even pace, but Perseus wasn't satisfied by this turn of events.

"I know not what I did to anger my father that he should punish me though," he confided to Pegasus. He waited for the horse answer him, but they walked in absolute silence. "You have no answers?" Perseus said humorously. "I'm not surprised." Then his smile was distorted to a frown. "I do not understand his absence."

Zeus had never been so furious in his life. He burst into the halls of the Olympian palace with small crackles of electricity streaming in his eyes. Hermes meekly followed him over to Hera who looked up at them from her bed of pillows. Her servant shivered at the very sight of Zeus. He was so scared he nearly dropped the plate of fruit he was feeding her.

"You are a monster!" Zeus yelled at his wife, with outstanding rage.

"How nice to see you too, Husband." She casually replied.

"If you find fault with Perseus, that is one matter, but to attack a defenceless babe? You are—"

"Hold your accusations." She warned him sternly. "What do you speak of?"

"Do not pretend you know not what I am referring to." Thundered Zeus. He hated liars and thieves. Wife or not, Hera was going to feel his wrath. "Perses, son of Perseus, was taken from his crib."

"Sounds like a negligent mother and an untrustworthy nursemaid." Hera disdainfully replied.

"Hera, you forget how well I know. Anything to try to sabotage Perseus, especially at this hour, when you know I cannot come to his aid—"

"Sabotage?" Hera said in confusion. "You think I have more idle time that I do. Perseus has enough mortal enemies to fight; I need not get involved."

"You are foolish."

"Am I?" She said with malice. "Perseus will fail, not because of my dislike for him, but because of his own stupidity. He has made enemies when he cannot afford to." Then she gave Zeus a look of caution. "Bide your time, and you shall see."

"I may not be able to protect Perseus," he sorrowfully admitted, "but whosoever harms his family shall spend all eternity in misery."

He stormed out of the chamber with Hermes trailing right behind him. Hera was left in the comfort of her collection of soft silk pillows to digest her husband's threat.

Andromeda moved through the palace halls in a very quick pace. Arsenios and Tellus were walking on each side of her, while Phineus slowly lagged behind.

"I do not care if your horses are tired or if your men are hungry." Andromeda said bitterly to her newly appointed officer. "You do not rest until you find him, Tellus."

"Yes, my Lady." Tellus nodded.

"No matter how far you have to search, bring him home."

"Andromeda—" Croaked Phineus, but Andromeda crudely waved him off, and then stopped to face Tellus.

"I do not need to reiterate the importance of your mission?"

"No, my Lady." Tellus replied, showing her confidence in his eyes.

She was able to conjure a weak smile. "My hope lies with you." She said, before departing.

Phineus stepped forward. "I shall show you out, Tellus."

Arsenios quickly glanced over to Tellus, but he said nothing.

CHAPTER NINE

The path bent and came to an end, which opened onto another smaller valley that ended in a sheer clearing. Pine trees crowned far from the cliff that looked as short as the grass.

Perseus and Pegasus stepped at the end of the canyon. Across the valley and atop of the cliff were the ruins of an ancient temple.

Once it had dominated the cliffs and all the land around it. According to legend, there was once a vicious prince who ruled from the impregnable fortress, which extorted tribute from all who came through his territory. Now the prince and his bandits were less than a faded memory and their wealth availed them to absolutely nothing.

Perseus stared up to a craggy grey tower that loomed up into the night's sky. He hadn't been around there in years. Not since he journeyed up the mountain to speak with the three witches on how to vanquish the Kraken all those years ago.

Perseus looked over to his noble steed. "Shall we then?"

Pegasus neighed in objection, and began to back up. Perseus petted his companion gently.

"Very well." He said softly to Pegasus. "So much for my loyal companion."

Then he proceeded to climb the mountain alone. The expedition was long and gruelling. The climb was a bit more different than Perseus had remembered. The luminous moon beamed on the face of the cliff relentlessly. While scaling the mountain, the climber could feel his strength was being driven from his body. He also felt his muscles tense and sweat was flowing out of his pores. He met the mountain half way and then he briefly looked down. The highland stretched for miles and miles below. He gulped when he stared once more into the mountainside. Then his foot slipped on a rock that knocked it loose from the side of the mountain. Perseus grabbed hold of the rocks as tightly as possible as the rock careened down below, until it finally smashed against the side of the cliff.

He lifted himself back onto the tiny rock ledge. Perseus looked down at his feet and began to step slowly along the path. His hands were gripping the rocks tighter than ever.

The remnants of the temple were devoid of the magnificence that had once ruled here. The building itself was all that remained. Though cloaked in grease and soot, the columns were unbroken. They were built as a grim homage to the slave workers who had raised them. But most of the interior wall was gone, and the faint light reflected not off marble or mosaic but bare rock.

The interior was home to numerous of rats. They swarmed in front of Perseus and closed in curiously behind him. Their constant chattering sounded like running water in very old rustic pipes. They watched the intruder out of ominous red eyes. Though they smelled blood they did not try to bite.

Perseus spotted the illumination of fire up against the far wall. A crumbling assortment depicted some unwholesome rites reflected some of the glow back into the centre of the temple chamber and provided enough light to see.

Crouched around the flames were three figures.

They moved slowly.

The three old hags who lived in the tower were severely disfigured, with long sharp fingernails that were the same length of their stringy grey hair. They were all blind and they had to rely on the use of a mystic eye that they would pass between them in order to get around their shambles of a lair. The tallest witch had it now, while the others sniffed blindly in the dark. Their fingers were twitching, as if they were waiting to grab anything that passed by them.

The one with eye inhaled the air very loudly, and smile ran across her wrinkled face. "So, you return to us, Perseus?" She gleefully asked.

The heads of her other two sisters rose to attention and followed the recognizable fragrance over to the tower's entrance. Perseus emerged from his hiding place, as all the witches smiled uncontrollably.

"No longer the meagre soldier," said the one with the eye, "but a valiant king."

"My ladies, it is an honour to be in your presence." Perseus respectfully bowed.

"Let me have a look at him." Said the short fat hag, sticking her arm out for her sister to pass the eye.

The tall one relinquished the eye, as Perseus stood unaffected by this tawdry transaction.

"Is he still as handsome as he always was?" Asked the third witch.

The short one held the eye right in front of her and saw Perseus as clear as day. "Indeed." She said immorally.

The tall witch stepped forward, using her sense of smell to face in Perseus' direction. "So why is it that you have come here? You are ruler of Argos now. Surely you need not the aid of three old hags." She said modestly.

"They say the Granae see and know all things before and all things ahead." Perseus answered. "So why do you question me, when you already have the answer?"

"Still as sharp as you once were." The short one enthralling said.

"I wish to see him." Demanded their youngest sister, who still hadn't a chance to use the eye. "Be not selfish with the eye."

The short Granae handed the eye to her neglected sister. She coveted the eye with greed and held it to finally catch a glimpse of the handsome young king himself. A toothless smile stretched across her deformed face.

"You wish to know where your son is and if he is still alive." The tall Granae said to Perseus.

"I do."

"Oh, he is so fair." The youngest witch favourably stated.

"I believe I know who took him from, but I—"

"Patience, young Perseus." Said the tall witch. "What gift have you for us?"

The one with the eye saw a disordered look on Perseus' face.

"I am afraid I do not understand."

"Your father has forsaken you for a time." The tall Granae revealed to him. "Without his power, even the 'mighty' must earn our knowledge."

"Forsaken me?" Perseus said in disbelief.

"Come child, you have not seen?" Retorted the short Granae, who seemed to be growing impatient. "He answers not your prayers. Nor will he."

"What have I done to lose his favour?" Perseus asked them.

"No favour has been lost." The tall one guaranteed him. "Now, there is a Cyclops who dwells in the swamps of Tartarus. Bring us his horn, and we shall tell you who took your son."

"Tartarus?" Puffed Perseus. Tartarus was in the lowest region of the world, as far below earth as Earth is from heaven. It would take at least nine days and nights to reach the underworld. "That is a lengthy journey. Surely you would not send me on such a senseless quest with my son's life."

"You have casted your family aside before." Snapped the short Granae.

"Your son is alive, but the longer you tarry, Perseus, the cloudier his fate grows." Advised the tall witch. "I urge you make haste to Tartarus." Armed with his knowledge, Perseus began to head toward the exit. "And Perseus, without your father's grace, you are not the warrior you believe yourself to be. Take care."

Perseus nodded dutifully to the three witches and left the dingy lair.

The youngest Granae looked over to her sisters. "He best take care. It would be a pity to lose so fine a man to Hades."

Andromeda soundlessly walked down the corridor in the Palace of Argos. Her heels were clicking very lightly on the marble tiling. Her eyes were set straight ahead, her jaw clenched with determination. As she walked, a cloud of delicate perfume trailed out behind her like a luxurious silk scarf. She had spent a good hour beforehand in her private chambers, styling her glossy blonde hair and applying subtle touches of paint to hide the dark circles under her eyes so she could create a façade of mental wellness.

She was in a position of great power—the leader for her entire kingdom—and it was only fitting that she was thoroughly prepared. She smoothed down her dress as she walked, trying to protect her trademark air of self-assurance. She smiled slightly at her own fears.

When she entered the royal court, all the attendants and delegates rose from their chairs and bowed their heads to their queen. After she took her place on her throne everyone took their seats and began their daily routine on managing the kingdom and its allies. The first item on the docket was the Argos army camp outside of Corinth.

Andromeda held court in the palace of Argos, wearing a beautiful thin dress, but her face showed much concern and heartache. Phineus sat beside her, and Arsenios stood behind them.

Charon, third in command of the army, stood in front of the queen and discussed his progress. "And with Corinth completely submissive to Argos, the men ask if they may return home, to prepare for the harvest."

"What say you this, Charon?" Andromeda asked him.

"My Lady, the Corinthians knew they have been conquered. I say let the men go. Keep a small army to be safe, but there is no threat."

All the attendants and members of the court nodded in agreement.

"You bring this matter to me after you have consulted others?" She said in wariness.

Charon's expression was candid. "I wanted to be sure my request was reasonable."

Andromeda rose from her throne to address the court. "In light of Argos' success, you all forget how difficult it was to obtain Corinth. Or am I mistaken? Was the battle won overnight?"

"Andromeda—" Sputtered Phineus.

"You are not mistaken, my Lady." Said Charon. "But none would challenge the power of Argos once under her rule."

"And has any kingdom acknowledged defeat already?" Irked Andromeda.

"There are varying degrees of—"

"Has any kingdom acknowledged defeat so readily, Charon?" She screeched in resentment. She found it quite irritating that she had to repeat herself.

Charon gave a defeated sigh. He knew this was a battle he was not going to win. "No, my—"

"The soldiers stay in Corinth." Andromeda firmly commanded.

Charon bowed to her. "Yes, my Lady."

Laughter around the court caused Charon's face to turn red from embarrassment. Before he could rise, Andromeda was already out of her seat, and she was striding down the corridor. Phineus nodded to Charon sympathetically and went after her. Charon finally rose up and then approached Arsenios, as the rest of the court cleared out of the throne room.

"The men will be displeased." He said to Arsenios.

"They have been before." He replied. "You know she made the right decision. And you shall obey her, as you do Perseus."

"And where is our great king?" Charon asked with anxiety. "It has been said that he has fled Argos in shame."

"You speak dangerous words, Charon." Arsenios strongly presaged his officer. "His matters are not your concern. Be silent, and accept your Queen's command."

Andromeda stood and walked to the balcony, which overlooked the city and the sea. The setting sun reflected off the water, a thousand different shades of orange and yellow and red, casting a fiery light on the marbled exteriors of the buildings that hit the sea. She leaned on the railing and broke down into tears. She couldn't look at her kingdom while she shut her eyes with pain.

"Andromeda?" Called out Phineus.

She quickly wiped her face and took several deep breaths. "Here, Uncle."

Phineus casually walked onto the balcony with the view of politics still being flaunted on his rosy face. "As far as Corinth is concerned, I believe it would have been better to…" Then he paused. He observed Andromeda crying. He hated to see her like this. "What ails you, my dear?"

"Tis nothing." She lied. "What say you about Corinth?"

"Waste not your thoughts on Perseus; he has abandoned you."

"No, Phineus, he searches for our son." She passionately argued.

"Searches in vain." Phineus elucidated. "Can one man find that which a score of palace guards cannot? A *fool's* journey. Arsenios fills your head with stories. Andromeda, I say this as one who cares greatly for you…Perseus is not returning."

"Then I have nothing left." Andromeda whimpered.

"You have Argos." Phineus reminded. "That should be enough for a queen. Child, let your eyes not cloud with tears, lest you become blind to your blessings."

He caressed her face, in a slightly lecherous way and then headed back inside. Arsenios entered the balcony from another door.

He had heard everything.

"My Lady, do not forsake hope." He comforted her. "King Perseus shall return."

"My heart hopes your words are true, but my head is not so romantic." She said, feeling weary. Even to her ears, her voice sounded weak and insubstantial, and she hated herself for it.

"If I may, listen not to Phineus. I fear his intentions are selfish."

Andromeda looked at him with discomfort. "That is treason, Arsenios."

"If you do not agree, have me arrested." He boldly professed.

The sky grew darker and the wind began to howl. Andromeda felt the hairs on the back of her neck stand up. She was distraught, but she was determined not to show it, especially not in the face of her guards and Arsenios.

Andromeda stared at him, debating whether or not to call his bluff. Arsenios stared right back at her, never blinking or saying a word.

"I thank you for your concern." She stated, before leaving him on the balcony.

Arsenios took a moment to count his blessings and gave a sigh of relief.

CHAPTER TEN

The underworld known as Tartarus was a deep, gloomy abyss that was used as a dungeon to torment the many villains of all existence. The Titans were condemned there after losing their battle against the Olympian gods and the hecatoncheires stood over them as guards at the bronze gates. When Zeus overcame the monster Typhus, he hurled it into the same abyss. The worst of these offenders were deemed to be those who had sinned against the gods themselves. The greatest crime of all was to abuse the gods' hospitality. All the more so since to be on familiar terms with the great deities was a particular favour, reserved for the elect.

Tartarus is also the kingdom of the dead and it is ruled over by Hades. He was a greedy god who was greatly concerned with increasing his subjects. Those calling would increase the number of the dead were seen favourably. The Erinnyes—also known as the Furies—were welcomed guests. They were a group who punished crime. They would pursue wrongdoers relentlessly, until death, often driving them to suicide. Hades exceedingly disinclined to allow any of his subjects to leave. For most, life in the underworld was not particularly unpleasant. It was rather like a miserable dream, full of shadows, without sunlight or hope. A joyless place where the dead slowly fade into nothingness.

Perseus and Pegasus trudged through the swamp. Large trees with low-hanging branches adorned with moss gave the swamp an eerie feel and made Pegasus nervous. Perseus dragged him through, as he swatted many flies that swarmed around him.

The trees of the misbegotten land were twisted as if they were in pain. Their leaves were hungry for the sunlight that rarely penetrated there. The bushes were crouched low to the earth, as though if they were ashamed of what this land had made them. There were no flowers. Even the reeds and the rushes looked unhealthy.

The water moved like oil, and in some places loathsome smells rose from the bubbling pits of sludge. From time to time something hid deep in this foul landscape that would emit a challenging, lingering cry. It was a sound as devoid of beauty or grace as its gloomy surroundings.

"Come, Pegasus." He urged the horse. But the horse was being difficult again. "Wretched horse." He muttered under his breath.

Suddenly Perseus was being pulled underwater.

Pegasus reared in fright.

Perseus flew out of the water and dangled from a tree limb. His ankle was caught in a trap. He struggled to collect himself, sputtering a crude mixture of water and mud.

All he could see was a huge knife being held by a huge hand. Perseus tried to reach for his sword so he could engage in combat. But before he could do so the assailant cut the trapped Argos king loose.

Perseus looked up at his attacker to see he was the largest man he had ever seen. The man was shirtless, revealing nothing but solid muscle. He looked wild with a distrusting and unpredictable stare. But Perseus could see through the stranger like a ghost. He seemed to carry the weight of the world on his shoulders.

The man stood at six foot-five, and weighed more than two hundred thirty pounds. He was an immense man with imposing dimensions. Despite his scale-tipping weight, this stranger was no way obese or out of shape. His huge upper body emitted confidence, power, and menace—all with good reason.

"Sheath your sword." Ordered the stranger. "I will not fight you."

Through the man's voice boomed throughout the swamp, Perseus did not falter. "You have not the choice."

"You hold no challenge, as I have already defeated you." The burly man motioned to the hanging trap.

"A coward's triumph." Perseus scoffed. "Hiding snares."

"A man is entitled to protect his home." The stranger remarked. "Surely you have a method of protection in…wherever it is that you are from."

"Argos," Perseus replied, "where I am King and General."

"I always believed generals were useless without their armies."

Perseus raised his sword, beckoning a challenge. "And I always believed those who lived alone and away from humanity had something to be ashamed of."

Atlas drew his sword and accepted the intruder's challenge. "What is your name, stranger?"

"Perseus."

"Well, Perseus of Argos; prepare to admit defeat at the hands of Atlas."

Atlas charged forward, leaving a stunned Perseus no time to react. He had been waiting for a long time for a worthy opponent that he could unleash his strength upon. Somewhere that he could channel his unbridled fury.

That opponent presented himself now. Atlas swung his fist like lightning and he connected with Perseus, hitting him so hard that—in Atlas' mind—Perseus' ancestors would die.

Perseus lunged at Atlas. The strong man met the attack with equal enthusiasm, and the two of them slammed into one another at full speed.

Perseus punched Atlas as hard as he possibly could in the face. Then he swung again, and this time Atlas just managed to yank his head out of the way.

Atlas chose that moment to drive a fist squarely into Perseus' stomach. It caught Perseus by surprise, doubling him over and brought his face close enough to Atlas that the burly fellow was able to punch his opponent in the eye.

Perseus staggered and Atlas closed in for the kill.

But he was slow.

Perseus was able to sidestep him and he brought the base of his hand slamming up into Atlas' mouth. Atlas' head snapped back and he tasted his own blood in his mouth. Perseus' hand thrust forward once more.

Atlas was able to block it…just barely.

He grabbed Perseus' wrist and slammed him back up against a tree, which shuddered under the impact. They grappled for a few moments and then Perseus shoved him back. But Atlas didn't let go and together the two of them crashed into the mud.

The two were engaged in a very fierce duel. Even though the stranger was both fast and strong, Perseus had him cornered against a tree in a matter of moments.

"You fight well," Atlas professed.

Before Perseus could even respond, Atlas kicked Perseus' legs out from under him that sent him back into the swamp. When Perseus looked up, the Atlas' sword was in his face.

Then he sheathed the blade and offered a helping hand to the defeated Argos king and general. Perseus refused and got up on his own.

"But you have not the age for wisdom." Atlas continued his critique. "Go home, young King of Argos. Tartarus holds nothing for you."

"I come for the Cyclops." Perseus blatantly stated.

"He hides well." Atlas replied. "You shall not find him."

"Then perhaps you could direct me to him?"

Atlas flashed Perseus a questionable gaze. "So that you may suffer the same death as so many before you? Nay, I will not."

"Those before me were not favoured by the gods."

"And you are?"

Perseus stared back in affirmation.

The man nodded, humouring the confidence of this foolish young man. "I am intrigued and shall lead you to him."

"Your assistance is not needed." Perseus said coldly. "Simply tell me where—"

"Then I shall come for my own amusement." Interrupted the walking man mountain.

Atlas loudly whistled and a large black horse appeared from the bog. Pegasus took an immediate fancy to the dark filly, and suddenly he was bestowed with the energy and courage to continue this lengthy journey.

Perseus scowled at his steed. "Suddenly you have gotten your second wind, eh?"

The dense foliage blotted out the sun, as the two travellers came up to a massive den. Perseus and Atlas stood in front of a large cave that was dark and mystical in appearance.

It was the lair of the Cyclops.

The entrance was covered with sticks and moss, but an opening was slightly visible. Atlas motioned over to Perseus with his torch.

"There you are." He boasted, as Perseus looked up in awe.

"He lives here?" Asked Perseus.

"That he does." Atlas answered. "Shall we retreat?"

"Nay, I will fight him, and I will be victorious."

He rode over with Atlas, and then took the torch from him. Then Perseus proceeded to light the den on fire. Within moments the fire consumed the den. Atlas looked at Perseus as if he were insane. The imprudent young ruler was setting a monster's home ablaze, and in the matter of moments he was going to be torn apart by the den's owner.

The fierce roar of the Cyclops filled the whole lair. The sound bounced off the solid stonewalls and came at full force at the two mortals.

"Did you feel that?" Asked Perseus.

At first Atlas didn't know what he was talking about. But then he himself felt it too. The ground was shaking.

There was a loud tremor and it seemed as though the earth was moving—like something was taking giant footsteps.

Perseus lunged toward the silhouette in the dark cave. But the figure that arose from the shadows was no human man. The massive creature that stepped out into the blazing sunlight and it was twice as tall as both Perseus and Atlas. The Cyclops' shoulders were as broad as the width of a horse-drawn cart.

Atlas couldn't blink. The sound got louder. The vibrations felt stronger. The Cyclops was about to emerge from its shabby dwelling to face them.

"You do not know the anger you awaken." Atlas said to Perseus, who didn't show any fear or remorse.

Perseus drew his sword and stared out into the den, which was filled with billowy smoke. "Then why do you not run? He may kill you too. Are you not afraid of death?"

"There are many things more frightening than death." Atlas lectured.

Perseus was thinking about a witty comeback until he saw a huge foot emerging from the shadows and stepped out right in front of them. The Cyclops finally ran out of his hiding place.

The beast stood tall with its single eye glaring down at Perseus. It shone an eerie yellow glow that resembled a cat stalking in the night. Its upper body was very rigid like a rhinoceros' hide.

Perseus looked up at him with the creature standing well over ten feet. The colour of the skin was not a normal human flesh tone. It seemed almost translucent, shifting from orange to bronze depending how the light hit it. It was impossibly muscled. Gargantuan, muscles rippling, it was a force of nature on feet. Its toes were cloven hooves that were as razor sharp as a stag's. As the Cyclops' upper body was extremely well proportioned, it moved with a lithe, skittering grace that seemed barely human.

It roared its challenge.

Atlas' jaw suddenly dropped. Perspiration broke out on Atlas' brow, and he felt a cold trickle of fear run slightly down his back.

Pegasus bucked by the very sight of it, and then prepared for the fight, as the Cyclops gave another impious roar.

The creature took three powerful strides forward, stepping out into the open field. Its eye was darting around, seeking its tormentors. Then it spotted Perseus on the ground, Atlas beyond, and it flexed its muscles and roared with rage, ready to fight.

When Perseus was a full stride away, he leapt for the Cyclops, bringing his leg up for a high kick to the beast's throat. The Cyclops took the hit hard, but it was faster than Perseus had expected as it grabbed his foot and gave it a sharp twist.

Perseus had to roll with it or have his ankle broken. He flipped to the side and shoulder-rolled back to his feet.

The Cyclops gave out another ear-splitting roar, even more furious than ever before, as if it were angry that the powerless mites sprinted around him had dared to try and inconvenience it. It occurred to Perseus that perhaps the sudden brightness of the pyre had flash-blinded the Cyclops, at least, but that wasn't going to deter it. That was just going to escalate the problem.

He was right again.

Then the Cyclops charged, counting on its brute strength to put an end to Perseus.

Pegasus skilfully maneuvered around the hulking monster, as he distracted him while Perseus began stabbing the Cyclops in the legs. The Cyclops snarled, but not in pain—only in frustration. Finally, he took a swing and knocked Perseus off of Pegasus.

Perseus fell hard into the swamp, and lost his sword.

The Cyclops stomped toward him, as Perseus searched for his sword in vain. The beast's eye narrowed, and its lips drew back revealing snarling teeth set into shimmering pink gums.

Without hesitation Perseus launched himself toward his enemy. He drew back his fist to deliver a knockout blow. His tightened knuckles flew at the Cyclops, who caught it easily with its bare hand, and squeezed it until the bones grounded together.

Grunting, Perseus attempted a gut punch with his other fist, but the monster effortlessly blocked the blow.

Then the Cyclops took its massive and powerful hand, and proceeded to push Perseus underwater. The beast tightened its grip around the warrior king's neck, as Perseus began to drown.

Perseus felt the dampness over him a weight as the water seeped into his bones, pulling him down to its icy depths. He pulled out a dagger from his side and stabbed the massive hand. But it didn't faze the oversized cretin, but only escalated the problem.

The world spun and Perseus' descent quickened as numerous images flashed in his mind. All of his earliest memories were as sharp as life.

As the Cyclops shoved Perseus further underwater, an arrow flew through the air, and it pierced the Cyclops in its eye.

It howled in pain and fell toward Perseus, who scrambled to get out of the way. He was too slow, and the Cyclops landed on him—dead.

Atlas lowered his bow and rushed over to the pond. He reached underwater and pulled up Perseus, who was gasping for air.

Then Perseus' eyes opened and he plunged out of the water. Ripples spread, then stilled before he broke the surface. Wheezing very heavily and painfully, Perseus stared up at Atlas—the man who had just saved his life.

"And you say the gods favour you?" He snidely asked Perseus. "You are mistaken my friend!" Then he let out a thriving chortle.

Perseus looked down, realizing how true this was. "I am indebted to you. I was not prepared—"

"You lacked your army, general." Atlas retorted.

Before Perseus could answer, Atlas swung his sword down. With that one stroke of his glimmering blade, he lopped off the Cyclops' horn and presented to Perseus.

"I believe you came for this."

Perseus took the horn from the Atlas' hand. "You are a gifted warrior. How did you come to Tartarus?"

"It was the only place that would have me, that did not know my name and did not know what I had done."

"You were banished for a crime?" Asked Perseus.

"I chose to leave." Atlas said abruptly. "And you? Why is a great king so far away from his city—and alone?"

"I chose to leave also." Perseus permitted to his brawny ally. "I search for my son. He was taken from me."

"Do you know who took him?"

"I have an idea, yes."

"That is good." Atlas said with contentment. "He shall soon suffer as you do now."

"Yes, he shall." Perseus grimly replied.

CHAPTER ELEVEN

The day was yet very early. The purple haze and a yellow streak in the sky proclaimed the sun was up. The skylark soared aloft, its song faded in the distant clouds, and the woods resounded with joyous bird-notes.

Perseus rose from his makeshift bed to greet the day. He was ready to continue on his quest. He climbed on the back of Pegasus and looked over to Atlas.

"You will not accompany me?" Perseus asked.

"I am not one of your soldiers, Perseus."

"Then come as my friend."

"I cannot." Atlas flatly refused. "I wish you well in your search. You shall find your son."

Perseus nodded to his new friend and rode off into the countryside.

As Perseus rode further, he heard a noise coming from behind him. He turned around, and he saw a large black horse galloping up to him. Perseus gave himself a smile.

Atlas finally reached up to Perseus, and then drew Pegasus to a walk.

"For my own amusement." Said Atlas jovially.

They both smiled at each other, and then urged their horses to take off in blurring speed.

Night had fallen on Mount Olympus. Zeus and Hermes sat in candlelight, as they held a secret meeting from the rest of the gods.

"Is there nothing that can be done?" Zeus whispered to his trusted advisor. "Can this agreement not be broken?"

"As lord over all, your will shall be followed, but you will lose much admiration."

Zeus waved his hand. "You are right, you are right, Hermes. I must simply watch as Perseus struggles."

"Unless…"

This caught Zeus' attention. "Go on?"

"Hera said nothing about communicating with your son." Stated Hermes.

"I cannot go down there."

"Not you, my Lord." Hermes schemed.

Zeus thought about it for a moment, and then he caught onto Hermes' plan.

* * *

The tallest Granae, now in possession of the eye, smiled at Perseus as he presented her with a cloth bag. Inside it was the horn of the Cyclops they had requested.

"It was difficult for you to obtain." She said to Perseus.

"And yet you hold it in your hands." He impatiently replied. "Now, I beg you, tell me who took my son."

Perseus leaned forward to hear what information the old hag was holding out. He deserved the answers on what he had to go through in order to pay the price.

"Princess Diona of Jobba acted as Perses' nursemaid, only to steal him from his bed whilst Andromeda slept." The Granae finally disclosed.

"Princess Diona?" Perseus replied in bewilderment. "I do not know her. Why would she—"

"Go and ask her these questions yourself." The tall old crone interjected, and showed him to the door.

Still confused, Perseus obliged the tall Granae and went on his way. Once he scaled back down the mountain he saw Atlas, who was waiting with the horses.

"We go to Jobba." Perseus said to him.

Atlas nodded and they saddled up on the road to Jobba.

Hera lounged amongst her attendants in the palace on top of Olympus. She saw Thetis entering the room, and noticed she was nervous. Upon seeing her, Hera raised her hand and the attendants left the private chamber.

"What news have you for me?" She asked Thetis.

Thetis hesitated for a moment. But the glare from her queen's eyes forced her to regretfully answer, "My Lady, Perseus has defeated the Cyclops."

"Impossible." Gasped Hera.

"Perhaps he does not need his father's help after all?"

Hera shot her a look, and Thetis looked to the ground in shame. "Do not be naïve, Thetis." She scolded the Goddess of Nature. "Of course he does. And yet, I can do nothing about it, for I am closely watched." Then she paused, as a sly grin spread across her beautiful face. "But you, he would never suspect you, Thetis?"

Hera was right. Thetis made a terrible habit on spying on Perseus from up in the heavens. And as she did so, she angrily thought of the punishment Zeus had inflicted on her own son. But there was little she could do about it because Perseus' future was now in the hands of chance.

She would love to use Zeus' amphitheatre of life again, and this time she would send Perseus to the ends of the earth with no way of ever returning. However, her powers were actually a pale fraction of Zeus' own. But there was the amphitheatre, of course. Thetis would give just about anything to saunter over to that little toy model and break that little statuette in Perseus' likeness in her bare hands. But it would truly bring the anger of Father Zeus down upon her.

If she wanted to fulfil her quest for vengeance, she would have to turn to other nefarious characters to succeed, and to promise her plausible deniability.

"What would you have me do?" Thetis asked softly.

Hera gently approached her and whispered, "Go to those who are loyal to you. Tell them they now serve you and your Queen."

Andromeda awoke from a deep sleep to find Phineus sitting at the edge of the bed, watching her. A nurse and two guards stood right behind him.

"Uncle?!" Andromeda wheezed in terror.

"I worry for you, Andromeda." Phineus said caringly. "You are restless, even in your sleep."

"Perhaps it was because of my audience." She conjectured. "I assure you I am fine."

"You are not, child." Phineus continued. "You do not sleep, you do not eat, and you pace through the palace halls like a lost soul."

"Uncle that is not—"

"I understand why." He interjected. "You have lost a child and a husband. That I cannot help you will. But I will not let you lose your kingdom. The people need their queen to be strong. To protect them. And there are some that feel you are not capable."

"Who might those be?" Andromeda curiously asked.

"It does not matter." Phineus quickly dismissed her query. "I shall handle them. I am here to help you, Andromeda."

"You are?" She said in amazement. "Here to help?"

"Of course. *Now*, your nurse has prepared a tonic. It will help you sleep."

Andromeda nervously sat right up and saw a goblet in her nurse's hands. "I am well rested. I do not need your tonic."

"You act like a child." Huffed Phineus. "So defiant."

He wiped a stray strand of hair away from her face, and smiled on her lovingly. He then turned to the nurse and reached for the tonic.

"Phineus—" Whined Andromeda, until her uncle roughly grabbed her face and forced her to drink the strange smelling fluid. She began to bat at his arms, but it was to no avail.

"Shhhhh…" Phineus hushed her as if she were a baby.

Andromeda was choking on the tonic, but Phineus held her tight. Within moments she fell back into his arms until she seemed to be lifeless. He eased her back down onto the bed and kissed her neck.

"Sleep well, my love." He whispered ever so tenderly. Once the bedroom door had closed, Phineus turned to one of the guards. "Do not let anyone enter. The Queen needs her rest."

"Yes, my Lord." Said the guard, escorting Phineus out of the bedroom.

Then Phineus turned to the other guard. "And see if Charon has left for Corinth. If he is here, I wish to speak with him."

Arsenios entered the hallway. "He set out this morning."

"I am sorry to have missed him. I only sought to wish him well on his journey."

"It is one he has made before."

"Very well then." Phineus nodded and then proceeded down the hall.

Arsenios watched him go and then he looked back to the bedroom door.

CHAPTER TWELVE

Perseus and Atlas yielded their horses, as they looked down on the city of Jobba.

"Shall we be welcomed or scorned upon our arrival?" Atlas asked his companion.

Perseus confidently replied, "Jobba is under Argos' rule."

"Therefore scorned." Atlas sighed, and then drew his sword.

"Sheath your weapon." Perseus ordered him. "They have flourished under our guidance and are grateful."

"So grateful that their princess snuck into your home and stole your child?" Atlas sneeringly remarked.

Perseus glared at him, but noticed that Atlas was now looking past him down the road. Perseus turned his head to see a beautiful young woman walking up the path, carrying a clay pot. She staggered in the heat, as her face brightened when saw the men.

Perseus quickly looked away and backed to his friend. "Come, Atlas."

The strapping man ignored the King of Argos. His attention was fixated on the approaching stunning creature. "Good day to you." He said to her politely.

The woman gave Atlas a modest smile, but nary any reply.

"What is your name?" Pressed Atlas.

"I am called Kallipso." She answered, her voice chimed into Atlas' eyes like it was sweet as bells.

"And you are from Jobba?" Atlas said it with a smile. It was the kind of harmless flirtation a convalescent can get away with, but Kallipso blushed all the same.

"Yes."

"What errand brings you this far from the city?" Perseus asked her, while taking control of the conversation.

"The river that runs through Jobba is dry." She confessed, holding her pot for him to see. "I come in search of fresh water. Alas, I did not find what I was searching for. When I heard your horses, I hoped perchance for a ride back to Jobba, as the day is hot and still long."

Perseus looked over to see Atlas who was enthralled with her ravishing beauty. Then he said to Kallipso, "I regret we have no horses to spare."

"Pay no heed to King Perseus." Atlas intermittent. She was the most beautiful thing he had ever seen. She was even the more stunning than all of the women in his entire life. He couldn't help staring. "You may ride with me, lest you die out here in the heat."

Perseus softly glowered at the strongman, but Atlas countered with a low growling snarl.

"King Perseus?" Kallipso asked in astonishment, and then she quickly kneeled before him. "Forgive me, my Lord. I was not aware that I was in your presence. It shall be an honour to walk before you and announce your arrival to Jobba, if you would grant it?"

"Nonsense, you shall ride with us." Atlas insisted.

"Atlas," Perseus softly said, "I do not believe that is wise—"

"I do not take orders from you." Atlas viciously snapped at him. Atlas leaned over to pull Kallipso up onto his horse. "It is not safe for a woman to travel the roads alone."

Kallipso flashed him a smirk. "Oh, I am not alone."

She let out a hideous shriek that would render any man deaf within a full-mile radius. Sweat protruded through her brow, as her face began to melt.

The horses reared back in fright, while the men froze at the girl's torment. She fell to the ground and held herself in pain. Perseus could hear the bones underneath her skin cracking and the cartilage reforming in a throbbing horrible reconstruction.

The woman almost burst out laughing. The moment had gone through drama nearly to tragedy and was now transforming mid-scene into a farce.

Kallipso was now kneeling on her belly, and Atlas saw two bulging nubs on her shoulder blades. They became larger and larger, like she was giving birth to something out of her skin. Then they burst right out of their back.

A pair of wings had sprouted out of her back!

Then her thighs contorted and her legs bent backward to give them an appearance of a bird's. Her toenails and her digits stretched out in to sharp talons.

By the gods! Perseus mentally exclaimed. *Was this much excruciating when Father turned Calibos into that repulsive being?*

Kallipso's face was now hollowing out. Her teeth became jagged and the pupils of her eyes became reptilian slits. They blazed with yellow fire and her smile revealed teeth that had suddenly grown long and sharp, and hungry.

She turned in to a harpy!

With a revolting shriek, she sliced Atlas across the chest with her knife-like fingers. Perseus drew his sword, and then saw a flock of six more harpies descending upon them.

They were all aware of was the metronomic beat of the harpy's wings as they grabbed great gouts of air and thrust out behind her. The feeling of her climbing ever higher and rushing ever faster through the afternoon sky excited her. The wind rustled across her face, which was flushed with the terrific demands.

Her heart pounded in her chest. Blood was rushing through her body like rivers of molten flame that sent her from crown to toes to the tips of her fingers—or in this case talons.

Atlas grappled with the demonic Kallipso, while he desperately tried to get his sword. Perseus quickly came to his aid and started slashing at the flying monsters. All of them gave the Son of Zeus a terrible shrieking that made his ears bleed.

Perseus used his shield to protect himself while he fought the harpies. One of them gnashed its teeth and emitted a hideous scream. It turned toward Perseus as if it meant to snap its bloodied fangs down on his throat.

But he managed to veer his body away from its cruel, hissing mouth. Then he lunged his sword through the centre of its chest and it gave out a wicked yell, and then started to spasm.

When he finally managed to kill one, he was shocked to discover the blood that stained his sword was black and rough like tar. Pegasus bucked up to the air, as the hideous birds pecked and sliced at him. Blood was being smeared all over his beautiful white coat.

After a gruelling battle with Kallipso, Atlas was able to pull out his sword. Once Kallipso caught a shimmering glimpse of the blade she flew back in defence.

Then a large shadow flew over them. Not only this startled the men but also the harpies as well. Perseus leapt off Pegasus and gazed up at the anomaly. He was prepared for another small army of monsters, but then he found himself smiling.

A large bronze owl descended down from the sky. It was no ordinary owl, but a metal one in fact. It had blades for talons and its eyes were a pair of whirring irises. As it flew down to slice through a harpy it gave out a whistling battle cry. An arc of black blood sprayed at Perseus and Atlas.

"What in the gods?" Asked Atlas, wiping the disgusting fluid off his face.

Perseus's smiled never disappeared. "Bubo!" He said thankfully.

Kallipso used this distraction to attack Atlas.

He ducked, and then she headed for Perseus. With a quick turn, the young king dodged her.

Frustrated with her miss, Kallipso left herself open for a counterattack. Her recklessness came with a hefty price. Perseus seized this window of opportunity to cut her wings off.

She fell to the ground, and shrieked in pain. Tears were gushing from her eyes, sobbing hysterically that he took away the one thing that made her special from everyone else.

Bubo struck at a few more harpies, however, with their leader defeated, the others fled.

Perseus smiled up at his mechanical avian friend, when he came to rest in a tree beside him and Atlas. "Good to see you again, my old friend."

Bubo tweeted happily in a series of harmonically sounded chirps and motorized whirls.

"You are familiar with him?" Atlas asked Perseus, sounding very flabbergasted.

"He belongs to my father."

Atlas raised his eyebrows, as he wiped the sweat and blood from his forehead. "You live a very strange life, King Perseus. Bronze owls, winged horses—what other strange creatures have you."

Perseus turned his attention to the writhing Kallipso. Without her wings, she had no way of escaping them. Perseus stood over her with his sword in his hand. He pulled the blade back over her head, preparing the killing stroke. Kallipso closed her eyes in fear, with tears streaming down her deformed face.

"Stop!" Cried Atlas, ceasing Perseus from carrying out the execution. "Let me, please."

Perseus relented immediately as Atlas rushed on over, brandishing his sword.

Kallipso slowly changed back into her beautiful human self with not as much pain as it took for her to change into that gruesome beast. She curled up in a ball, like a defenceless baby and cowered about her forthcoming fate. She hid her face inside her eyes bawled uncontrollably. Atlas looked down upon her with such pity. His furious expression had softened. He felt absolutely sorry for her.

"Atlas…" Perseus prodded. He looked at his eyes—something was strange about them. He suddenly felt that the harpy had enchanted him with some sort of hypnosis or excreted some kind of pheromone that affected the senses of men.

"I cannot." Atlas crumbled under emotion, lowering his sword.

He looked at Kallipso in awe. Her bosom was heaving, and her eyes went flashing. Fierce fingers of wonder caught at Atlas' heart. She was slender, yet formed like a goddess: at once lithe and voluptuous. Her rich black hair, black as the night itself, fell in rippling burnished clusters down her supple back. Her dark eyes burned on him.

Perseus sighed and took his place once again, towering over the helpless demon with his sword in the air. "Then I shall—"

"No!" Atlas exclaimed, grabbing Perseus' arm with his huge mighty hand.

"We must!" Perseus asserted angrily. "She will only attack us again."

"I shall watch her." Debated Atlas, who sounded like a child who had just brought home a stray dog and he was trying to sway a parent's approval.

"You are mad." Perseus contended with a passion. "She is a monster—a wild creature. A harpy will never before a man in honesty." Then he looked down to her to see she was still grovelling for life. "She does not deserve to live, Atlas."

"Neither did I." Perseus' muscular friend replied.

"You have become my friend, and for that I am grateful. But your foolishness endangers our lives. That I will not tolerate."

Perseus sheathed his blade and then mounted on top of Pegasus. He gave Atlas a very stern look, and then turned his head to face the city of Jobba. With the kicking of his heels, he set forth to conclude his venture.

Atlas watched his friend go, and then he noticed Bubo was staring at him. The dome of the owl's expressionless face wasn't giving any sense of emotion. But Atlas could hear several angry responses in the guise of bells and whistles.

"What are you looking at?" Atlas said to the oversized judgmental contraption.

Bubo chirped at him obscenely, and then proceeded to fly after Perseus. Atlas shook his head, and turned to Kallipso, offering her his hand.

"Come." He said to her. "I shall not hurt you."

Kallipso nervously accepted his hand and looked deeply in his eyes. She could feel a spark igniting in every fibre of her being. He went out of his way in order to save her—after what she had done to him and his friend. She asked herself on how it was possible for someone to feel such romantic feelings for a despicable creature like herself. Then she quickly remembered the verbal exchange between him and Perseus.

What did he do to make him feel that he didn't deserve to live?

Then she was recapped by an old saying: misery loves company.

There they were—two kindred souls from two different backgrounds. One of them was a mortal and the other was a demon. They were definitely going to turn some heads when they arrive in Jobba.

Aphrodite was lying in the garden with her lover Diamon, whispering affectionately into his ear. From the moment he first saw his mistress, with her long, gleaming blonde hair hanging all the way down her back, Diamon wanted her. He always had a fancy for women with gorgeous hair, and Aphrodite had a passion for showing hers off. She tossed her head when she laughed, letting the light glint off her shining tresses as she leaned backward, her hair forming a beautiful cascade that had Diamon completely enthralled.

When Aphrodite was looking for volunteers to tend to her lovely garden, Diamon didn't hesitate at all. They spent the whole morning flirting and, occasionally kissing before it was time for a rest. Their liaison was also dangerous, but also thrilling with the fear of getting caught. Diamon continuously looked over his shoulder to see if Zeus was lurking about. To the king's knowledge Diamon was appointed to weed and nurture the vine, but all he did all day was play in the garden.

Aphrodite sank down onto Diamon as her hair caressed his cheek. Leaning backward, she nuzzled her face into his, her locks practically covered Diamon while he arched up against her.

Before they could advance any further in their romantic seclusion, the young man cringed in fright of Hera standing over them. Her arms were crossed and impatience manifested her face.

"My Queen…" He gasped, backing away from Aphrodite.

Diamon was discovered in a very compromising position with one of Hera's beautiful daughters. And he knew the severe punishment for committing such a lecherous affair. He feared Zeus more than he did the queen. But he couldn't deny his mistress Aphrodite's sensual requests.

Hera looked at Diamon hardheartedly. The young man feared the next thing that was going to come out of her mouth would be the harsh sentence she would bestow upon him.

"You," Hera finally spoke, sending a chill down Diamon's spine. "Leave us."

It took a moment for Diamon to process his queen's command, and then he slowly backed away from Aphrodite and shivered to his feet. He briefly stumbled, like a fawn that was learning how to walk for the first time, then he finally found his balance and ran off before Hera could change her mind.

Aphrodite looked over her shoulder to see Hera. "Oh, Mother, why do you torment me so?" The Goddess of Love moaned in annoyance. "And I liked him, too. You are so much worse than Father Zeus."

Aphrodite hated to be interrupted from her playtime. She had a tiresome day of arranging marriages and creating new relationships for the lovers all over the mortal world. All she wanted was a little pampering. But Hera was still her queen and she needed her services.

Aphrodite was waiting for a witty retort from her mother, but Hera's face was consumed with such anxiety.

"I must speak with you." Hera said to her urgently.

CHAPTER THIRTEEN

Drums and horns filled the main square of the fair city of Jobba. Many people came out of their stores and homes to catch a glimpse of their long absent ruler. For most of the way Pegasus' hooves thudded dully on hard-packed dirt. But when they began clattering on stone, Perseus glanced around the heart of the city and slightly shuddered by the sight of the large number of palace guards waiting for them. Despite they all bowed like the other peasants, Perseus, however, could feel their disdain and resentment toward him.

The village of Jobba was small and rustic. Nothing seemed to have changed in the last time Perseus had visited this kingdom. The thatched houses still sat at odd angles to the road as if the inhabitants didn't want to be reminded that their neighbours were a short stone's throw away. Gardens were well tended and embowered by low stonewalls overgrown with a creeping vine, and smoke drifted prosaically from each chimney. As the soldiers led Perseus into town, he caught the eye of several villagers, some of which tapped their companions to notice their ruler had returned.

There was an indisputable strangeness in Perseus which something frightened people who met him. He gave the impression of someone who did not think logically, but with all his senses.

Perseus tried hoisting a genial smile onto his face, but the scaffolding of grief wouldn't support it and each grin collapsed into a brooding scowl. It was all the same to the villagers, who give him only calculating stares and suspicion.

Atlas couldn't take his eye off the strange mechanical device that flew like a real owl. He wanted to know what kind of dark magic was used to bring such a thing to life. Then he realized the only logical reason was this bizarre owl was actually created by the very gods.

When Perseus was off on his journey to seek counsel from the Stygian Witches Zeus ordered Athene, the Goddess of Knowledge, to give Perseus her owl Bubo so it can supply him with advice when it would be required. However, Athene refused to part with her wise lifelong companion and had Hephaestus create a mechanical clone of her beloved pet. The idea of thwarting her father's command without disobeying it was too tempting for the slightly mischievous Hephaestus to decline. He worked with all his skill and speed to finish the task before anyone else might learn of the intended deception. Bronze and iron were no substitute for feathers, but Hephaestus was very proficient and ingenious.

In place of feathers Bubo boasted rectangular metal plates, which overlapped his wings and they were very highly polished. Tubular legs ended in metal talons, and the great rounded eyes flashed and spun with energy derived from a non-biologic source. They gleamed bright red, like tiny windows in the night. Bubo's body clanked perceptibly when he moved and the sound he made was cousin to a normal owl call. But it was much throatier and decidedly metallic.

"Perseus," Atlas called and pointed to Bubo. "What is that creature flying over us?"

Perseus looked up into the sky and waved for Bubo who was hiding under the sun.

"Bubo! Come down here now."

Bubo sliced through the clouds and appeared once more. He shimmered in the rays of the sun as he once more was visible to all the people in the crowd who were watching the travellers passing through the city square.

Atlas watched, amazed at the sight of this mechanical wonder.

"Who is Bubo?" Asked Atlas.

"My owl." Perseus replied. "He is mechanical and helps me in my times of need, just as I am on finding my son. Bubo's a marvel, but don't tell him that. His ego will grow to an unbearable size."

Bubo landed on top of Perseus' shoulder and clicked and whirred.

"When he is ready, Bubo will show you something that no other owl—no other kind—can do."

Bubo began to slowly hover above both Perseus and Atlas. The bronze owl's head was spinning around in circles.

The children in the crowd were all clapping and laughing in delight. Never in their young lives that they have witnessed such a spectacle. Bubo zipped past them as he sang a merry medley assortment of harmonic clicks, whirls, and chirps.

Perseus looked on, smiling. "That's not all. Keep watching."

The bronze owl stopped spinning his head around and rocketed quickly to the sky. All eyes continued to watch Bubo as he nearly broke the sound barrier as he soared up to the heavens.

"And here's the best part." Perseus told his brawny ally.

Bubo shined brighter than the sun as he got closer and closer to his friends below. Perseus stood perfectly still as Bubo entered his line of sight.

"Here he comes."

Bubo stopped immediately before standing on the top of Perseus' head. The people in the crowd shouted and applauded at this fantastic sight. They all began to chant Perseus' name as their ruler smiled broadly.

Humour briefly saved him. It was always there, flickering into life at unsuspected moments. He was amused with the world and with himself. Often his humour took form of complicated evasions of the troubled times that he had recently endured.

Atlas stared at the bronze contraption with such scrutiny. Bubo crept off Perseus' head and then perched on his broad shoulder. The owl shifted his head over to Atlas. The irises of his huge eyes were fixated on him. Bubo couldn't smile, but all he could do was chirp a friendly hello.

Atlas looked over to Perseus, an awestricken expression occupied his face. "You live a very strange life, Perseus." Then he looked at Bubo, who was bobbing his head. "And have very strange friends."

Bubo responded with a flat disgusted tone. Atlas stared in wonder as Bubo spread his beautifully crafted metal wings. They creaked slightly. Then the wings became a blur while a loud humming resounded, and the marvellous manifestation shot skyward with a speed no flier of flesh and bone could have matched. Perseus looked on to see his friend soaring higher than ever before until he had vanished from sight.

"Was it something I said?" Atlas asked Perseus.

As Pegasus walked through the several guard formations, Perseus looked up to the palace to see Queen Leda standing in her balcony. She was a young ruler, but the years of reigning over Jobba had aged her several years. Perseus quickly dismounted his horse and climbed up the stairs to greet her. A group of guards stood watch around the Queen.

In person Queen Leda was even more beautiful than the townspeople had suggested. She was young and lovely in a way that made all of the goddesses Perseus had worshipped suddenly seem plain. Her fair skin was not the product of powder and paint, her cheekbones were sharp and angular, and her eyes were bottomless. They were ice blue with an equally dour demeanour. She was dressed in a thin elegant gown, but it was beautifully cut and did nothing to divert Perseus' attention from her beauty.

"Queen Leda..." Perseus began, but was taken aghast by her security detail. "It seems Jobba is ruled with a tight fist, not the way I had intended."

"Regretfully not all cities are as obedient as Argos, King Perseus." She replied. The tone in her voice was quite aloof. "To what do we owe the honour of your presence?"

"Tis an urgent..." He started to answer, but paused again due to the imposing armed squad. "And private matter to be discussed only with you and your King."

"I'm afraid Manasses is no longer with us." Leda regretfully reported. "He now holds court in Elysium."

"I am sorry for your loss." Perseus said dolefully. "He was a good man."

"Yes." She spoke sombrely. "A private matter, you say?" She asked, motioning Perseus to enter the palace.

Both he and Leda walked through the dimly lit corridor. It was a bit unnerving and Perseus felt his skin crawl. At first he thought Leda was going to spring a trap on him in some form of coup d'état. But then he realized if this were indeed a devious plot, he would have been killed on sight as soon as he first set foot on

Jobba. All he wanted were answers to the whereabouts of his son, and prayed to Zeus it didn't lead into some outrageous political incident.

"It involves your daughter, Diona." Perseus finally spoke. "Is she here?"

"What do you know of my daughter?" Twitched Leda.

"Nothing." Perseus replied, taking notice of his hostess' sudden change in behaviour. "I seek only answers from her."

Leda muddling stared at him. "Answers?"

"The Granae told me that she is responsible for the disappearance of my son."

Leda stopped their trek and gawked at him very hard. Perseus could tell she was highly offended by the expression on his face. Her eyes narrowed in contempt against him. Then he observed her tiny hands forming into fists. Her knuckles were turning white.

"You have not set foot in Jobba since the day you conquered it." She gruffly reprimanded him. "And yet now you ride into our city accusing my daughter of such an action?"

"I ride into *my* city, searching for your future king." Perseus abrasively retorted, stepping closer to her. "I urge you not to forget that you only hold the title of queen because I was gracious enough to let you keep it."

Leda's throat was jumping, like she was drowning and desperately searching for air. Her eyes widened in terror and felt her heart skipped a beat. This wasn't the same subjugator that took her late-husband's kingdom from him. She was talking with a totally different person.

"Forgive me, my Lord." She curtsied, paying tribute to Perseus. "Sorrow clouds my mind."

"Sorrow?" Perseus said in bewilderment. "What ails you?"

"It is the very one you wish to see." Leda declared, leading Perseus in front of a door with two armed guards standing watch. She waved to them to let her and Perseus through, and they swiftly obliged.

Inside the bedroom was a collection of attendants in each of the four corners, while several nurses and doctors quietly confer. All eyes were fixated on a young woman whose arms and legs were bound to the bed, as she gave out terrible gut-wrenching moans.

Perseus stared down at her in shock of confusion. Her features were sunken and hollow—numerous cuts and claw marks were all over her face and body as if she were involved in a horrifying animal attack. She was hardly recognizable. The gashes were so deep that they will leave permanent scars. But her mind was beyond repair.

Perseus examined the poor woman closely. He knew her from somewhere, but he couldn't remember where. He carefully strode closer to the bed, but was taken back by the agonizing howl the girl made when one of the nurses was cleaning one of her open wounds.

"Diona!" Perseus cried, recognizing the victim.

Some terrible and savage claw had eviscerated Diona. The flesh of her belly had been slashed as if by swords, but the tears were much too jagged to have been made by edged steel. These were definitely claw marks, but nothing short of a lion or a bear could do such horrible damage. Diona's skin was bloodless and white and hung like strips of canvas, and in the gaps of the wound Perseus could see striated muscle and jagged ends of shattered ribs.

She should be dead. Her wounds were terrible, her bed beneath her where she'd lain was soaked with blood, and the bandages the palace's attendants had put on her were already drenched.

Her features were drawn, her skin was grey and it was also streaked with sweat and gore, her eyelids fluttering open every now and then but there was no sense or understanding in her eyes. Diona was dying—should *be* dead.

Unnatural wounds. Thought Perseus. *They are most unusual. Some feral creature made these lacerations. She wasn't attacked by any mere animal.*

"She did flee Jobba." Leda told him. "The guards did not see her, and I did not realize her absence until the morning. I sent an army out to find her…" she briefly paused and fought back tears, "…and find her, they did." Leda mellifluously wept. "They found her hanging from a tree—her limbs were tied to different branches. She had such beautiful skin—blessed by Aphrodite Herself…but now…"

She winced by the sight of her daughter's current condition and it broke her heart. Perseus put his hand on her shoulder and she embraced him.

"I cannot imagine what my daughter did to deserve such treatment, but every day I pray that she dies, so to free her from the evil that has overtaken her."

She let go of Perseus and looked down at her daughter. Leda felt something had taken her breath away, as Diona looked at her weakly. She had all the power in the kingdom but still felt so damned helpless. Perseus expression changed into a sign of sympathy. He felt terrible about what had happened. Leda's daughter was dying and his son was missing.

Diona could not have been the mastermind behind this plot. He thought, staring at the girl's gruesome injuries. *She was merely the accomplice, and whoever devised the kidnapping needed to silence her because she knows his true identity.*

Leda said to Perseus, "Perhaps this monster that has infected her did steal your son, but not my Diona…"

The princess moaned again, this time letting out heart-wrenching sobs. Her whole body convulsed then lied limp. The outburst startled Leda, rushing to her daughter's side. She knew it was time for Diona to go.

Perseus knelt beside her and looked at her with soul full eyes. "Diona?"

"She is unresponsive and has not uttered a single word since her return." Leda vindicated.

Perseus took Diona's hand in his. Tears were forming in his eyes. She was his only clue to his son's whereabouts.

"Diona, tell me, did you take my son?"

"King Perseus, please…" Leda begged him not to press any further.

"Diona, I must know." He pressured the dying princess. "Did you steal him?"

Diona began to moan.

It was sad and low.

She seemed to be very cognizant of the situation. She gruellingly tried to keep her eyes open to face King Perseus—the man who she had wronged. Her beautiful brown eyes were round and moist, and they were also glassy as marbles. They struggled to focus on Perseus—the father of the baby boy she had stolen was just several inches away from her. Tears of pain and anguish were flowing off her check and onto her pillow. She tried to speak, but it caused her enormous agony.

He has to know! She screamed in her brain. *He has to know what I did! Please, Zeus, let me live long enough to tell him where they took Perses.*

"Do you have him still?" Perseus pleaded.

Diona rolled her head to look at him. Her eyes were fluttering like a pair of butterflies in flight. She tried to move, but she had lifted her wounded arm no more than one inch with pain exploded through every nerve…and she screamed. Her eyes opened wide and Perseus saw that the pain had awakened her mind. She stared at him with clear comprehension of what had happened, and the reality of it was close to unhinging her mind.

"Of course, she doesn't have him!" Yelled Leda. She didn't know how much Diona could take anymore. This interrogation was hurting her, and it was torturing Leda more than it was for Diona.

The doctor motioned for one of the nursemaids, a young woman was not yet twenty-one but who was already deep in the practice of the healing arts.

"Hold her, Talia," the doctor ordered. "But have a care."

Diona was thrashing and screaming, but the young nurse pressed the ailing princess gently but firming down, whispering soothing words to her. Diona jabbered at her in nearly incoherent English, which the woman did not understand. Her panic was like a storm in the narrow confines of her bedchamber.

Perseus ignored Leda. "Where is he, Diona? Is he alive?"

Diona began to sob. Her whole body was shaking. She felt more than half-dead. Her eyes were sunken into very dark pits, her hair was greasy and it was pasted to her skull, and her lips were rubbery and slack. There was a foul taste in her mouth, and an ache that was sunken deep into the core of every muscle and bone in her entire body. She hung her head and shook it slowly back and forth like a sick animal, trying to clear her brain of the layers of fog and cobwebs. Her shoulder throbbed strongly. Not quite pain, but not a comfortable feeling. It was a strange sensation, as if things were moving beneath her skin. She rattled her bounds with unfathomable strength where everyone thought she was going to pull the bedposts apart. They could hear several bones breaking like they were made of glass.

"King Perseus, you must stop." Leda implored him. "This is too much for her!"

But Perseus kept on badgering. "Diona, did you give Perses to someone?"

Diona nodded in all directions.

"Who?" Perseus distressingly asked. "Who took him from you?"

Diona began to wail loudly like a demon that crawled its way out of Hell. Her limbs were twisting in their bindings. Leda tried to pull Perseus away, but he shook her off.

"You are killing her!" Leda bawled wildly.

"And she is killing my son!" He hollered. "Must both of our children die?!"

Diona suddenly grabbed Perseus' arms. He jumped in surprised, and then saw Diona was trying to tell him something.

"'There is no honour in death…'" She finally answered.

Leda was petrified by her sickly daughter's response. It was the first thing she had said since she was brought back to the palace.

But that wasn't her voice.

It was something inhuman.

Her natural voice was being overridden with something ghostly.

"What?!" Leda shrieked. "What, my child?"

Leda feared that some demonic force had sought refuge in her daughter's broken body. It was tearing up her insides and fighting for control like a vicious parasite eating its host on the inside.

She tried to squeeze in between Perseus and Diona, but the girl wouldn't let go of the young king.

"'No ill fortune befalls the son of King Perseus…'" She moaned; this time her voice was becoming more masculine.

"What is she saying?" Leda asked him, feeling her hair turning white.

"She is telling me who forced her to do this." He answered, trying to figure out what it all meant. He suddenly frowned. "I know these words…"

"'Mighty and Noble Perseus.'" Diona softly mocked in pain. "'Mighty and Noble Perseus.'" She said again, with someone else's voice fighting for control. "'MIGHTY AND NOBLE PERSEUS!'" A man's voice had replaced Diona's.

Leda almost fainted after she heard the ghostly wailing.

What could it all mean? She thought. Her hands were shaking and her knees felt weak. *What was she speaking of? And why does Perseus look so afraid?*

Perseus froze in his place, as he recognized both the voice and its weary rueful tone. His mouth went dry, and he had to swallow hard before speaking. The last time Perseus heard someone taunted him like that was after his raid against the Corinthians days ago back at the Argos army camp.

Someone who had a motive to make Perseus torment like this.

Someone who wanted to make Perseus what it's like to lose a son.

He now knew who had taken his boy.

Diona opened her eyes and looked directly at Perseus. They held each other's gaze before Diona let go of his arm and dropped back onto her bed.

Nurses and attendants rushed to her side, pushing Perseus back. He couldn't take his eyes from Diona's lifeless body.

Leda wailed like the damned, and jumped onto the bed and tried to wake Diona up. The attendants were pulling her back, but Leda put up a sturdy fight. The guards had to force her out of the bedchambers along with Perseus just when the doctor pulled a blanket over Diona's motionless body. It was a merciful act and Perseus nodded her mute thanks. Leda turned away to blink tears from her eyes. She held onto Perseus and breathed with great care until she was sure that she would not disintegrate into tears.

CHAPTER 14

Perseus sadly walked into the palace courtyard in the balmy night. He saw Atlas sitting on the steps while Kallipso cleaned and bandaged the wounds she had given him in their battle earlier.

She bent close to examine the wound. Atlas could smell her perfume.

Also, there was the faint trace of the natural fragrance of her very own smooth delicate skin.

The scent of her was so lovely, so compelling that he could almost taste it. More sweat beaded his face.

Perseus had caught them right in the middle of a private moment where Kallipso pulled Atlas to her and her was filled with such urgency and a passion unlike anything Atlas had ever experienced. Perseus looked away from the loathsome scene. This union was very blasphemous and he failed to understand why Atlas would spare such a hateful thing. Even the damning thought that this soulless creature tried to kill him.

The intensity of it was fuelled by the honesty and freedom with which the gift was offered, and he took her in his arms and the kiss became a scalding point of contrast that spread its heat down through every other place at which their bodies touched—breasts and hands and hips and thighs moving toward each other, discovering the place where they fit and the ways in which they were welcomed. Their hands explored each other, running over bare flesh.

Kallipso's hot mouth moved from his lips to his cheeks and then his chin, and ears and throat. Atlas felt little fires ignite under his skin. Her burning line of kisses trailed lower to his chest.

Atlas began to unfasten her gown as Kallipso began to unravel his robes. They shared a smile before Atlas looked up to discover Perseus.

"There you are!" He said, standing up to greet Perseus. Atlas adjusted his robes while Kallipso blushed with embarrassment and took a moment to compose herself. Atlas looked around Perseus, trying to find something. "Where is your son? Did you find him?"

"No, is he not in Jobba." Perseus gloomily replied.

Atlas was in alarm. "But the hags said that the princess—"

"Yes, I know, and she did have Perses. But she gave him to another."

"That little thief!" Atlas spat in hatred, and threw his fist anger, which caused the bandages Kallipso had tended to unravel.

"Atlas, please!" She said, with a worried look on her face. "Be still."

Perseus looked at her with great disparagement. "Why is she still here?"

Kallipso rose up without looking him in the eye. "King Perseus, I know you do not approve of my presence, but I assure you I mean no harm."

"Do you think I am that naïve?" Perseus replied unkindly. "You would as quickly lie with a man as you would stab him in the heart."

Atlas pushed Kallipso behind him. "You speak with authority that you do not possess. And in insulting her, you insult me."

"I hope to insult your intelligence, so that you may realize the gross error that you have made." Perseus argued, trying to talk some sense to his delusional comrade.

"You speak as though you have never done wrong."

"I have made mistakes, but nothing so foolish—"

"Nothing so foolish?!" Atlas loudly snarled. "You leave your wife and babe in the care of strangers, and yet you are surprised when they are not as you had left them."

"You have fallen under a harpy's spell!"

"And now you hastily make amends by traveling halfway around the world, searching in vain—"

"I DO NOT SEARCH IN VAIN!" Perseus yelled at the top of his lungs.

The two men stared at each other and collected themselves. Perseus and Kallipso locked eyes. His gaze was cold and penetrating. It caused her to retreat further behind Atlas, hoping he would protect her.

"She will love you and then kill you in your sleep!" Perseus strongly warned Atlas. "I only try to save a friend."

"Save your son." Atlas viciously replied. "If that is to be my fate, I happily accept it."

Perseus couldn't believe what he was hearing. "You are blind."

"No, it is you who cannot see." Atlas quarrelled. "Let me remind you that every time you leave for battle, in search of *glory*, you have a woman who prays for nothing more than your safe return and a son who shall eagerly await the day he marches with you. You are a blessed man, Perseus, and yet, you refuse to realize it." Then he put his arm around Kallipso and then pulled her in tight. "Life is too short for solitude. Bother us no more."

Perseus stared at the both of them. He struggled to understand on why Atlas would engage in a liaison with a bride of Hades. Perseus believed all that time alone in Tartarus had affected his mind. And then he felt the sharp barbs Atlas had told him about his recent behaviour with Andromeda and Argos.

Perseus took a breath to steady himself. "We leave for Seriphus at first light."

Atlas nodded to him, and Perseus left the courtyard. He needed to be by himself for a while and plan what he was going to do next.

Perseus leaned against the balcony looking out over the dark city. He reached into his pocket and pulled out Andromeda's golden ring. He stared long and hard at it.

"What misery you have sustained on my account?" He said out loud. "If your heart can forgive me…"

He waited for several moments, as if he were expecting the ring to answer him. Then there was a knock on the door, followed by two guards entering the balcony. Perseus turned to face them. A suspicious look ran across his face.

"My Lord," one of the guards gently bowed, "Queen Leda requests your presence."

"Can she not wait 'til morning?" Perseus asked, his mind being elsewhere.

"She said it is urgent and that we not return without you." Said the other guard.

Perseus nodded and ambled to the guards. He looked at his sword and considered on taking it, but he didn't.

The guards escorted Perseus to Queen Leda's quarters. She sat with her back to the door. The guards bowed down before her.

"King Perseus, my Lady." The leading guard announced to her, as both he and his comrade kneeled before her.

Leda waved them away so she and Perseus could discuss her matter in private.

"Leda, I do not think it is wise to meet here at such an hour." Perseus gently advised her.

Leda rose from her chair and sauntered over to him. Tears streamed down her face on each step she took.

"It seems my prayers have been answered." She said sombrely. "Diona joins her father in Elysium this evening." She broke down, choking on sobs and sunk her face into Perseus' shoulder.

Taken back from this, he awkwardly consoled her. He felt very uncomfortable.

"I share in your grief." He said sympathetically.

"The gods have a morbid sense of humour, do they not?" She asked him. "Taking away those who are dear to us, that we should spend the rest of our mortal days alone." She looked up Perseus imploringly. "And I am so alone, Perseus."

Perseus averted his eyes and led her to her bed. "Come, you should sleep. I shall call for your attendant."

"No!" She forlornly refused. "Do not leave me, I do not wish for my subjects to see me in such a state. Rulers must always appear strong."

"You are a strong queen, Leda." Perseus said to her. "Your people admire you."

"As do yours." Leda replied, caressing his cheek. "Let us mourn our children together and then start anew. I shall bear you a strong son."

Perseus moved back. He was offended and uncomfortable.

"I already have a son…and a queen."

Leda stepped forward to the light and shed her clothing. Perseus looked to the ground.

Her body was lean and finely made, with full breasts tipped with delicate pink nipples. She had no scars, no flaws, and Perseus could only imagine the purity of her beauty.

"I can please you in ways your wife cannot." Leda said to him seductively.

Perseus slowly bent down and picked up the robes. He looked at her square in the eyes—only her eyes—and covered her back up.

"You are a queen. It would do you well to act as such." He instructed her before heading for the door. Then Leda rushed after him, grabbing his arm.

"Perseus, I implore you to reconsider my offer." She begged and looked at him rather sternly. "Do not take it lightly."

Perseus tried to gently push her away, as he opened the door. But to his surprise there were six guards standing in the doorway with their swords drawn. Leda shook free from Perseus, pulling her robes up to cover her exposed flesh.

She turned to the guards. "Arrest this man!" She ordered them. "He is an imposter! He pretended to be our noble King Perseus so that he may enter my bedchambers and have his way with me!"

Perseus whipped himself around. "What?! Leda, you are mad!" He faced the guards, who were moving in closer on him. "Take no step closer."

"Sir," said the captain, "do not resist."

They closed in on Perseus. He looked to where his sword should be, only to remember that he does not have it. The guards tackled him to the ground. Perseus struggled with them, but he grasped at the stark reality that he was no match against six men.

"I am King Perseus!" He cried in defiance.

"That is blasphemy!" Leda thundered with rage. "The gods shall judge you!" She loomed over to the guards who were waiting for her next command. "Imprison him. Tomorrow all the citizens of Jobba shall bear witness to his challenge. If this man is indeed the Son of Zeus, he shall have no difficulty defeating his opponent."

The guards chained Perseus and took him away. He turned his head to see Leda smirking an evil smile.

"I offered another way." She scornfully reminded him.

"I will return for you." Threatened Perseus.

"A meaningless threat." Leda casually shelved. "I shall see to it that you do not survive the day, Perseus."

With that, the guards dragged Perseus to the dungeon.

CHAPTER FIFTEEN

Perseus awoke knowing that sometimes in his sleep, he had made the decision to kill.

When his eyes opened, he briefly experienced some disorientation in which he feared he had awakened somewhere in the afterlife. Then he remembered he was in Jobba. His jaw clenched. He had been sleeping sitting up, with one side of his face flattened against the wall of his cell.

As far back as he could possibly remember he couldn't sleep on the cot in his own private tent.

His tongue had the taste of dry wool. It stuck to the inside of his cheek, and he winced as he tugged it away.

The pain awakened his anger. He had been dreaming of Polydectes just then, and he could still taste the bitterness that had filled him in his dream.

He felt the anger for Polydectes leaving him and the Argos army. Then there was the soul-burning surge of vengeance for he had discovered that the ruler of Seriphus was the one who truly orchestrated the abduction of his son Perses.

Perseus lonely sat in his messy prison cell with a single guard keeping watch over him, fast asleep. Perseus wasn't in the domicile reserved for political prisoners, but the same dingy cell where they threw common criminals. He lay on his bed and stared at the blackness of the ceiling. He felt old and used and damaged in a hundred ways. He even felt an insufferable dryness in his mouth, and there was also a sickness in the pit of his being.

He heard the snapping of fingers that echoed throughout the dungeon. The guard woke up to see his replacement with his arms crossed in exasperation.

"You worthless, lazy cur!" The new guard scolded the jailer.

The soldier pushed his replacement away jokingly. "Shut your mouth." He chuckled. "You never would have made it until dawn." The substitute guard looked over to Perseus, who turned his head to the side in insolence. "Oh, he has not uttered one word, nor moved at all."

"Scared is what he is." Teased the other guard. "Queen Leda doesn't deal lightly with prisoners."

He noticed his friend was looking past him. The lethargic guard seemed to be in a trancelike state. The armoured proxy turned around to see woman seductively striding toward them. The men couldn't help but to stare in awe.

Perseus squinted his eyes in order to see through the dark. The woman's figure was very familiar. He glanced further until he could make out her face.

Then his eyes were spread wide open.

Kallipso!

She stopped in front of them and suggestively pulled the hem of her skirt above her knee. Then she gave them an amorous smile.

"Who…who are…you?" Stammered the loutish guard.

Kallipso put a finger to her lips to silence them. The guards stood motionless as she neared. They were undressing her with their wandering eyes—looking her up and down—but they were obsessing over her lovely face. She was much more beautiful than Queen Leda. Maybe it was because she had a much more toned body and was several years younger.

Her face quickly changed into an image of an old hideous hag in a flash. But soon she returned to her flawless visage.

The soldiers recoiled in terror, and then looked at each other in confusion.

"Did you see that?" One asked the other.

While they were distracted, Kallipso quickly pulled out two knifes that were hidden from behind her back.

The soldiers didn't even get a chance to draw their weapons, as Kallipso systematically subdued the both of them. She stabbed one in the stomach and slashed the other's throat in the same fluid motion. The knife whooshed through the air, and it was followed by a disturbing squelch. Her recent victim dropped dead instantly. Then she looked over to the guard she gutted. He was clutching his stomach in pain and looked up at his murderess with watery eyes.

Kallipso gave him a look of empathy. She knelt down to meet him at eyelevel and caressed his pale sweat covered face.

"It will be over soon," she said amiably. The dying guard looked at her in misperception. Kallipso softly scuttled behind him holding her knife. "Close your eyes and go to Elysium to claim your reward." She gently whispered, before she mercifully slit his throat.

Atlas emerged from the shadows and nodded to her, while she placed coins on the slain guards for them to pay Charon the Ferryman's fare through the River Styx. Atlas offered his hand to her, and she woefully accepted it. They both approached Perseus' cell, but he didn't get up from his cot.

"Come, Perseus." Atlas proclaimed. "Let us waste not time." Perseus refused to move. All he did was roll over his side on the uncomfortable bedding. Atlas looked at him as if Perseus was stricken deaf. "Come on then." Atlas urgently articulated.

"Go without me." Perseus solemnly replied.

"But your son?" Atlas asked in puzzlement. "And Polydectes of Seriphus? Have you forgotten your quest so soon?"

"Not for a moment." Perseus said in strong conviction.

"Then let us go now. There is talk—the Queen means to kill you today."

"She will not." Perseus guaranteed his rescuer. "I shall defeat any man or beast she challenges me with."

Atlas looked at him for a moment and then shook his head. "Your pride and youth mislead you."

Perseus sat up on his cot and stared at Atlas seriously. "I did not become a general through cowardice. I shall stay and fight."

"Then you and your son will perish. Do not be so foolish as to use this moment for glory."

The imprisoned king angrily elevated himself from the bed and stomped toward Atlas and Kallipso. "So, I am supposed to flee in the darkness from a kingdom *I* control? What would my people think of their King?"

"That he was smart enough to recognize a battle he could not win alone." Contended Atlas. "No man can defeat an army, Perseus. And that is surely what Leda will send."

Perseus lowered his eyes from him, carefully contemplating on what he had just said. Then he raised his head up to face Atlas. "Ready the horses," he ordered his friends, "I shall join you after the fight."

Atlas looked sadly at his friend.

Too much pride can kill a man, Atlas thought, escorting Kallipso out of the dungeon. *I wager his father had not taught him that lesson. Soon Perseus will have to learn it the hard way.*

CHAPTER SIXTEEN

The people of Jobba—Leda's people—thronged the sprawling courtyard below. By the hundreds they filled the open plaza before the magnificent palace that Leda had inherited when her husband, the king, passed on. The pellucid waters of a reflecting pool mirrored the palace's graceful domes and arches. Mosaic tiles, adorning almost every inch of the place, and it also had elaborate geometric designs.

Queen Leda smiled down on her people from her private dais. A large crowd was forming around the courtyard. Many citizens were craning their necks to get a better view of the upcoming battle. People emerged from the neighbouring walkways and verandas that surrounded the enclosure. They all were busy clamouring, placing bets, but mainly they were all gossiping about the "imposter" who posed as King Perseus and how he assaulted their Queen.

Although the dais was significantly higher than the bleachers, the massive stone pillars that supported the roof above had the potential to block one's view of the action on the courtyard. On the raised dais were three chairs; one of them was a grand throne that was obviously reserved for Leda. Her royal advisor occupied the seat at the far right, and the one at the opposite side belonged to the late Princess Diona. The backrest was decorated with a sympathy reef and bouquet of beautiful red roses.

Leda was dressed, as was customary, in a long white silken tunic. Its pleats fell softly across the curves of her powerful body. A violet robe, pinned at the shoulders with golden brooches, flowed down her back. Her hair glistened when the fragrant perfume she often wore smoothed her abundant tresses. She wielded her sceptre with casual grace, but it remained, as always, a potent reminder of the queen's authority and position.

With a wave of her hand, Leda ordered the music to be silenced. Her people looked up at her expectantly. Like the rest of Greece, they had suffered much after Perseus conquered the city, but Jobba endured. The soldiers automatically raised their arms in salute. Their fists were thumping against their chests simultaneously to produce a dull thunderclap that echoed across the makeshift arena.

Kallipso sat on top of Atlas' gigantic black horse, as she held onto to her lover. Pegasus stood right next to them, snorting in disgust.

The sound of drums announced the arrival of the prisoner. Everyone in the crowd rose up to get a better observation of the charlatan. Perseus was escorted into the courtyard by a group of soldiers. They stopped in the middle of the square and the crowd fell silent. Perseus gazed out to the throng of citizens who were all staring at him.

"Citizens of Jobba…" A voice resounded from the royal terrace.

Perseus looked up to see Leda's court advisor addressing the people. However, the Son of Zeus ignored him and stared at Leda with such quiet rage.

She returned his scowl with a derisive smirk.

"Last night a criminal entered our city, claiming to be Perseus of Argos, in order to take advantage of our Queen." Leda's advisor continued his proclamation. "Fortunately, the brave soldiers of Jobba arrested this man, and he stands before you today." Then he paused and raised his arms in presentation. "For your entertainment, the Queen has ordered that this man's punishment shall be a fight to the death with Jobba's most fearless soldier—Leandros!"

Atlas and Kallipso looked at each other in great worry. She held him very tight.

"We have to do something, Atlas." She said, getting off the horse.

"We cannot do anything." He replied, holding her back. "If we storm through there right now, we will be outnumbered by Leda's soldiers."

Kallipso became vexed. "We just can't let him die." Then she clutched Atlas and said softly, "By the gods, that monster is going to kill him…he's dead."

Atlas held her close. "He is not going to die." He said firmly to her. "You will see. That's not how this ends. Perseus is no ordinary man. He is the Son of Zeus. Everyone is aware of that. I feel sorry for the poor fool who is going up against him because he is about to enter a world of trouble. He just doesn't know it yet"

The crowd erupted as a large, brutish man emerged from the palace's doors. Perseus sized up his opponent. Leandros was no taller than he, but his girth was much larger. Leandros was a large, muscular man. His nose had been broken too many times to count. Despite that, his dashing features still held a hint of the good looks he had enjoyed in his youth. On his good days, one could briefly see the streaks of grey creeping into his shaggy, light brown hair. He constantly flexed his muscles and glared menacingly at Perseus.

"As you see, it will be a fair battle." The advisor announced. "Leandros carries no weapons."

Leandros removed his robes to show his very well-proportioned physique. He was at least six-feet-nine inches tall and three hundred pounds of pure muscle. His massive chest was glistening with sweat.

The soldiers ripped off Perseus trappings to disgrace him in front of his people. Both combatants engaged in fighting stances and stood in the ring motionless like statues.

"Let the fight begin!" The announcer loudly decreed.

The soldiers quickly backed away to the sides of the courtyard, while Perseus and Leandros walked around each other—trying to anticipate each other's first move. The crowd was rendered silent and watched the two warriors in awe. The two men stood facing each other. Perseus took his opponent's measure, noting how fast his chest rose, up and down, up and down, his nostrils flaring, and his breath making steam in the chilly air.

Leandros took a step forward, his fists cocked, and silently felt sorry for the poor bastard. Perseus was still carrying all kinds of grief over the disappearance of his child.

He's the enemy. He attempted to take the Queen's life. He must pay.

Suddenly Leandros lunged forward and struck Perseus in the chest.

Perseus stumbled back but managed to dodge another blow. Leandros charged forward again like a raging bull, but Perseus moved back in defence.

After watching Perseus retreating from several more punches, the crowd began to boo. They assaulted him with venomous harangues and pelted him with rotted fruit and vegetables. Perseus shook it off and kept his eye on his hulking enemy.

Finally, one punch connected with Perseus' face. Atlas jerked forward at seeing blood drip from Perseus' nose, but Kallipso held him back.

"Atlas, no!" She said, as he struggled. "This is *his* fight. Let him go!"

Leda gave herself a smile, while she watched her champion thrashed Perseus. "So, the god-son does bleed."

Leandros was twice Perseus' size and much faster. His mind was swathed by a cloud of choking despair, Perseus barely saw him coming. The crowd gasped in astonishment as Leandros struck Perseus again with a vicious uppercut that dropped the Son of Zeus in a matter of seconds.

His skull was ringing, while his bruised profile laid flat against the soil. Perseus wondered if he should even bother trying to lift his head. Then the image of his son Perses flashed before his eyes. Then out of nowhere he found the power to get back on his feet to resume the fight.

Perseus wiped the blood away, and then stared at Leandros who was smiling. He was looking cocky, as if he had already won the fight. He was running on nothing but the sheer pluck and stubbornness. He had Perseus trapped in a corner, but now Leandros was dancing exuberantly on his heels, wasting energy while he showed off his fancy footwork.

"Come, you coward." Leandros baited Perseus. "Let's not drag this out all day."

Pile-driver fists hammered Perseus' face and body, shattering bone and cartilage.

Not so tough, are you? Leandros taunted silently. His knuckles punished his enemy's ribs. *Without the gods' help!*

Perseus winced as his tongue probed the cut on his bottom lip. A gooey string of blood hung suspended below the split lip for a second before thinning enough to drop onto the ground, joining several other drops in a smeary mess right under him. His eyes narrowed as he looked down at his own bloodshed.

Then he stampeded at his oversized opponent and delivered a hit to Leandros chest before the burly gladiator tossed him to the ground. Leandros walked around Perseus and spat on him. The crowd cheered at the insult.

"I cannot watch this." Snapped Atlas, as he prepared to dismount his horse. "I must help—"

"This is not your battle to fight, Atlas." Kallipso reminded him.

Perseus slowly got up and wiped the spit from his chest. In one quick move, he was in Leandros' face. He finished a few quick punches to the face with an elbow to the nose.

Blood sprayed everywhere. Leandros grabbed his broken nose and saw Perseus was smiling.

"Now *this* is a fight!" Leandros exclaimed with delight.

Then he punched Perseus in the stomach and the kidney. Perseus ducked behind him and tackled him to the ground. Everyone watched as the two men rolled around in the dirt, trading punches.

Determined to put Leandros on the defensive, Perseus lunged at him as he struck him with his fists and boots. But the famous soldier smoothly countered Perseus' attacks.

For a seemingly immovable object, Leandros moved with unexpected speed. Unfortunately, mass was winning. Perseus' furious blows bounced off Leandros' gigantic head and shoulders with little effect. Leandros shrugged off the trouncing attacks as though they were more substantial than falling snowflakes.

Perseus blocked and parried, repelling Leandros' blows as best he could, while he reached down inside himself, marshalling what remained of his strength, as he waited for the overconfident brute to give him an opening.

There!

Perseus ducked under Leandros' right and countered with a left uppercut to his big man's chin. The blow caught Leandros by surprise, and Perseus took advantage of the other fighter's confusion to block Leandros' hasty counterpunch and rolled off a smooth left hook. Powered by Perseus' pivoting back and hips, the hook knocked Leandros backward for a few steps, almost toppling to the ground.

Now it was Leandros' blood dripping onto the arena, and Perseus spotted a flicker of uncertainly in the lummox's once conceited eyes.

Atlas gripped the reins of his horse, as he nervously watched.

Leda changed positions in her seat to get a better view of the fight.

The crowd howled with delight, while Perseus caught a glimpse of genuine annoyance on Leda's lovely face. Perseus raised his fists before his face and taking the fight back to Leandros. He rushed into the giant's strike zone, tossing jabs and counterpunches at Leandros like they were going out of style.

Perseus intended to do more than rough this man mountain up. Leandros charged right at him to finish Perseus off, but in his impatience, the gladiator didn't see the left hook coming right at him. Perseus' knuckles slammed into Leandros' jaw, catching him off guard. Blood flew from the champion's pulverized lip.

Then Leandros made his big mistake: he got mad. *The nerve of this imposter!* His body language positively screamed. *Why didn't he just fall down like he was supposed to?!*

His face was flushed with anger, and he ran over to Perseus like an enraged bull, flailing wildly with his fists.

Bad move, my arrogant friend. Perseus thought, calmer and more in control than ever before. He knew that he had nothing left to lose except for the respect of his people and the safety of his only son.

Perseus blocked Leandros' frenzied blows with ease. The furious gladiator left himself wide open, and Perseus took advantage of his carelessness to pummel Leandros' body with combination after combination until Leandros looked as woozy and uncoordinated as a common drunkard stumbling out of a tavern.

Perseus swung a fast double-punch combination, and this time Leandros didn't allow the blows to cause any further damage. Instead he used the force against Perseus. The King of Argos stepped back, shaking out the pain in his hands from the impact, and Leandros brought his fist around and up. He caught Perseus just under the chin, sending the demigod up in the air.

With a quick move, Perseus leaped down and grabbed Leandros as he passed. Bracing his feet, he hauled Leandros into the air despite his much greater weight and threw him as hard as he could.

This has gone on long enough, Perseus decided.

He dropped his left, luring his opponent in. As Leandros lunged forward, taking the bait, Perseus bent his knees, dipping beneath Leandros' headlong punch and swinging up from below with a rocketing upper jab that knocked Leandros right off his feet.

The giant hit the ground with a gratifying thud. Perseus stood by, fists raised and ready. The entire crowd erupted in a thundering roar except for Leda and the rest of her court.

Then Perseus landed on top of Leandros and punched him in the face several times. It was effective on further bashing his nose. Any normal enemy would already be out cold, but Leandros just absorbed the blows until Perseus took a moment to catch his breath.

But Leandros didn't give up and then he head-butted Perseus in the face. Perseus doubled over and fell to the ground.

Leandros leapt up and threw his hands in the air, working the crowd. No one seemed to be put off by the blood gushing from where his nose used to be.

"Can you believe this man proclaimed to be King Perseus, Son of Zeus?!" Leandros yelled to the crowd. The people reacted with yelling and waving, and cheered for Leandros. "He is nothing but a pathetic weakling."

Perseus couldn't take anymore.

He kicked his leg at Leandros, blowing out his kneecap.

Leandros screamed out in pain and crumpled to the ground. Perseus stood and began pummelling him. The crowd and Leda watched in awe.

Perseus stepped back and stared blankly at Leandros, who tried to stand. After a few failed attempts he managed to do so and limped toward Perseus.

"It is over." He said to his battered nemesis. "Can this not end?"

"One of us has to die, my friend." Leandros hoarsely answered.

Then a sword was thrown into the courtyard. The blade laid several feet away from Leandros' feet.

"Kill him!" Shouted a citizen. "Kill him, Leandros!"

Perseus and Leandros both stared at the sword and then at each other.

Leandros stepped over to it, heading for Perseus. Rushing forward, he managed to get his hands around Perseus' neck and began to strangle him. Perseus tried to push him off but settled for a knee to the groin.

Leandros doubled over and then Perseus threw a wild blow to the side of his head that sent Leandros to the ground. Perseus stood over him, breathless. Out of the corner of his eye Leandros saw the sword and struggled to grab it.

Perseus saw his hand reaching for it, but he was too late. Leandros turned around and sliced Perseus across the chest, with the sword.

Perseus gaped in shock, as did the citizens at this "fair fight." Leandros used the sword to stand and charged at Perseus, who ducked and retreated from the blade.

Atlas couldn't take any more of this brutality. He leapt off his horse and began pushing through the crowds. Kallipso was right behind him. They managed to get up to the fight, but several soldiers stopped them.

Leandros took another swing, and Perseus grabbed his arm. He twisted Leandros' arm to make him drop the sword. Perseus took it away from him, while everyone in the crowd waited breathlessly to see what he was going to do with it.

Perseus threw the sword down and grabbed Leandros, pulling him into a stranglehold. Leandros weakly protested, as Perseus began to drain him of his life.

Leandros' body made a deafening thud when it hit the ground.

Everyone stared at Perseus in trepidation. The fight wasn't supposed to end this way. Leda squirmed nervously in her seat when she saw Perseus glaring at her. She whispered to her advisor who quickly disappeared.

Perseus grabbed the sword and then raised it in the air. "I am Perseus of Argos—"

He was cut short by the sound of thirty armed soldiers entering the courtyard. They surrounded Perseus with the tips of their swords pointing to his neck. The crowd began to boo and demanded the soldiers to let him go, but the guards pressed on further. As they descended upon Perseus, Atlas and Kallipso raced out into the court with their weapons in their hands. All of the soldiers turned their attention toward them.

"We fight this one with you, Perseus." Said Atlas.

Perseus, who was tired from all of the fighting, nodded appreciatively.

The citizens truly got a show when the three renegades took on the soldiers. Perseus tiredly swung at the soldiers. Even though he was exhausted, he was still a very skilled fighter. He was kept untouched though by Atlas, who struck down anyone who dared came near his friend. Kallipso impressed everyone the most. Her wings weren't fully regenerated, but she was able to leap into the air and glided down on the soldiers and frightened many of the palace's guards and citizens.

Leda sat riveted in her seat and watched hopelessly as her soldiers were being slaughtered. She looked over to the next group and waited in the doorway.

"Go! Help your comrades!" She yelled at them. They stood rubbernecked and didn't move. "I order you! Kill him!" She pointed to Perseus, but they were still stationary. She glowered at them and saw her advisor approaching. "What are you doing?!" She yelled at him. "Send them in!"

He looked her very earnest. "They say they will not fight the Son of Zeus."

Leda looked up in time to see Perseus yank his sword out of the last soldier.

Thirty dead bodies joined that of Leandros in the courtyard. The dirt was now a rusty colour from all of the blood.

Perseus stood before the crowd, brandishing his sword. “Do you still question who I am? If so, come forward.”

The crowd was silent. One by one they knelt before him, recognizing their king. Perseus looked triumphantly down on them.

He turned to face Leda, who stood speechless. She knew she had lost. Then returned to his faithful followers.

“Shall I kill anymore citizens of Jobba, or have I won my freedom?”

Leda didn’t answer. All she did was lower her eyes, still feeling baffled on how he could have won. She had an army, while he had two other cronies—one of which was a demon.

Perseus walked through the crowds, as each passing member quickly dispersed allowing their king a clear passage. He reached Pegasus who was happy to see his rider. He ruffled the feathers in his wings and whinnied thankfully. Perseus patted his four-legged companion affectionately and slowly got on his back. Atlas saw him struggle at first on trying to get his leg over the horse’s side. He marched over to help, but Perseus held his hand up to stop Atlas in his tracks. With a grunt of effort Perseus managed to hobble over Pegasus’ bareback.

Atlas wrung a small smile and mounted his horse. He extended his arm for Kallipso to climb aboard and wrapped her arms around Atlas’ well-built torso.

Perseus rode over to the terrace until he was before Leda. She leaned over to the side, waiting for him to speak.

“As for you, my Queen,” He said sneeringly, “I shall return with my army and watch you beg for forgiveness as your city lies in ruin.”

Her eyes widened in horror. “Perseus, please have mercy.”

“You deserve none.” He snarled, as Leda felt dread in her heart.

Perseus turned to face his two companions and then proceeded to ride out of the city. Bubo flew over them, leading the way. As soon as the three warriors faded from sight, the citizens of Jobba looked at their queen in revulsion.

CHAPTER SEVENTEEN

Zeus walked with a spring in his step and a song in his heart. He was even whistling a lively tune. His attendants and the rest of gods looked at him in astonishment when he passed by them. They all agreed their father and king was in rare form this very day. As he turned a corner in the palace corridor he saw Hera and swept her off her feet. He leaned in for a kiss and she gaily obliged, and then quickly untangled herself away from him.

"You are in a jovial mood." She said to him, still feeling her lips tingle. For a moment she could have sworn she had seen sparks igniting before her very eyes. "What pleases you so?"

"Can a man not simply delight in the beauty of his wife?" Zeus replied, without a care in the world. This had probably been the first time he truly felt free. He felt proud of his son Perseus who survived on his own without interfering in his life.

"Not you." Hera chillingly replied.

Zeus' smile unfolded. "Hera, I care not for a cold bed. Let us end this wager between us."

Hera smirked and leaned into him. "And why is that, Husband? Losing faith in your son?"

"On the contrary, I do not wish to see you humiliated when he prevails."

"How kind of you," she jeered, "but I am not worried."

"You should be." Zeus heavily cautioned her.

Hera left her husband to his boastfulness to seek refuge on the balcony. She found Thetis and Aphrodite in conversation. Hera's eyes narrowed in anger and stormed over to her sisters.

"Can you do nothing that I ask?" She hissed at Aphrodite.

Thetis was taken off-guard by her queen's sudden outburst. She was afraid to face her. She knew Hera was angry, and Thetis feared the penalty.

"My Lady?" Aphrodite timidly asked Hera, who was fuming with rage.

"He's mortal!" Hera screamed at the both of them. "He should not be that hard to kill!"

Aphrodite shivered in her queen's presence. She held onto Thetis, who was also trembling in fear. They didn't deserve to look at Hera in the eye. They turned away from her in embarrassment and failure.

Arsenios was grooming his horse in the stables, humming cheerfully on each stroke of the brush. Unbeknownst to him he was being watched. As he was cleaning his brush someone appeared right before him. Arsenios jumped back to see it was Queen Andromeda who scared him.

"My Queen?!" He cried in fright. Andromeda motioned to him to lower his voice. "How was your…rest? Are you feeling better?"

"I am fine." Andromeda replied, feeling unease. "But there is another who is ill, drunk off of the power he seeks to obtain."

Arsenios gave her a questioning look. "My Lady?"

"I fear your assumptions of Phineus are well-founded. Every day Perseus is away, he grows bolder. I suspect he will stop at nothing to gain control of Argos."

Arsenios pondered for a moment. "What does my Queen suggest be done?"

"I do not know…"

"As always, I wait for your command, and should certain actions be necessary, I will practice the upmost discretion."

"Thank you, Arsenios," she said gratefully, but then she became despondent. "But I do not believe that is the only solution. Perhaps if I speak with him…"

"My Lady," Arsenios mildly interjected, "may I speak honestly for a moment?"

"Yes, speak."

"You are wise enough to already see his intentions and that he will stop at nothing to achieve them." Began Arsenios, looking at Andromeda with kindness. "Why do you let the fire continued to burn throughout your home, infecting those around it with its viciousness and disregard? Why not extinguish it when you have the opportunity?"

A young horseman galloped across the countryside. "Faster, girl." He urged his horse, and the filly ran faster.

The man looked over to the left and something in the distance.

Tellus was riding with his men and saw the lone horseman heading toward them.

"Soldiers of Argos!" He called out. Tellus turned to see the horsemen in curiosity. "Please! I bring word from Jobba!" He cried again, he wasn't slowing down. "It is urgent!"

Tellus rolled his eyes. "Oh, bother…" He groaned, as he and his soldiers reined their horses and waited for the messenger to catch up.

The boy leapt from his horse and bowed immediately.

"Speak, boy," commanded Tellus, "we have not the time for this."

"I speak for Jobba." The boy stated, unravelling a scroll, and began reading the message. "'We seek to make amends with King Perseus. We do not wish the wrath he promised us. Leda has fled, leaving us helpless. The people of Jobba beg forgiveness from our Mighty King.'"

This captured Tellus' attention. "Perseus was in Jobba?"

"Yes, two days ago." The messenger confirmed.

"Where did he go?"

"I know not."

Tellus sighed as he took in the boy. The young man's hair was a mop with brown curls. He strangely resembled Perseus in the most unusual way. Tellus stepped forward to the messenger, who suddenly felt the hair on the back of his neck standing up.

"Well, come then." Tellus gestured over. "Let us escort you to Argos. You may tell Queen Andromeda yourself."

The boy looked at him in disbelief. "She would grant me that honour?" He said, feeling awestruck.

"She would insist seeing you." Tellus replied, patting him on the shoulder.

The boy's face lit up like the night's stars, and nodded excitedly. Tellus pulled a robe from his saddlebag and presented it to the young messenger.

"What is…?"

"All members of the court must wear a robe of Argos."

"Member of the court?" The boy was amazed by the splendour he was receiving. The corners of his face were already aching from smiling so much. "I cannot wait to see the Queen."

Tellus put the robe around the boy, and then smiled at his eager face. "And she cannot wait to see you."

Steel glittered in Tellus' hand and with a heave of his great dusky shoulders he drove the dagger in the boy's stomach.

The young rider's high thin squeal broke in a strangled gurgle and he felt the strength of his knees deserting him.

The boy's eyes bulged in shock and he looked at his killer with sad eyes. His mouth gaped for a yell, and his hand leaped to the hilt of the knife. But at that instant his eyes met those of his murderer and the cry died in his throat, and his fingers went limp.

With one swift motion, Tellus pulled the knife out of the boy's body, and then quickly slit his throat.

The boy's eyes became glazed and vacant, and then he slid off his horse and fell into the dirt.

"Tie him to your horse." Tellus ordered a solider, while he produced a small cloth to clean his knife. "His face must be unrecognizable."

As the soldiers followed Tellus' orders, he chased away the boy's horse. The whole company turned around and rode back towards Argos. Tellus looked behind to see the boy's body being dragged across the rocks.

Son, you are doing your country a great service. I promise you that your sacrifice will not be in vain.

***

Perseus, Atlas, and Kallipso sat around a campfire, eating their supper. Perseus picked at the wound on his chest, attempting to clean it.

"You are only making it worse." Kallipso said to him.

Perseus snidely whipped, "But you could heal me?"

"Perseus," huffed Atlas, "She fought beside you this day."

Perseus paid no heed to him, and continued to pick at his wound.

"Very well." Kallipso boiled. "Let it get infected, but I cannot help you when the fever takes hold."

Perseus sighed impatiently. "Alright then, will you help me?"

Kallipso smiled to Atlas and began to clean the wound properly, by cauterizing it.

"Quite a fight you had," said Atlas, "But I didn't know you were that skilled."

"How quickly you forget then." Perseus scoffed at him. "It was not long ago that I pinned you."

Atlas snorted. "Tell me, good friend, was that before or after I saved you from the Cyclops?"

The men burst out laughing. Atlas took it a step further and playfully tackled Perseus, who let out a very low groan.

"Atlas!" Kallipso yelped, trying to fix Perseus' bandages.

"Yes, easy…" Perseus said, holding his ribs. "You forget your size."

"Nonsense," Atlas boldly denied, "Leandros was twice that of me."

"No ordinary man would have stood a chance against him." Kallipso bravely stated. "But Perseus, Son of Zeus, prevailed."

Atlas threw his hands in the air, triumphantly.

Perseus sat upright, his back rigid. He breathed evenly, telling himself over and over that there was no pain, no pain. He felt nothing, only numbness.

"Hold still now," said Kallipso.

"I *am* holding still." He took a deep breath, exhaled, and sent a message to his side that he would feel no pain. He knew he could control pain.

He held up his soiled white tunic, which was raised above his wound. Slowly and carefully, Kallipso applied a forest remedy that she'd mixed together in a wooden bowl.

Perseus didn't like the look of the discoloured paste, so he turned his attention over to Atlas.

"Ow!" Perseus yelped, staring down at Kallipso. "Don't press so hard."

Kallipso rolled her eyes. "Did that sting a little?"

Perseus shot her an irritated look, and then turned to the side. Kallipso brought her hand up, covering her mouth to hide her grin.

Then he stared at her, who was just finishing tending to the wound. She looked up to him and gave him a shy smile.

"It was on no account of my father." He said to her.

"You surely cannot deny his assistance?" She asked in reply.

"I can with the upmost certainty." Perseus said, his face was now laced with sadness. "He turns his back on a son in need. If he has forsaken me, then I shall forsake him."

All three of them sat in silence. This was a serious ordeal. Perseus had given up on his father and the rest of the gods. Atlas came to the conclusion that the reason why Perseus' father is not helping him because he wanted Perseus to find his son himself.

All this torment and frustration was all a test.

Perseus sighed and looked at his friends. "Come, let us rest for a few hours."

CHAPTER EIGHTEEN

Andromeda and Arsenios passed by the great hall but noticed Phineus meeting with several delegates from the royal court. Andromeda stopped and entered the room with a stunned look on her face, with Arsenios in tow.

"There is no need to discuss this with her." Phineus said to a townsperson. "I am approving it."

"Uncle?" Said Andromeda, emerging from the hallway.

Phineus looked up to see her. He felt mildly embarrassed at being caught. "Do not look so worried, Andromeda." He gently told her. "I was only handling the tedious affairs that you should not be troubled with."

Andromeda looked him with abhorrence. "As Queen of Argos, I am to be involved in all affairs, tedious or not. While I appreciate your assistance, it is not necessary."

Arsenios smiled proudly. Phineus leapt up and stalked over to her. While Andromeda flinched, she also stood her ground.

"You are as grateful as your father was." Phineus complimented her. "If he had followed my advice, Argos would be twice the city it now is. I will not watch you squander this state's reputation, as you wait in forlorn for a man that does not deserved to be king!"

Andromeda heard her uncle, but it was as if he was speaking from then of a long tunnel, and moving away from her. She wrinkled her nose in disgust and then her shoulders sagged.

"You are family," Andromeda she began, holding back her irritation, "and because of that, I have tolerated your rants and accusations until now, but I will do so no longer."

Phineus looked at her if she were jokingly.

But she wasn't.

Andromeda felt a small weight in her chest. She had enough of her uncle meddling in her affairs. He had forgotten that this is her kingdom. She was the queen and he was only a subject.

"Is that so?" He replied, trying not to laugh.

"Unfortunately for you, it was I who was crowned ruler over Argos. You must either accept this or leave."

"Those are bold words, my Queen." Phineus replied, feeling relieved his niece finally had grown a spine. "You are right, I am no ruler, but I do possess a certain influence that I am sure you would not want against you."

"Argos does not bow to threats and neither shall I." Andromeda contested.

Phineus gave her a crafty grin. "We shall see about that." He said, storming out of the room.

Arsenios excitedly turned to Andromeda, who desperately tried to hide her emotional state.

"You are right, Arsenios." She confided to him. "The fire must be extinguished."

"And it shall be, my Lady."

Zeus paced back and forth on the balcony of the palace on Mount Olympus. Hermes stood before him watching in worry. He had never seen his lord so angry before. Not since Thetis tried to kill his son out of revenge for turning her son Calibos into an unsightly satyr creature.

"Insolent son!" Zeus roared furiously. "I curse the day I brought greatness upon him!"

Hermes docilely said, "He is troubled, my Lord—"

"I am troubled!" Yelled Zeus, as Hermes raised his hands in defence. "Do you think it does not pain me to watch him struggle, while I can do nothing? All his life, I have watched over him, never letting him suffer, assisting in his glorious conquests. And now, the first time he must go through the pain and hardships most mortals experience, he curses my name!"

"I am sure he did not—"

"I am done, Hermes." Zeus vexingly concluded. Hermes couldn't believe what he was saying. Just earlier Zeus was praising Perseus and now he was cursing his son's name. "Speak no more of this matter to me!"

The night was hot and humid, with a tense of electricity that made Andromeda's skin tingle. She sensed a thunderstorm was approaching and felt the temperature suddenly drop. And just like that lightning cracked across the heavens and she felt the first few cold drops of oncoming rain. She welcomed it and then stretched her arms out in a lovely wingspan like a bird about to take flight. She silently prayed that the rain would cleanse her of all the pain and suffering she had endured in this vile tribulation. Her skin broke out into tiny goose pimples and breathed into the cold refreshing air. Within seconds her beautiful silk gown she was wearing was soaked through. Then she watched the rain poured down on Argos. It was coming down in sheets in the city. The coming night cooled the water as it blanketed the trees surrounding the palace. The moon stayed high and hidden above the clouds of the storm as if it wanted to avoid the sadness within her own house.

Thunder slammed a fist against the walls and the whole palace shook. The storm had brought wind with it and it howled through every crack in the walls and under every door. The wind rose and rose until it was a piercing shriek and Andromeda wanted to cover her ears, but at the same time she felt drawn to it. It called to her and screamed at her and tore at the night.

Lightning flashed so brightly that the corridor was suddenly stark whites and blacks, and it outlined every curl and twist in the ornate wrought iron of the balcony door.

The driving rain beat against the palace's walls. The howling wind drowned out the gentle sobs that filled the master bedroom. Fiery red lightning cracked the night, throwing the marble columns and roofs into sharp relief.

Andromeda's face was tense as she moved further onto the balcony. Storms like these really set her servants at such discomfort—fearing that the gods were plotting a much brutal retaliation on when Perseus slayed the monstrous Kraken years ago. She filed the thought away, like so many others, to gather dust until it was forgotten. The day-to-day running of Argos demanded all the time she had. Even to these long seven months where Perseus was way conquering the rest of the kingdoms in the land.

More thunder, and the wail of the wind was white-hot need in her brain. She could tell Zeus was angry about the atrocious plot against her family. Andromeda heard very little of Perseus' mother Danae. According to Perseus she was very beautiful. So beautiful that her own father kept her closely guarded from the eyes of men and constantly locked her behind iron doors like a caged commodity. But it was not enough to keep the eye of the all-mighty Zeus away. It was said Zeus had transformed himself into a glittery shower of gold and visited her. Then he loved her as a mortal man, and Danae was understandably receptive to his sympathetic advances. When King Acrisius learned Danae had given birth to son who was sired by the King of the Gods, he looked upon Perseus as an abomination, he sealed both his daughter and child in an iron casket for them to drown at sea. Zeus ordered Poseidon to save his lover and child, and then he sought retribution by unleashing the Kraken on Acrisius and his kingdom. Not only Acrisius was punished for his savage jealously and cowardly revenge, but most brutality he was condemned to a lingering death for his incestuous desires toward his own daughter.

On what made this storm even more personal was the victim was Zeus' own grandson. And she thought Perseus was furious when he first heard the news about Perses' disappearance. He was ready to declare martial law on Argos and perform scorch earth. But now Zeus—Ruler of Olympus—is up in the heavens venting his frustration. It is known that when the gods are angry, the storms that rolled atop the mountain were more violent than anywhere else in the world. Less is certain about the weather when the immortal inhabitants of that mountaintop dimension are mostly irritated and confused.

Hera, help the fool who decided to cross us. Andromeda silently prayed.

Suddenly the bedroom doors were thrown open, and out of the halls came Arsenios running to his queen.

"My Queen, come quickly." He said urgently.

Andromeda couldn't say anything. The next thing she knew she was quickly following her faithful servant. They raced down the hall, while Andromeda's robes were billowing behind her. She looked on ahead and saw Tellus and a few of his soldiers were standing in the court, sopping wet. She stopped in the entry and saw a large canvas bag resting on the floor in front of them.

Andromeda already knew what was in it.

She couldn't breathe. She fell to the marble floor and was choking on her sobs.

Tellus advanced several steps towards her and kneeled. He gave her a look of sadness and grief. He took a moment to compose himself on how he should break the news to Andromeda.

"We found King Perseus…" He said, looking at the body bag. He could see the hand of the boy he murdered hanging out of its opening. Then Tellus said half-heartedly, "I am so sorry, my Queen."

"No," she whispered, "no…it cannot be!"

Phineus passed by the doorway, but entered upon seeing the commotion.

"What's going on in here?" He asked.

Andromeda didn't even acknowledge him, and he remained there silent in the archway.

"Where did you find him?" Arsenios asked Tellus.

"In the countryside, near Jobba. He was alone."

"Let me see him." Andromeda slowly got up from the floor.

Tellus became uneasy. "My Lady, I do not suggest that. The sight that will greet you…it is best to remember him how he was."

"I don't care, Tellus." She said, making her way to the covered corpse. "I wish to see my husband."

Arsenios motioned for Tellus to open the bag. He sighed and undid the knots.

Andromeda let out a terrifying scream.

Even Arsenios and Phineus looked away. Their faces winced in the horrid discovery of the mangled body. The face was unidentifiable, as very little of it even remained.

"My God…" Phineus lost his breath.

Tears were gushing from Andromeda's eyes like they were waterfalls. "Who could have done this? Why?"

"If you wish, my Queen," Tellus offered, "my men and I can leave at once and track down these barbarians. But we thought it best to bring you word of this terrible action first."

Andromeda nodded feebly. "You were right in doing so."

Tellus nodded accordingly, and then exchanged looks with Phineus and Arsenios before he left with his small squad of soldiers.

Phineus was at a loss for words.

His niece was an emotional wreck.

She had loss her child and now her husband—all in less than a week.

"Andromeda, I..."

"Please, not now, Uncle." She distantly murmured.

Phineus hung his head in shame, and vacated the room.

"Shall I have him brought to the tomb?" Arsenios gingerly asked.

"Don't you dare touch him!" Andromeda fiercely berated him. "He is not going anywhere."

As Andromeda wept over the cadaver's chest, Arsenios placed his hand on her shoulder.

"He called me his 'closest friend.'"

Andromeda raised her head to see tears in Arsenios' eyes. She embraced him.

"Why is this happening, Arsenios?"

Ares, the God of War, leaned over the large grindstone in his armoury to sharpen his blade. Sweat beaded on his brow and he never even blinked when those little rivulets got into his eyes. He noticed Hera lurking about, but he didn't stop. He kept to his sword, watching the sparks flying off from the friction.

"For whatever purpose you are here, I want no part." He said, never turning his head to look at her.

Hera turned her scowl into a smile. "When has a great warrior ever refused a battle?"

"Not if it involves your husband, or his son."

"I understand you do not wish to anger him."

"You agreed to certain terms; I bore witness." Recalled Ares, examining his sword. "He believes you to be faithful to them, and yet, you conspire against Perseus."

"The agreement was that only he could not involve himself in Perseus' affairs." Hera corrected him.

Ares polished is blade and then brought it back against the grindstone. "I have no ill will against this mortal." He said, peddling the huge stone wheel. "Why should I assist you in his demise?"

Hera replied, "My husband is selfish, bestowing blessings on his own children, but neglecting ours."

"I have none." Ares said abruptly.

"But you *will*, and then you shall watch as your own offspring stand idly by, watching those like Perseus succeed."

"Tis no concern of mine."

"Very well then." Hera blandly responded. "When your children fail to achieve honour and glory on the battlefield, I shall remember your words."

Ares stopped sharpening and then looked at her with much trouble. Hera smiled to herself, knowing she got him where she wanted him.

The deep forest seemed endless and swallowed Perseus and his friends entirely. It was dark with tropical foliage. The trees hung heavily with buds, and the ground was wet and messy. Daylight could be seen only from the tops of the trees, the carpet of the forest was cool and clammy under their feet. What struck Perseus first was how intensely silent it was. There was no sound existing outside of the small twitter of their very own movements through the brush.

The sun beat very hard down upon Perseus. It was hot, and there were no trees with enough leaves to give him shade. He didn't care about the heat. He didn't care how scruffy he looked with his stubbly chin and dusty clothes. He was interested in only one thing—Perses.

Meanwhile, Atlas crunched his way through the brush in another part of the forest, squeezing his way through the trees. He stopped to scratch his back against the side of a thick trunk, rubbing himself as the leaves fell around him.

Their surroundings were thick with undergrowth in the valley and the sun was beating down relentlessly. The group came far enough to sweat-soak every inch of their clothes as they laboured through the foliage.

The lush tangled forest was closing in on them with every mile they travelled. Perseus imagined that if they stopped, he would actually see the vines and branches growing and slowly reaching out toward the warriors. If they stayed in one place for long, the horses and their riders would be completely strangled—victims of the dark and strange forest.

As they were all trekking through the path in the hot afternoon sun, Perseus was disturbed by the very faint noises that were lurking about in the bushes. He continually looked over his shoulder, hoping to discover what was there with them.

"Listen." Perseus said to his friends. "Do you hear that?"

Atlas and Kallipso listened, but heard nothing. They both shook their heads, and looked at Perseus, thinking that the journey had finally taken its toll on him.

"I hear nothing." Reported Atlas. "Let's carry on."

Perseus hesitantly nodded and then resumed walking. But he stopped yet again, hearing that perturbing racket.

Atlas looked back at him, a worried look ran across his face. "Perseus, we waste the daylight. We have not seen any other living being for miles. Your mind is playing tricks on you."

But Perseus knew something *was* here. And he wanted to investigate, but all he did was nod in agreement over to Atlas, and took a step forward.

Suddenly a spear was thorn into the ground before him.

All of them drew their weapons and looked up at the trees to see where the projectile had originated.

Perseus' eyes widen in unspeakable discovery to see what was hunting them.

There were over thirty wood nymphs perched in the branches, with their spears aimed at the three warriors. The creatures were all humanoid in nature, but they had a tinge of green to their hair and skin. They rebuffed the intruders with sneers and brandished their weapons violently.

"Drop your weapons." Perseus ordered Atlas and Kallipso.

Atlas gave him a surprised look. "Are you mad?"

Perseus shot him a look, as he threw his sword to the ground. Then Atlas and Kallipso each followed suit.

Perseus looked up to the nymphs, holding his hands in the air to show them he was unarmed. "We mean you no harm." He said to them, never taking his eyes off the tips of their spears. "My companions and I only seek passage through your woods. We are on our way to Seriphus."

One of the nymphs leapt down to the ground like a blossom from the tree, and landed before Perseus. The young king deduced this one was the leader because the creature's age had no correlation with his physical condition. His body was sleek but muscular, and he stared hard at Perseus.

"You and your fellow man may pass." Stated the nymph elder. His voice was resounded with the wisdom of the ages. Then he turned to stare at Kallipso and cringed. "But the harpy cannot."

Atlas stepped forward to challenge the forest spirit. "Who are you to make such demands?"

The nymph stared at Atlas coldly, feeling insulted. "I am Euripides, King of the Wood Nymphs."

"Nymphs?" Atlas said in disbelief.

"Please let us pass without incident." Perseus beseeched the forest king. "We shall make no trouble and will not rest until we are clear of your kingdom."

"As I said before, you and he may continue." Euripides severely repeated. "We do not allow harpies in out forest—they are bad omens. You would do well to rid yourselves of her company."

Perseus looked over the diminutive ruler to bare witness of Atlas' graphic fury. The burly man's face was turning red with anger. It was a much darker shade when he argued about the matter of Kallipso in the courtyard back in the palace of Jobba's.

"How dare you—" He growled, balling up his fists.

Perseus quickly silenced him, and then turned back to Euripides. "You are sensible in your caution, but I assure you, she is no bad omen. Kallipso has proven her loyalty."

Euripides gave the silver-tongued leader a doubtful grimace. "Why should I trust your word?"

Perseus sighed. "Because I used to feel as you do now." He said, while Kallipso peered over Atlas' shoulder. "But I swear to you, no harm shall come to your people while we pass through."

"You speak in ignorance." Euripides replied, noticing Perseus' bruised face. The nymph king came to the conclusion that the battle Perseus recently fought must have affected his common sense. No one in their right mind would ally themselves with a foul creature such as a harpy. "Have you not heard of the Minotaur and his army?"

Perseus stood perplexed. "I have not." He subserviently confessed to Euripides.

"The most merciless beast the gods created." Euripides explained. "He thinks nothing of feasting on the flesh of humans and nymphs alike."

"He lives in the forest?"

"Indeed," Euripides reluctantly replied, "with his army of centaurs. They hunt at night, descending like a dark cloud on hapless travellers. All must seek cover before the sunsets. Daylight is your only protection."

"Can we make the journey to Seriphus in one day?" Asked Perseus.

"No," Euripides spiritlessly answered. "Even without rest, it is two days. I am sorry."

"Very well then." Perseus said, while he signalled to his friends to head on out. Then he turned back to see Euripides. "We have wasted valuable time. If you will excuse us…"

Perseus began to lead Pegasus past the nymph ruler and his people. Atlas and Kallipso did the same with their horse and followed him. Kallipso looked overhead to the small spear-equipped warriors. She never felt more afraid in her life. This was much scarier when Perseus was standing over her with a sword over his head and was about to deliver the fatal blow until Atlas saved her. Kallipso looked at each and every one of the nymphs, who lowered their weapons and allowed her through the path.

Euripides stared at Perseus in confusion. "You wish to continue despite my warnings?"

"I appreciate your concern, but I must reach Seriphus." Perseus said in conviction. "Your Minotaur and his army shall not stop me.

Euripides had never met man who was just as stubborn as Perseus was. He couldn't decide either to call this man a hero or a fool. But there was something about Perseus that made the ancient king reconsidered this current predicament.

"I shall take you to the most direct route." Euripides informed them. He pointed upward at a vast network of ropes, vines, and nets hanging from the trees. Here and there, faces were visible—watching them.

Perseus smiled in appreciation, and turned Pegasus around while Atlas and Kallipso followed Euripides. They set out once again, moving much deeper into the forest as rapidly as their strength allowed. The day had turned heavy with dampness and chill. Earlier their progress was slowed in the tangle of the underbrush and the wet leaves was a tad struggling. The rest of the wood nymphs tailed Perseus and his friends by leaping from branch to branch in the trees to provide surveillance for the traveling party below them.

CHAPTER NINETEEN

Queen Andromeda was cold.

It wasn't simply a physical sensation—it went far beyond that, encompassing every aspect of her body and mind and spirit. She was cold in a way she always imagined how the continents in the north must feel.

She bundled herself in blankets, but it wasn't enough for her. The cold was in the core of her. It scrapped her will and it made her a shadow of the woman she'd been.

She knew she looked terrible, and she simply didn't care.

She waved on her bed, with her mouth ajar in a frantic quest for air while her mind shrieked the utter wrongness of that action, because there was no air to breathe. Andromeda trembled, rubbing her hands, keeping her eyes shut tight as she rubbed her face. She realized as she did that she wouldn't feel quite so hollow anymore.

Andromeda sat alone in the safety of her chambers, crying in desperation and despair. There wasn't anyone around and she felt a little relieved that she didn't have to hide her feelings. After a few moments, she looked up to see her Uncle Phineus lingering in the door. As he approached his poor niece, Andromeda tensed immediately.

"Please, Andromeda," Phineus said to her calmly, "I do not wish to argue. I come only to share in your grieving."

"Is that so?" She said in denigration.

"Harsh words have been said, but we both know they were out of anger." He continued, feeling ashamed for his recent behaviour. "My actions were only in concern for your well-being." He said in that pompous voice.

"I appreciate your concern." Andromeda replied, clearing her throat. "It has been difficult for me, and now with Perseus gone…"

"He was a good man." Consoled Phineus. "But I am here for you, Andromeda, and I shall make certain you are protected."

"Thank you." Phineus embraced her affectionately, but Andromeda still felt cold. "But, Uncle?"

"Yes, my child?"

"Who shall protect me from you?"

Phineus pulled back with a crazed confused look on his face. His jaw dropped as if at some horrific realization. "What do you mean, my dear?" He faltered.

Andromeda stared at him gravely. Phineus could tell by her eyes that she was angry. "Why do you pretend to mourn with me?" She asked, her voice sounding raspy from all the crying. "Surely, you do not think I am that naïve to believe your sympathetic words are genuine and not an attempt to get closer to the throne?"

He let the words linger and then looked steadily up onto Andromeda's eyes. Beyond the sternness, he could see the concern and even the fear.

Phineus shook his head sadly and left his chair. "You are troubled…"

Andromeda leapt to her feet. "Since your arrival in Argos, you have done everything possible to usurp Perseus' position. Now you stand here, pretending to grieve, when it is quite possible that you were involved in my son's disappearance and my husband's murder!"

"How dare you accuse me of such actions!" Phineus bellowed, feeling the sting of her vicious barbs. "That is preposterous!"

"Be sensible, Uncle!" Andromeda shouted, sending Phineus back a couple steps. "You are more than capable of those charges. I only wish I had seen your true intentions sooner and not let such a snake into my home."

Phineus stormed over to the balcony and motioned to the city. "I was only trying to protect Argos! You have been irrational since Perseus' departure. I was doing what I thought was best for the city and its citizens."

Andromeda took a breath. "I believe I know what is best for my people—"

"Other states already question the capability of a female ruler." Phineus interjected. "I did not wish for them to take advantage of your fragility at this time."

Andromeda felt a flicker of irritation, like the striking of a match within her soul. It heralded a flash of temper that was coming more and more often lately, more and more intense. No matter how hard she tried to keep it under control. She couldn't no longer grin and bear it. She gave Phineus a cautionary scowl that sent him back several small steps.

"Do not mistake femininity for weakness." Warned Andromeda. "I did not expand the Argos empire by merely seducing my enemies. You believe there to be frailty where there is none. These other states have learned not to underestimate my power. You act not for Argos but for yourself!"

Then Phineus reached out and started to pugnaciously shake Andromeda's shoulders. "I act for *us*, Andromeda!" He yelled right at her face. Andromeda stared at him in horror. It was as if he were another person. He reminded her of the two-faced Janus who had just revealed his true intentions. He kept on braying, "For our name, for our family, for our city!"

Andromeda could tell from the sound of his voice that he was already getting absorbed in the task.

"Argos is not your city—she is mine!"

Andromeda roughly shoved Phineus back. He lost his balance, and as Andromeda watched in horror Phineus fell over the balcony.

Phineus plummeted; his arms and legs were pin wheeling. He helplessly fell down to the rocks, screaming at the top of his lungs.

Andromeda covered her face in fright when she saw Phineus' body finally hitting the bottom. Shaken by what she had done, she backed up from the balcony and fell to the ground, holding her knees. Then she brought them right under her chin. Tears formed in the corners of her eyes as the anger and guilt swelled in her stomach. She might as well have been a statue because she was totally immobile.

Yet for all the mysterious creatures that supposedly inhabited these woods, none were as powerful as the infamous Minotaur that was lurking about. The fading sunlight barely penetrated the sheath of trees as Perseus and the rest of his party made their way through the forest, oblivious to the awesome sight of the ancient growth around him.

Perseus and Euripides walked through the ceiling of the forest, while the rest of the wood nymphs followed behind them, along with Atlas, Kallipso and the horses. Bubo was flying over them as well. The gears shifting in his mechanical wings gave out several gentle clicking sounds.

At one point of the trek, Perseus looked down and noticed a small boy walking next to him. The boy stared up at the Son of Zeus in such admiration that Perseus cannot help but smile.

"And what is your name?" He asked the boy.

The only response the boy gave was his smile. It never left his face. It was as if it was carved onto his smooth visage.

Euripides leaned over to Perseus. "He cannot hear you." The nymph king said solemnly. "His name is Nikias. His mother left this world bringing him into it."

"And the boy's father?" Perseus asked in concern.

Euripides lightly shook his head. "Unfortunately, he left, seeking glory and fame. He found the Minotaur."

Perseus observed the boy with more tenderness, which was returned with the same innocent smile.

Euripides looked up to the sky and slows down on the march.

"We shall stop here for the night." He announced.

"We can make it further." Perseus persisted.

"No, Perseus." Euripides stopped him. "We'll continue for Seriphus come morning." When Perseus was about to object, Euripides stood up. "My people's lives are not yours to risk."

With that Perseus stopped where he was and heeded Euripides' words. "Forgive me, Euripides. You know these woods far better than I. Where shall we make camp?"

Euripides smiled and pointed up to the trees. The wood nymphs were busy making lodgings among the branches. They threw down several ropes for Perseus and his friends to climb up the trees and join them, leaving the horses on the ground.

The entire group of nymphs reclined sleepily in the branches later that night. Kallipso rested against a very uncomfortable Atlas. They were both doing their best to get some rest. Bubo sat on a nearby branch, as his eyes were sealed shut. Perseus was the only vigilant one of the whole lot. He watched Nikias who was sleeping peacefully, and then turned his attention to the ground. Thought it was dark Perseus was able to make out Pegasus' body, while the horse casually munched on a field of tall green grass.

Euripides made his way through the branches with ease and swung onto the one next to Perseus. "You are not tired?"

"I am." Perseus wearingly replied.

"Yet, you do not sleep?"

"I choose not the vulnerability that comes with sleep."

"We are mortal, Perseus." Said Euripides. "We are always vulnerable."

Perseus was focused on Pegasus. "They will not attack the horses?"

"They consider them one of their own." Euripides assuredly replied.

"The Minotaur has surely been tracking us." Perseus observed.

"No doubt."

"Why did you agree to help me?" Perseus asked the kindly wood nymph. "Knowing it could bring you such danger?"

Euripides smirked at him. "There is a strength in you that I have not seen in many. I thought your resolution might help me to overcome my cowardice."

"You are no coward." Said Perseus, wondering what was going through Euripides' head. "You only wish to protect your people."

For a moment Euripides looked despondent. "Yes, but what chance have they for happiness when they must live in fear every day of their lives?"

Perseus suddenly took this thought in, while Pegasus snorted up at them.

Perseus' non-vacant stare—the closest he would ever get to sleep—was broken by several loud footsteps below. He looked down and saw nothing but the cloudy sky blocking the moon. It drowned any light it illuminated. Then Perseus heard some sticks being broken under several unseen figures. The occasional snort and grunt are the only other sounds he heard.

Perseus quickly looked over to see Euripides who was also studying the sounds. He had heard them many times before.

Suddenly Pegasus and Atlas' horse whinnied and ran away. Perseus strained to see in the dark but cannot. He waited, but no one seemed to give chase. He sighed with relief.

All the nymphs woke up, and all shrunk back in fear.

This was their nightmare—every night.

Atlas slowly unsheathed his sword.

Nikias looked to Perseus in utter terror.

The sound from below eventually subsided, and then everyone began to relax.

"It's alright, they have passed." Euripides reassured everyone.

Nikias scrambled through the branches toward Perseus. Before the boy could make it to Perseus, the branch under Nikias snapped.

He locked eyes with Perseus, who lunged toward him.

But Perseus was too late, and Nikias fell into the darkness below.

The boy hit the ground with a horrible thud.

Perseus looked over to see a very grave Euripides. They watched as Nikias struggled to sit up, but the boy was blinded by the darkness. Finally, the clouds moved and the moonlight beamed down on him.

The first thing he saw was feet.

Shaggy boots gave way to very shaggy legs.

Nikias looked up in horror to discover the Minotaur looming over him.

The fiend was even more monstrous than imaginable. The thing was covered in brown fur and as it rose up muscles flexed under its skin. It stood on two legs, but the feet were gnarled and twisted parodies—part animal, part human, with claws that tore ragged lines in the hard-packed earth. It had a deep chest and shoulders that sloped upward to a bull neck and giant muscular arms that spread wide as if to gather and crush Nikias. The hands were dreadful, with long fingers tipped with claws that curved into wicked points. Fresh blood streamed from the tips of each wicked claw.

But the worst thing was its head, its face. Tufted ears rose above a knelt brow beneath which were cold bloodshot eyes. It had a narrow muzzle that wrinkled back as it opened its mouth in a snarl of primal animal hate. Teeth like daggers dripped with hot saliva.

Nikias could not move. Could not think.

His heart slammed against the walls of his chest. He could not blink or swallow or scream. All he could do was behold this monstrosity.

The Minotaur threw back its head and the massive muscles of its chest and sides fleeced as it let loose with an alarming growl so loud that it threatened to break the fragile scaffolding of the boy's sanity. The sound was too loud. It exploded inside his head and though Nikias was aware of the approaching footsteps of the Minotaur's horde of centaurs all around him, the Minotaur in front of him had muted them to meaningless noise.

It had the strong muscular legs of a bull, with an even more built torso of a man. The head was a mix of a bull and a man—truly hideous. Horns rose up from its head and they gleamed in the light. The eyes shone an eerie gold glow, and when it snorted its breath lingered in the cold air. The Minotaur stared down at Nikias menacingly.

Nikias was too frightened to drop the stare between him and the vile creature. He didn't even notice he was completely surrounded.

Perseus and the rest of the company had a bird's-eye-view of the horrific scene. Centaurs surrounded the tree in which the wood nymphs took up sanctuary. They stared up hungrily, feeling excited for the forthcoming bloodshed that was about to happen.

The Minotaur laughed at Nikias. "Surely, Euripides does not think you will satisfy my hunger?" Nikias gulped in fear, as the Minotaur took a step forward. Then the horned behemoth looked up to the trees in a frenzied search. "Show yourself, Euripides. Or do you mean to cower behind this child you sent me?"

Perseus couldn't bear to watch anymore. He readied his sword, but Euripides grabbed him, shaking his head.

"Nothing can be done for Nikias." He told Perseus, who in return gave him a look of distrust. "Facing the Minotaur means death. Let the boy go."

"Here is your chance for happiness." Perseus urged him.

Euripides looked away. Perseus gritted his teeth and dropped out of the tree and landed on the back of a centaur. Perseus immediately held his sword to the creature's neck, while staring straight at the Minotaur.

"I am King Perseus of Argos." He introduced himself before the monster, which didn't seem to be impressed. "Go now, or be prepared to face my army."

Euripides looked down from his hiding place. He was frightened but also enthralled.

The Minotaur looked up at the nymphs and at his own soldiers. He gave Perseus a smile.

"We will gladly face your army, King."

Perseus drew his blade across the centaur's neck, slicing its jugular.

The battle had started, as both Perseus and Minotaur ran for Nikias.

Suddenly an arrow flew down, striking the Minotaur in the back.

This distraction allowed Perseus to grab Nikias. The Minotaur looked at the arrow curiously, and then looked up to the trees to see Euripides lower his bow. The nymph king turned to his people, who also had their bows drawn.

"Fire!" Euripides exclaimed.

The nymphs let out a cloud of arrows that rained down on the centaurs. Some were hit, but most of them were able to retaliate by throwing their spears into the trees. Chaos broke out, as several nymphs were impaled and sent screaming to the ground.

Atlas prepared to leap down, but Kallipso held him back. "This is my fault."

"No—"

"I am cursed." She blurted out.

Atlas shook his head and then tenderly grabbed her face before he descended on the centaurs.

Perseus fought his way through the centaurs, pulling Nikias along with him. He slashed and diced each centaur that ever came near them. Perseus remained calm, even though he could barely see.

Euripides looked down on his people, getting slaughtered by centaurs. He heaved a heavy sigh, and jumped to the ground. He was surrounded immediately, but he fought with such vigour that was very unaccustomed of his age.

The Minotaur mercilessly took down any nearby nymph. The beast was so big and powerful the nymphs didn't even stand a chance. The Minotaur ripped one of their arms out of its socket. Bright crimson blood spurted from the nymph's shoulder as he shrieked in complete agony.

Atlas fought a group of centaurs that encircled him. Suddenly they all heard a horrifying shriek. The centaurs looked up to see Kallipso in her harpy form and she was swooping down upon them with her talons and knives drawn. Her true self took even Atlas aback, as she viciously fought the centaurs. Atlas was also surprised to see Bubo the bronze owl slashing at the creatures with his sharp metal talons.

Perseus pushed on through the woods with Nikias. Finally, he spotted what he was looking for—Pegasus. He whistled to the horse and Pegasus galloped toward him. Perseus looked down to Nikias who stared at something behind him.

Nikias opened his mouth to scream, but nothing came out.

Perseus turned just in time to see a centaur swinging a club at him. It hit Perseus in the ribs and sent him to the ground. The centaur towered over him, while Perseus struggled to find his sword in the darkness. He endured another blow and a hoof to the face. He looked over to see Nikias crouching on the ground, holding his sword. Perseus reached out, and Nikias quickly gave it to him.

With newfound strength, Perseus slashed at the centaur, which fell dead on top of him. Perseus looked up to see another of the fallen creature's brethren grab Nikias. Perseus lunged for the centaur and stabbed it through heart—just inches away from Nikias' face. Blood spurted out all over the boy.

Nikias screamed again, but all that emerged was absolute silence.

Perseus grabbed the boy and turned to Pegasus, who had approached cautiously to them. Perseus tossed Nikias on top of the horse.

"Bring him home!" Perseus commanded Pegasus.

Nikias shook his head. Perseus stared at him for a moment. The boy was covered in blood. His face no longer showed the innocence it once had. He looked scared and profoundly sad. Perseus shook himself out of the daze and slapped Pegasus' rear. The horse took off in a hurry. Nikias looked over his shoulder at Perseus and the massacre was escaping.

Euripides looked around at the dismal sight. He was getting tired and disillusioned by how many wood nymphs laid dead. Suddenly, he heard a voice behind him. He knew exactly who it was.

"So, you've finally come down to face me yourself, Euripides."

Euripides turned around to see the Minotaur. He was even larger when he was face to face with him. The Minotaur kicked Euripides back with his front legs, sending him and his bow flying. Euripides landed hard and barely had a chance to sit up before the Minotaur was upon him.

"You will be unrecognizable when I am through with you." The Minotaur growled.

The mighty Minotaur let the wood nymph king come right at him. The massive beast backed away a few steps to give the impression that he was afraid.

Euripides leapt when the Minotaur was ten feet from him, arms outstretched; mouth wide open, and the horned fiend stood to his full height and swung his fist.

The king's jaw shattered under the impact.

Euripides howled and fell at his feet, scrabbling for refuge in the heather. He was astounded by the Minotaur's actions and confused at the strength of his attack.

Then the beast began beating Euripides into a bloody pulp. The Minotaur was strong and unrelenting. Soon the nymph king could barely raise himself up. The Minotaur loomed over him, preparing for the last blow.

"For happiness…" Euripides gasped, before the Minotaur bashed his skull in with his massive hoof. The beast kept stomping on it again and again until it felt the bone rupture.

Perseus watched helplessly at the grisly act from a distance. He tried to make his way over to the Minotaur, but he saw Atlas being tackled by a centaur. They proceeded to wrap him around in chains, while their brothers kept Kallipso at bay, by throwing their spears at her. She let out a piercing cry when she got hit.

Atlas looked up to his wounded lover, feeling powerless. "Go, Kallipso! Get out of here!"

She didn't answer and never retreated.

Perseus looked around in his surroundings. He was stunned. This was the first battle he was going to lose.

"Perseus!" Atlas yelled, striking the young king's attention as he motioned to another direction.

Perseus whipped around to see more centaurs galloping toward him from all directions.

He was surrounded.

Perseus was managed to take out a few before the Minotaur arrived. With one swing of his club, Perseus was down. He couldn't fight anymore—no matter how much he wanted to.

Perseus the Mighty had finally been defeated.

The Minotaur stood over him proudly, and surveyed the woods in a victorious demeanour. The numerous corpses littered the clearing. Atlas, a few remaining nymphs, and then soon Perseus were all about to be taken prisoner.

Then the beast reached out and grabbed him like a child choosing a toy. One hand was wrapped tight around Perseus' neck. The Minotaur began to raise him high into the air.

Perseus didn't even bother to struggle. The Minotaur's strength remained constant and unmoving. The creature maintained its savage grip on the broken human and continued to rise him higher and higher into the air.

"We shall eat the dead for dinner." The Minotaur grimly declared, and then stared down at the humiliated survivors. "The rest can be breakfast." Then the beast effortlessly tossed Perseus over to one of its henchmen.

The centaurs laughed as they dragged Atlas and Perseus behind them. Atlas was able to turn his head to find Kallipso, who had escaped the murderous raiders' clutches, perched in a tree. She had returned to her beautiful human self, except her wings were still spread wide. She looked hauntingly beautiful as she watched the scene before her.

Arsenios entered the great hall to find Queen Andromeda pacing back and forth. A distracted expression was imprinted her pale and flustered face.

"It has been taken care of, my Queen." He informed her.

Andromeda nodded to him absentmindedly. "What is it like, Arsenios, to take a life on the battlefield? Do you feel remorse?"

Arsenios hesitated for a moment. "It is my duty to protect my King and my city. I feel no remorse. Nor should you, my Lady."

"Oh, no?" Andromeda looked at him as if he had no soul. "Surely killing a member of one's own family is worse than an enemy soldier?"

"You could not distinguish Phineus from such." He replied. "My Queen must not let remorse cloud her initial suspicions of him."

Andromeda's face was now filled with anguish. "Remorse reminds us that we still have a heart."

CHAPTER TWENTY

Perseus and Atlas sat in defeat as they were chained together to a tree just outside of the Minotaur's camp. In the distance, they could make out by the light from the bonfire that the vile creature and its centaur cohorts were feasting on the wood nymphs. Perseus shuddered by the screams and groans of the few who were unfortunate to still be alive. He vividly imagined a centaur's jaws biting down hard, crushing its victim's larynx. Its eyes glinting with cold glee as the monster released its grip on the nymph's throat, and blood gushed from his wound. While this encouraged Atlas to struggle with his chains even more.

"Wretched chains!" Cursed Atlas, trying to break the handcuffs. "Perseus, see if you can reach—" He stopped to Perseus sitting beside him motionless with his eyes closed.

The young king was still sulking on his first and probably last defeat.

"Perseus?" Atlas asked him again, but the only reply the strong man had received was a pitiful look on his friend's face. "Perseus!"

Atlas hollered in Perseus' ear. This time it snapped his young friend into attention. Perseus grunted in surprise, finally acknowledging Atlas.

"Oh, did I disturb your sleep?" He mockingly asked Perseus. The Son of Zeus opened his eyes to glare at his fellow prisoner. "Good, you're awake. Now help me to get out of these chains. I do not intend to be some horse's breakfast."

Perseus looked at Atlas in despair. "There is no point in trying to escape. We will be killed as soon as we stand." He said with inconceivable bitterness.

"Maybe *you* will be." Atlas said, feeling disgusted by Perseus' sour attitude.

"It is hopeless, Atlas. Just accept—"

"I will accept nothing!" Atlas bellowed, deciding it had enough of this "oh-woe-is-me" garbage. "You are mad. Do you not see what good fortune we have?"

A sombre look of doubt shadowed Perseus' eyes. "Fortune?"

He looked at Atlas in mystification.

Maybe he is the one who is truly mad. We were outnumbered and beaten. And now he thinks we still have chance to escape?

"You still possess the strength to fight, as do I." Atlas said, rattling the chains that bound him and Perseus. "Those hideous beasts rely on the strength of their iron and thus leave us unattended. There are enough weapons here to—" Then he saw Perseus shaking his head in disapproval. "Why do you shake your head? I am not finished…"

"We were defeated, Atlas!" Roared Perseus, hoping his bull-headed friend would take the hint and face the bleak reality of their situation.

"In one battle!" Atlas hollered right back at him. "We have seen victory in many others, and we will see it again."

Perseus quietly replied, "I have never lost a battle."

"You never had to fight one on your own." Atlas amended him. "You have always had your father's vigilance and protection. In the real world, Perseus, you lose most of the time. It is through perseverance that you finally achieve success."

"Not for me!" Yelled Perseus, now sounding like a spoiled child who had just a game. "'Perseus the Mighty'? I win; it is what I do. It is how everyone knows me. I do not surrender! I do not sit in chains, Atlas! What would my people think?! What would Andromeda—"

"Your sense of self-worth is going to smother me before the centaurs do." Rebuked Atlas, while Perseus scoffed in anger. "Stop acting like the spoiled child of a god-king, and recognize who you are."

"And what is that?"

"You are only a man, Perseus." Addressed Atlas. "You cannot give yourself standards meant for immortals. You will fail. Victory is not given to you; it must be earned. And that is why men, not gods, achieve glory."

Candles provided the only light in the Olympian palace. Zeus slumped on his mighty throne, feeling despondent about this recent turn of events. He wished he could help his son, even though he was still angry that Perseus had renounced him but the boy was his own flesh and blood. There wasn't anything Zeus could without forfeiting the wager to Hera. Then he noticed Hermes was humbly approaching him. The gods' messenger walked up to Zeus slowly, like he was trying to conceal himself from a sleeping dragon. He didn't want to worsen his lord's mood.

"My Lord?" Hermes peacefully said to Zeus, similar to the melody of a child's lullaby. Zeus stared up into space, barely noticing his old and trusted friend was standing before him. "Is there anything…you wish for me to do?"

Zeus tediously stroked his beard, hoping by doing so would give him more power. "No, Hermes, you are dismissed."

Hera walked by the throne room with several of her attendants. She concealed herself behind a pillar to survey the scene. It looked like Zeus and Hermes were engaged in a very important meeting. She could tell by the distressed expression on her husband's face that it wasn't anything good.

"All hope is not lost." Hermes said to his master. "Perseus may still prevail."

All Zeus could do was to smile weakly. Hera looked on from her hiding place and felt quite pleased.

I've won. I've won!

* * *

The first rays of sunlight illuminated a very different vision of the Minotaur's camp. It was much better than the night before. The fire had burned out, the laughter and screams had subsided, and the centaurs were scattered across the camp, sleeping off their night of merriment and mayhem.

Atlas continued to struggle with his chains, while Perseus sat around in a daze. Atlas gathered one last surge of strength, and in one big stretch he shattered the links in his chains and he was free.

He turned to face Perseus in disbelief and began to laugh in amazement. "Perseus! Did you see that? I broke though iron!"

"No, I did." A woman replied from behind them.

Atlas looked over his shoulder to see Kallipso emerging from a tree. She had Atlas' sword in her hand. He looked at her with a mixture of love and admiration.

"I told you…you didn't have to—"

Kallipso quickly hushed him. "I think it best not to waste time here, come." Then she moved to cut Perseus' chains.

"Don't bother with him." Atlas protested. "He is still mourning his loss."

Kallipso ignored Atlas and saw Perseus, who was still feeling melancholy. "Do not mourn the nymphs for too long, for they died admirably."

"Kallipso," said Atlas, "he is not concerned with the lives that have been lost, only his ruined winning streak."

She was busy slicing through the chains. "I do not believe that Perseus feels nothing for the men who have fought beside him." The metal links sprinkled onto the ground. Perseus was free. "Come, Perseus, let us find your son."

Instead of getting up and running out of the camp with his comrades, Perseus remained seated. He didn't even look at Kallipso or Atlas. He crossed his arms and felt he was leaving this world and entering into another.

Atlas looked over to Kallipso. "What good is finding his son if he can never show his face in Argos again." He approached Perseus, making sure the sullen king was within earshot, and sarcastically said, "His people could never forgive a king who was defeated."

Kallipso was repelled by all of this. "Come, Atlas. Let us continue on to Seriphus. Perseus can join us when he is ready."

She handed Atlas his sword and motioned to his horse. Atlas scoffed at Perseus, and then proceeded to his stallion. Kallipso kneeled down to Perseus to meet him at eyelevel.

"Pay no heed to him."

"I was wrong to judge you so harshly." Perseus finally spoke. "But there is a truth in Atlas' words. All who know me will be disappointed with my defeat."

"Your soldiers, and your citizens, and your queen do not follow you because you win battles, Perseus." She comforted him. "They do so because they respect your bravery, they find comfort in your good heart. As their king, you owe it to them to be the man they believe you to be."

Kallipso rose up to her feet and joined Atlas at his horse.

Perseus closed his eyes and thought back to Hesiod's face. It was filled with excitement and admiration. It was the boy's first mission and he was very overwhelmed to be fighting under Perseus' orders.

Perseus could still hear Hesiod's soulful voice, as if he was sitting right next to him. "May I say it is a great honour to fight beside you on this on day..."

Then there was a shot of Andromeda staring lovingly at him in the Argos palace. "My love, come back to me..." She said hauntingly.

There was the image of a sad smile that belonged to Alexion, who was in chains. "You are just, Perseus..." He said in a low raspy voice.

And Perseus saw his loyalist friend Arsenios, who was trying to accompany him on the journey. "Then I come as your friend."

The last flash was Euripides sitting in the tree with Perseus the night before. "There is a strength in you that I have not seen in many..."

Perseus shook off his chains and swiftly got onto his feet. He could see Pegasus waiting for him in the distance. The beautiful white winged horse whinnied to him, beckoning his rider to come to over. But Perseus shook his head over to his steed and went off to a different direction.

Perseus crept through the camp, being absolutely careful not to wake any of the dozing centaurs. He stepped on a piece of metal and looked down to see Bubo—in pieces.

It looked like the centaurs took him apart to see how he worked and ripped off his metallic wings. Then it appeared they used him as ball for some kind of game and spiked poor little Bubo to the ground. Gears and sprockets were shattered everywhere.

His mechanical eyes were shut and the light that once powered them with life was nowhere to be found. Perseus looked down at him with great sadness.

"I'm sorry, old friend." He said mournfully.

Perseus continued on, as he pilfered a centaur's club and shield. After a few more paces, he saw something that caught his eye. Past the sleeping creatures Perseus could see his sword glittering in the morning light. Besides the centaurs being in his way, the main obstacle was that the tent where the sword was located belonged to the Minotaur.

Perseus' jaw was set in determination when he headed for his sword. He reached it without disturbing any of the neighbouring centaurs. When he leaned down to pick it up, the Minotaur's tent flap quickly rose, and the hideous creature emerged. It wasn't even surprised to see Perseus standing there.

"Good morning, King." Grunted the beast. The centaurs woke up to the sound of its booming voice. Slowly they got up and made their way to their master's tent. "Have you come for breakfast?"

"No," Perseus replied, "I have come to kill you."

The hulking monster looked at Perseus if he were joking. "An impossible feat, though many have tried." Boasted the Minotaur, giving him a cruel smile. "I admire your confidence, but after your performance last night, it is quite unwarranted. I will not stoop so low as to fight you."

Perseus took this blow with stride. "You have not the choice."

"Oh, don't I?" The Minotaur replied, surveying all its minions who have awakened from their slumber. "I have hundreds of soldiers here that would gladly rip you to shreds."

Perseus took a moment to size up all the centaurs, and then locked his eyes with his prong headed nemesis. "If I must kill all of them in order to fight you, I will do so with pleasure."

The Minotaur suddenly appeared to be disenchanted. "What is this fascination with fighting me? Is it to mend your wounded ego? Or perhaps you seek to avenged the death of your friend Euripides?"

"I want to know what it feels like to kill a monster who preys on the innocent without mercy." Perseus frankly replied. "I want to see what the blood of Hades looks like."

The Minotaur tried hard to hide its annoyance. "The only blood you shall see today shall be your own."

"Then fight me." Goaded Perseus. "If you are that sure of your abilities, then you will have your breakfast."

Eager to prove its ungodly strength and superiority once again, the Minotaur threw off his robe and picked up a spiked club. The centaurs cheered the beast on, as he closed in on Perseus. The Son of Zeus quickly discarded the centaur club and took his sword.

Perseus braced himself against the shield for the Minotaur's first blow. The spikes hitting the bronze shield made a deafening sound.

All the centaurs backed away, giving the fighters more space for combat. The Minotaur was fast and strong. It charged toward Perseus, who went for a quick stab.

But the beast dodged it and returned the swipe with another blow of the club. Perseus managed to block the hit once again, but the impact caused him to stagger backward.

This enraged the Minotaur. It dug his hooves to ground, picking up speed like its bovine brethren before a wild charge. It raced toward Perseus, but the human leapt out of the way at the last second, as he sliced the Minotaur across the back.

The centaurs gasped in shock.

They had never seen anyone wounded their master before. They had underestimated this king. This man was fighting without fear. This quality had at least given him an advantage.

The Minotaur looked over its shoulder to see the deep slash on its back. Dark red blood trickled over his muscles. It smiled back to Perseus.

"You accomplished one of your goals." It said to the King of Argos. "Congratulations."

Perseus kept his sword up, and circled the Minotaur. "I shall accomplish the other."

The Minotaur charged at Perseus, this time swinging the club at his legs. Even though Perseus was able to jump over it, the spikes caught part of his leg. He stumbled back and the beast threw another heavy blow. The spikes were stuck into Perseus' shield. The Minotaur pulled the club back, ripping the shield from Perseus' arm.

The Minotaur was unable to pull the club out of the shield. Frustrated, he threw away the weapons over his soldiers. The centaurs hastily dodged the debris.

The beast advanced on Perseus. It brought its hands up slowly, mimicking Perseus' defensive posture. The young king circled his prong-headed adversary, feinting, punching, trying to get into or at least an opening to deliver a quick punch to the face.

The Minotaur watched him carefully and whenever Perseus tried to land a blow, the monster brushed aside his attempts. But that didn't deter Perseus as he dodged and weaved, staying just out of reach of the Minotaur's return punches.

A massive fist suddenly struck him directly to the chest, knocking the breath right out of him. Perseus swung wildly, missed, and before he could recover the Minotaur punched him in the face, throwing him backwards and nearly tearing his head off.

Perseus, dazed, reached back and swung a leg over. The Minotaur stopped where it was, cocking his head, clearly puzzled by the move. Nature's abomination probably thought that Perseus was willingly to commit suicide rather than continue what was clearly a hopeless fight.

The Minotaur's powerful legs lashed out at him, kicking his face and stomach. The creature's iron-laced hooves dug into his flesh.

Perseus rolled away on instinct, grunting in pain. Somehow he managed to spring back onto his feet even as the Minotaur circled him menacingly, keeping up his attack. A rapid-fire series of bone-jarring strikes and kicks drove Perseus to the other side of the fighting circle. A driving fore fist punch made his teeth rattle, but when the beast threw a spinning kick at his head, Perseus caught the oncoming foot in an ankle-lock. The Minotaur was able to break free and leaped over the puny mortal's head in a single bound.

The spiked club whooshed over Perseus' head, and the Minotaur dropped out of the sky and landed directly in front of Perseus. He cursed under his breath and dropped, skidding on his backside, as he got a good look at the monster in front of him. It charged at Perseus even as the stone and earth scraped against the back of his legs. The Minotaur targeted Perseus' abdomen as he got closer, and the horde of centaurs kept cheering for their master to prevail.

Then Perseus realized he had stopped skidding on the ground and was right under the Minotaur.

Not good.

The Minotaur pivoted on its waist and bent over Perseus. A massive arm slammed down, straight for the demigod's face. Perseus rolled right, and another arm slammed down. Perseus rolled left, and then he was trapped right between the two abnormally muscular arms, with the Minotaur's sharp claws digging into his shoulders. Perseus kicked out, pushed off the ground, and started to squeeze himself through the arms, just as he became aware that somewhere nearby the spiked club was in his peripheral vision.

Better act now.

Perseus pushed his palms against the ground, bracing himself, and then kicked up with all his strength, planting both his sandals squarely in the monster's crotch. Perseus wasn't counting on the Minotaur having a weak spot, but it did slow the villain down.

As of now, Perseus had leverage.

Perseus arched his back, and thrust up with all his strength.

Suddenly several spikes were an inch away from his face.

"Unnnhhh!!!"

Perseus arched higher.

The Minotaur lifted an inch off the ground, and the spikes moved with the beast.

The Minotaur pivoted, looking confused. It was unbalanced now, its arms flailed for a second, and then it toppled over Perseus' head, and smashed to the ground, holding its arms out in front as it fell.

Perseus jumped to his feet, his leg muscles quivering. That thing had to weigh over three hundred pounds, and Perseus would need something to drink when this was all done.

But it wasn't done yet.

The Minotaur rose up again to face Perseus. It snapped toward him, scuttling on the ground as if it were a giant spider with many nimble legs. Perseus barely had time to get his hands up before he could parry the Minotaur's club with his sword.

Metal sparked and clanged.

Perseus was on the move and winced only before bull rushing the Minotaur. Fighting in close quarters once more, it was fist against fist as steel battled stone. The creature's right hand proved to be mightier as it made contact with Perseus' face.

Perseus roared in frustration and anger. The Minotaur took advantage and gathered all of its energy on trying to deliver a vicious uppercut, but Perseus dodged it with the utmost of ease. The beast snorted in hatred and the grip on the handle of the club was in tightened like he was going to strangle the life out of it.

The club came for him again, and Perseus thrust forward and just barely got his right hand up in time to block it. He was halfway through an eagle strike, so he came all the way around, swinging his leg, kicking the Minotaur on its side. But the beast's chainmail absorbed most of the impact. Perseus' foot bounced, but the recoil threw the Minotaur off balance again. Now Perseus was on the attack, legs and arms thrusting forward, driving the monster left, right, right, and then right again. The behemoth righted itself, and charged again.

Its right arm came up, and Perseus centred. He backed away and maneuvered out of its destructive path. The Minotaur moved with a hitch now, and it seemed to be as concerned with keeping Perseus from escaping as it was with killing him.

Time to end this little dance. The Minotaur grinned with cruel delight.

Perseus kicked out. The Minotaur took a kick to the shoulder, and wobbled, raising its arm, which was a mistake. Perseus had moved away, and now his foot was coming around again. It caught the Minotaur on the shoulder, and it spun all the way around. In the split-second Perseus leaped on its back and wrestled with the beast.

The Minotaur snarled and wailed. It was screaming at Perseus to get off. The Son of Zeus held on to as long as he could until the Minotaur threw him off and sent him crashing to the other side of the impromptu arena.

Teeth gritted against the pain, Perseus came in close, ducking and weaving to avoid the Minotaur's greater reach as he fired punch after punch at the creature's midsection. It was one of the few large areas on the beast's body not protected by its armour.

Believing in pain, the Minotaur lashed out and kneed Perseus in the chin. Perseus stumbled, and the monster pressed on and delivered a slashing left that laid open Perseus' cheek. The Son of Zeus could feel the blood flowing again, but even more he felt energy surging through him.

Perseus grabbed hold of the Minotaur's fists, forcing the beast back. He lashed out hard with the heel of his boot. The monster bellowed louder, staggering back, but Perseus did not let up. He pressed on, using blows he'd never before dared used on any living being. The Minotaur returned the attack, but the power of its blows seemed to be waning.

Both warriors were swaying on their feet. The Minotaur's eyes appeared dull, cloudy. Perseus' face was so swollen that his eyes were barely visible, but they were clear.

Then the Minotaur turned back and rushed Perseus with his horns down. He managed to connect with Perseus' side, and the human warrior cried out in pain. The pain was sharp, bright, and excruciating. Perseus grabbed the wound and the creature slammed his elbow into Perseus' jaw. He fell to the ground and felt around for his sword, while the Minotaur's spit and snot dripped down on him.

"You put up a good fight, King." The beast said to him. Almost sounding grateful for the exercise Perseus had generously provided. "It is a shame that you must die. You would have made a great addition to my army."

Perseus was choking on the pain. Searing pain erupted from his side, radiating out along his screaming nervous system, as over a foot of sharpened steel pierced through leather, skin, and muscle. Perseus bit down hard on his lower lip to keep from crying out in agony. He dropped to his knees on the blood-soaked grass, as blood flowed down his torso.

"No…" Perseus could feel his hand finally connecting with his sword.

"No?" The Minotaur replied, with disappointment in his voice. "Very well, I shall enjoy my breakfast."

As he leaned over to bite Perseus' neck, the young king swung his sword and decapitated the unsuspecting Minotaur.

The centaurs stared in disbelief and fear when Perseus stood up and lifted up the Minotaur's head for all to see. He held it high in the air as the blood dripped down on his face and arm. Perseus looked as equally terrifying as the Minotaur did. He let out a horrifying scream in which the veins bulged in his neck. The centaurs were too afraid to move. They simply stared at this human who killed their captain in this unbelievable spectacle of mortal combat. With another scream, Perseus threw the head at the crowd. They all ducked to avoid getting hit. Then Perseus used his sword to hack apart the body of the Minotaur.

"Are you hungry?" He yelled over to the centaurs. "Here is your meal! Come, eat!"

Perseus' madness frightened the centaurs. They all turned and ran, unsure of what this crazed human would do next. Perseus watched them go and within moments he was alone in the camp.

He was surrounded by the dead of the wood nymph tribe, which had been laid all over the outskirts of the camp. Over a dozen nymphs were brutally killed. Some were missing arms and legs. The centaurs scoured the woods to find the missing pieces, but even if this grisly task had been completed what had been assembled did not add up to twenty of the little folk. The Minotaur had fed as it killed. And Perseus made very damned sure that each and everyone one of them were avenged.

Pegasus slowly crept toward him. When Perseus saw him, he dropped the sword and signalled for the horse to come closer. Perseus caught his breath, pressed a hand to his injured side. He had lost more blood than he cared to think about. His head started to spin again, and black stars were exploding in the corners of his eyes. He knew he was about to pass out. He dropped to his knees and leaned against Pegasus.

He wanted to close his eyes and sleep for a while, but he knew that would be a big mistake. He might never wake up. With an effort, he pulled himself to his feet. He felt disoriented and tried to focus his mind and reach into the depths of his stamina. But his knees buckled and the collapsed against the white horse again. When Pegasus finally reached him, Perseus hugged him and broke down into tears.

Perseus hadn't wept so grievously since he first received word that his mother died. For many days he moped and felt bitterly toward the whole world. But at so much length he took courage and kept telling himself that she was the one who died, not him. And she wouldn't want him to live in pain and alienation. Her final wish was that he should restore her honour and claim his birth right. As time passed, his grief became less sharp and he succeeded on claiming the throne of Argos. However, now he realized on what cost it took for him to get accomplish his goals. Especially on what it took just to survive.

"No more." He sobbed, holding the horse's neck tight. Bile rose at the back of his throat. He clenched his teeth to keep from throwing up. "I can take no more. Have I not killed enough?"

His voice was broken, pathetic, like a child's. Then finally, in the outpouring of grief he'd tried so hard to deny, Perseus broke down and cried.

Perseus did not squawk or bleat. He spoke with tenderness to the horse, and Pegasus hung on to his words. Their senses were entirely given over to the soft voice of the King of Argos. His words were clear evidence of the tortured pain within his troubled soul.

Blood from the Minotaur was smeared over Pegasus white coat. The horse didn't mind. He stood there patiently, as Perseus cried into his mane.

Arsenios sombrely stood before the court made up of influential citizens of Argos. Andromeda sat behind him in her throne. Her head was lowered, as if she wanted to hide from the meeting.

"I speak on behalf of our grieving Queen." Said Arsenios. "The gods continue to test her strength. Phineus of Thebes is no longer with us, having died in his sleep this past night."

Gasps filled the hall, followed by indistinct murmuring among politicians and members of the elite. Andromeda began to choke on a sob.

"He seemed to be in good health yesterday." Said one citizen.

"I know." Arsenios replied, trying to keep the court in order. "It came as shock to us all."

Another citizen approached. "Will he be taken back to Thebes?"

"Phineus will be laid to rest here, in the family tomb, per our Queen's wishes." Answered Arsenios. "Arrangements have been made and a messenger dispatched to Thebes to inform his loved ones of this terrible news."

Andromeda stood up, which caused everyone to bow. She headed for the door, until a citizen reached out to grab her hand.

"I am very sorry for your loss, Queen Andromeda." He expressed his condolences. "Phineus was a good man."

"Thank you." She replied tearfully." The palace guards let her through to the hallway, while everyone else in the court looked at Arsenios with concern.

"She looks frailer by the day." One person spoke from the galley.

Another worried member of the court came forward. "She has had to deal with so much. More than the gods should allow."

Arsenios took in the sentiments of the crowd. "That is all you were called her for. You are now dismissed."

As people began to file out, one citizen walked over to Arsenios.

"Will the Queen be alright?"

Arsenios casually answered, "Of course." After everyone had left, he looked over to the palace guards. "Our Queen's resolve weakens with each tragedy that befalls her. Watch over her, see that she does nothing rash."

The guards each nodded in obedience and headed out of the court.

CHAPTER TWENTY-ONE

Atlas and Kallipso carried a small paddleboat into the calm waters. The Island of Seriphus loomed up from the sea in the distance. Polydectes' castle sat on top of the cragged isle like a beacon. As Atlas steadied the boat, Kallipso heard a noise coming from behind them. She gently touched Atlas' shoulder, and he turned to see Perseus riding toward them on the back of Pegasus. Perseus smiled sheepishly at the two and dismounted.

He never completely recovered from the wounds he received from the Minotaur, and they were etched into his flesh by the long journey to Seriphus. He managed to stop the infection from spreading through his wounds, but he was unable to stop it from spreading it into his mind. Now at last, despair became one of his weapons. He cultivated it; toiled over it; sharpened it; and it was his constant companion on the road to Seriphus.

"Glad you finally decided to join us." Atlas said to him. "I thought we'd be heading to Seriphus without you, and I have no idea what your son looks like."

Perseus lowered his head in shame. He had to make amends to the only two people who had helped through this epic journey. "I am sorry to you both. I am ashamed of my foolish behaviour. While defeat does not make for an admirable king, self-pitying is a far worse affliction."

Atlas and Kallipso smiled at each other, and then to Perseus.

"Save your breath," Atlas ordered. "You'll need it for rowing."

Perseus smiled, advancing toward them. He looked over to the island, observing the castle with such scrutiny. "How peculiar Polydectes leaves the only access to his city unguarded."

Atlas scornfully looked over to Kallipso. "He does not even appreciate our hard work."

Then he pointed to a tree where four Seriphian guards were tied up and gagged. Perseus shook his head in admiration. Kallipso climbed into the boat, as Perseus and Atlas pushed it out a little further. Finally, the two jumped in and grabbed the oars and set out for Seriphus.

While the two men were progressively rowing toward the island, Kallipso fell asleep at the bow. Perseus couldn't help to see Atlas admire her.

"What will become of you when our journey has ended?" He asked Atlas. "Will you return to Tartarus?"

"I suppose so." Atlas answered, not breaking his gaze on the sleeping beauty.

"Will she join you?"

"I would not subject her to the isolation that comes with Tartarus."

Perseus was surprised by his reply. "You are both welcome in Argos."

"An outlaw and a harpy living amongst your citizens?" Atlas asked in bafflement. "They will think their great king has gone mad."

"They will welcome you, as I have." Perseus promised him.

"I cannot." Atlas rebuked his offer. "If any of them were to learn of what I have done—"

"What have you done?" Perseus asked in a very ire tone. He demanded answers. This has been hanging over his head the whole time they became travelling companions. "To where you feel compelled to hide yourself from all humanity?"

Atlas turned away from Perseus. Whatever his secret was, he couldn't bear to look Perseus in the eye. "I do not wish to speak of it."

"I will not judge you." Perseus vowed.

"Everyone judges, whether they have a right to or not."

"Well, why do you continue to punish yourself when you are already remorseful? Surely your crime cannot be the reprehensible—"

"It is." Atlas interrupted.

"I do not believe it." Retorted Perseus. "You are not a bad person, Atlas."

"You know nothing of who I was, or the things I did—"

"But I know you now!" And I can see that you—"

"**I KILLED MY SON, PERSEUS!**" Blurted Atlas. Perseus went silent. He couldn't hide his shock from this ghastly revelation. "I deserve an eternity in Hades for that." Atlas turned away, looking so ashamed.

The two men didn't speak to each other for several minutes. Perseus looked over at his direction, trying to muster up the courage to follow through in this difficult time.

"Were your actions intentional?" He finally spoke.

"That is irrelevant." Atlas sharply answered.

"No…"

Before Perseus could finish, something had hit the boat. Kallipso sprang up in alarm as the boat was struck again. All three of them looked into the waters suspiciously.

The boat began to pitch as a loud, violent shockwave swept over the entire body of water. The passengers grabbed on to the sides of the old wooden boat, their voices rising, and fear was clouding their thoughts. The boat tripped and fell, as the sea was now a torrent of waves, tossing the vessel about like a toy. Cold water sloshed into the boat, seeping through the clothes of the terrified warriors. Their eyes were stinging. A loud rumble grew in their ears and in their terror they envisioned the boat tearing itself apart. The noise escalated to a crescendo, loud, booming, and crackling. The sound was turning almost physical as it blew across their clothes like the wind.

The boat suddenly lurched to a halt, the wood creaking and shrieking as loud as those it carried. Perseus and his friends held on as tightly as they could. The wood was splintering in their calloused, trembling hands, drawing blood across their fingers and palms.

However, Kallipso had nothing to hold on to but the narrow bow—where the wood was thinnest. It was already cracked and falling into the water. Atlas held on her so she wouldn't be thrown overboard and into the rapidly turning water.

Suddenly eight large tentacles spurted out of the water, surrounding the boat. At the end of each tentacle was the head of a piranha. Their jaws were wide open and were ready to strike. Each head let out a terrifying shrill when they lunged at the three passengers.

Kallipso ducked, while Perseus and Atlas drew their swords. They strike at the heads, but the creatures dodged each swing. They pulled back to regroup.

"Hurry, paddle!" Perseus said to his comrades.

Kallipso grabbed an oar and tried to get the boat away from the chilling creatures, as they swooped in for another attack. Perseus quickly sliced off one of the heads, while another one dove in and bit Kallipso on the shoulder. Atlas heard her agonizing cry and swiftly beheaded that one. The rest of the monsters retreated and disappeared back into the water.

"What in the gods…" Atlas said in awe. So far he considered this the worst beast they had fought so far in their sojourn.

Kallipso was nursing her shoulder, as Perseus picked up the other paddle. "Come," he said to his friends, "they are only regrouping."

They only have gotten a few yards away until the tentacles returned with a vengeance. Despite only two were slain, eight heads popped out of the water. The only difference this time was that the two that were lopped off had now have little heads growing back.

"What are these things?!" Kallipso said in fright.

Kallipso had her knives prepared. When the creatures attacked, she and her two male companions decapitated six of the piranha heads. Being affected by the pain, the remaining tentacles submerged back into the abyss.

Then the water around them began to bubble. The heads reappeared, but now they are rising to the air.

There was a movement in the air about them. Such a swirl as is made in water when some creature rises to the surface. A nameless, freezing wind blew on all of them briefly, as if from an opened door. Perseus felt a presence at his back, but he did not look over his shoulder. He kept his eyes fixed on the Island of Seriphus, on which a tenuous shadow hovered. This shadow grew in size and clarity, until it stood and distinct and horrific.

Finally, the body that controlled the tentacles started to surface.

The Scylla finally revealed herself.

She was half woman and half sea monster.

Her presence was frightening. She grinned menacingly at the three trespassers, as her tentacles descended upon them. Perseus and Atlas swung wildly as the monsters, as Kallipso diced the ones that came her way. While waiting for the heads to grow back, Atlas and Perseus grabbed the paddles and tried to get away.

Kallipso protected them by changing into her harpy form. She scared some of the piranha heads away using nothing but her demonic looks. Launching herself off the boat, Kallipso flew straight at the Scylla with her talons stretched out. She sliced the vicious sea monster across the chest. The Scylla roared out in pain, sending some of her tentacles after the flying harpy. This granted Perseus and Atlas a chance to get away.

The Scylla was not distracted for long. When she saw the men escaping, she slammed down four of her tentacles into their boat—breaking it in half. The men were tossed into the water.

A tentacle was wrapped around each of them. They both struggled to get to the surface, and they sliced through the gigantic limbs, and were freed. They made it to the surface to see Kallipso circling the Scylla's head, like the bird of prey she was. She dove toward her and attacked with her beak and talons. She looked down to the men and directed them to the Isle of Seriphus, which was only a hundred yards away.

"Go!" Kallipso yelled to the men. Perseus started swimming, but Atlas remained. He wanted to help Kallipso fight this damned abomination. Kallipso looked down at Atlas, realizing his intentions. "Atlas! Go!"

As soon as he turned to swim, he heard a shriek and discovered the tentacles now wrapped up Kallipso. They dragged her down to the water so she would drown. Atlas immediately turned back, swimming as fast as he could.

Perseus looked over his shoulder, but as soon as he stopped swimming more tentacles attacked him. They were all trying to drown him as well.

Atlas dove underwater to see Kallipso struggling with the heads. He swam over and hacked them to pieces. Kallipso could feel the tentacles losing their strength, and then she shot back to the surface and into the air. Atlas headed for the Scylla's body as well. Kallipso looked over to see Perseus being dragged underwater, and she swooped right in after him.

Perseus wrestled with the monstrous tentacles underwater. They had his arms trapped, which made it useless for him to use his sword. Just he was about to give up struggling, he looked over to see Kallipso dive into the water. With her sharp talons she sliced through the tentacles like a hot knife through butter. Perseus caught his breath and watches as she soared back to help Atlas. Perseus could see he wasn't too far from shore. The best bet was to go on ahead, but his friends needed his help.

Atlas was able to scale the Scylla's large body. The monster noticed just in time to watch the brawny mortal drive his sword into her heart. The oversized sea creature screamed out in pain, while all of her tentacles attacked Atlas. He fell back into the water and the tentacles followed closely behind.

Perseus swam toward Atlas, bringing him to the surface. He strived to drag his friend to shore. Kallipso bore down on the Scylla fearlessly, a look of grim determination on her angular features.

She was fast, and nearly as strong of arm as Atlas. Her sharp talons slashed through the air, never striking from the same angle twice. Kallipso finished the job by slicing across the monster's throat with her claws. The Scylla writhed in pain and began to sink into the sea.

Perseus was almost at the beach, but he was getting tired. He began to swim slower and he was going under. Kallipso flew down and picked up Atlas with her talons like an owl hunting for field mice.

"Perseus, can you make it?" She asked him, who felt relieved that she took quite a weight off his shoulders.

Perseus wearily nodded in response, watching her take Atlas to land. Moments later Perseus flopped onto the sand.

Kallipso gently dropped Atlas on the beach.

He didn't even move.

She had eyes only for her lover, as she draped herself against a nearby tree for support. All that strenuous activity against the Scylla had wiped her out. Atlas lay unmoving, all crumpled, bloody and broken.

Kallipso reverted back to her human form and crouched down beside him. Sobbing, with her face twisted in denial, she dropped to her knees. Her hands were trembling as she reached out, but she did not issue a sound from her lips except for Atlas' name—although every animal in the forest claimed later that they heard her piercing scream of anguish and horror. She repeated the name over and over, like a mantra, as if simply by saying the word she could anchor spirit to flesh and to keep her beloved from slipping away.

Then, she heard Atlas call *her* name.

She could feel her strained lungs finally beginning to relax as they drew air again. Her breathing was starting to slow down. She was finding it difficult to reclaim her composure. She could not shake the distressing implications of what had just happened.

Instinct guided her to take a hand in both of hers, and Kallipso cried out again with a hoarse coughing exclamation that gave voice to all the pain balled up inside Atlas.

There were bursts of ice and fire alone one side. Scrapes and busted ribs and a burning within one arm that told Kallipso it too was broken. There was even more pain where he had cracked his skull from the Scylla's thrashing, originating the source of the blood that painted his face.

"Atlas?" She asked nervously, but he didn't say anything in return. "My love?"

She tenderly took his face, searching for life. Blood seeped out from numerous cuts on his body. She tried to prop his head up and wipe some of the blood away. She stroked his brow and tried to kiss the pain away.

"Do not leave me." She said in grief. Her eyes were now misting. "I cannot bear the solitude."

Perseus stumbled toward them. He knelt next to Atlas as well. He studied his chest and saw that Atlas was slightly breathing. There was a dull ache near the bottom of Atlas' back, a gaping hollowness in the centre of his chest. With a start, Kallipso realized she'd forgotten to breathe, and with a frantic gulp of air comprehended to her horror that atlas couldn't.

His back was broken.

She couldn't bear to look anymore and closed her eyes—only that didn't help. Instead, it simply took her somewhere else.

Her own heart was pumping too hard and fast for her to separate the beats. Her breath was coming in narrow gasps that matched its cadence, like an animal that had been entranced. She stood there helpless as if a predator was in front of her, seeking her life. That made her angry; she hated being afraid and refused to be a victim, even of fate itself.

She thought at first she'd blacked out because all around her all was darkness. And then, of course, she assumed everything was blurring in the distance, while it resolved as she moved closer to Atlas.

After a few moments he opened his eyes.

Then he called for Kallipso.

She grinned in excitement, but Perseus had seen too many die and knew that Atlas didn't have much time left.

Kallipso knew what was happening. But she wouldn't dare to say it aloud.

"My friend…" Perseus said sadly.

"You have got to hold on, my love." Pleaded Kallipso, as she guided his one good hand along her cheek.

Atlas tried like to hell to keep his eyes open to see his ladylove. "I'm broken, Kallipso." He said with a quiver. "There is nothing I can do."

"**Stop it!** Don't you dare talk like that, I won't let you go!"

The passion surprised both Perseus and Atlas. Kallipso's face was disfigured with grief she'd never imagined or never thought could possibly be endured.

Atlas had difficulty on grabbing Perseus' hand. Perseus took Atlas' hand and squeezed it. "I did not mean too…" He said weakly. Sweat coated his face, and he had to force himself to take deep, slow breaths in a vain attempt to calm his racing heart.

Kallipso looked at him in awe. "Did not mean to what?"

Atlas turned his head over to Perseus, who knew what he was talking about. "I did not mean to kill him."

Perseus sighed, holding his hand. "I know you didn't."

Atlas shook his head. "Perseus, listen to me. I did not mean to…he was so small. I did not know my own strength…"

"The gods have forgiven you." Perseus said. His voice was filled with sadness. "Let peace take hold of you in your final moments. Do not enter Elysium as a tortured soul."

"Final moments?" Said Kallipso, not coming into terms of this dreadful reality. She felt the burning sting of the first tear falling down her face.

Perseus looked at Atlas with great respect. "You have been a true friend, and I shall not forget you."

Atlas nodded appreciatively to Perseus. Nothing else needed to be said. He stepped back, and immediately Kallipso hovered over Atlas.

"My love…" He said to Kallipso with kind words. She leaned in further to hear his final words. "You have warmed my final days in a way I could not have imagined."

"Do not speak words of death." Kallipso replied, holding his hand in a vice grip. She hoped it would be enough for his soul to stay on this earth. Atlas tried to touch her face, but he couldn't lift his arm. She rested her head on his chest, as he feebly touched her hair. "You have found the heart I did not know existed." Then she whispered, "Stay with me…"

Atlas smiled at the thought. He had never felt this way. His heart was full to bursting with the brightest and best of emotions and yet, at the same time, on the verge of breaking. How could any moment seem so wonderful and potentially terrible, all at once?

Kallipso leaned in to kiss him like a cobra going for a quick strike. She didn't merely kiss him, but forged a connection between her essence and his. He was hard, she was soft, he was soft, she was hard—the lines of isolation blurred and reformed so that he lost track as if there stretched, expanded, turned back upon itself, and enabled them to live an entire lifetime in an instant.

He couldn't breathe while he suddenly felt a sense of being incomplete. He could feel her discovering all the truths he had carefully hidden away. She saw the blood in his past and what it had cost him.

Before this moment, Atlas had never known the true meaning and nature of love. He still wasn't sure he had the answer. But what he found here—what he and Kallipso were sharing—was just as fundamental. It had changed his life by showing him possibilities he had never dared to imagine.

It was intimacy.

Then he closed his eyes, and they would never open again.

Kallipso sat up and looked down at him. She began to cry.

Perseus bowed his head in respect, and then reached out to Kallipso. "Come, I will take care of him."

Kallipso didn't move. Her tears burned scalding hot against her cheeks, scaring channels that would mark her always, of that she was sure. She couldn't stop crying. In part it was because of her slain lover, lying so still in her arms. A look of peace was on his face, replacing the one of shock and outraged disbelief that had been there before. But also, it was for what had happened to Kallipso herself, and for all that was to come.

When Perseus leaned toward her, she backed away.

"Leave me." She said, cradling Atlas' lifeless body.

She looked up to Perseus, and her expression forced him to obey her wishes. He nodded and receded backward. "Please join me, when you are ready."

He reluctantly turned and began to ascend the rocky staircase that was built into the mountain.

CHAPTER TWENTY-TWO

Perseus was breathless when he reached the top of the staircase. A dozen armed guards greeted him. They all drew their weapons on him, but Perseus raised his hand in front of them, while he caught his second wind.

"I am…Perseus of Argos…" he panted, feeling his chest was on fire, "…I come to speak with Polydectes."

The captain looked at Perseus' belt to see the hilt of his blade. "Sir, I will need your sword."

Perseus looked at him in query. "What?"

"You cannot be armed." The captain of the guards explained, motioning for Perseus to relinquish his weapon. "Give me your sword."

"I will not." Perseus sneeringly refused.

He paused to slowly withdraw his sword, which reflected the faint sunlight, the glimmer bounced off several of the guards. Then he pointed the sword's tip against the captain's throat, his expression hardened despite their years of alliance of both their kingdoms. Perseus could not afford to appear weak, not when his time had come.

"He has my son…"

"Please, King Perseus," the captain continued, unfazed by the danger touching his skin. "I will not ask again. This is your final warning: surrender your weapon or we will be forced to defend our home. You do not wish to cause an incident that would ignite a war, do you?"

"It began when Polydectes stole my son!" Perseus said with firm conviction. His eyes were fixated on the guards, all of whom shared puzzling expressions. They had him surrounded and even cut off his escape.

"What are you talking about?" The captain asked the crazed king.

"Don't you dare try to trick me!" Roared Perseus. "I know you have him somewhere in your castle. If he is harmed, I will swear on the name of Zeus—my father—I will burn your city to ground and make you, your friends, and your own family disappear. It would be like they if they have never existed and your bloodline would flow no more."

There was savagery in Perseus. It was a fierce flame that consumed his soul. When aroused, he thought savagely and acted savagely, and he rejoiced in massacring the Minotaur who had massacred all those defenceless wood nymphs.

The captain noticed the blade before him started shaking. He could see the desperation in Perseus' eyes that he was willingly to die.

The rest of the guards held their weapons ready. They were all waiting for the intruder to make his move.

"I will bring you to see King Polydectes." Said the captain. "We will get to the bottom of this heinous crime that has accosted you and your wife. But please, in the name of everything that is sacred you have to lay down your arms. You don't want your son to grow up without a father."

The guards closed in on Perseus. He was no much for all of them in his exhausted state. He could feel his knees suddenly go from all the strenuous activity he had recently engaged. All he could do was stand his ground.

He contemplated heavily on the captain's words. With a world-weary sigh Perseus lowered his sword and gave it to the captain. The guards lowered their weapons and two of them took Perseus by each of his arms and prepared to take him to see Polydectes.

"You have made the right choice, King Perseus." The captain said, in relief.

Perseus took a breath, and then proceeded to plan on how he was going to handle this situation with his former friend.

Kallipso cried over Atlas. The black blood from her open wounds was dripping all over him.

"I am a monster." She sobbed. "I was not supposed to be loved." Then she looked at Atlas, thinking he was asleep. She pounded on his chest and shook his body, hoping it would wake him up. "Atlas, come back."

She sat up with determination chiselled on her lovely face. She reached into her belt and unsheathed one of her knives. She stared at Atlas very closely. His face was being drained of its healthy colour and slowly changing into an ashen pallor. Tears streamed down from her eyes as she gripped the handed of the knife firmly. It was as if she was choking it with such brutal retaliation. She imagined it was one of the Scylla's piranha-headed tentacles that were trying to take a bite out of her.

"Then I shall go to you." She said to her dead lover with such fortitude.

Kallipso quickly slit her throat and remaining expressionless as the black blood poured from her neck in a hot shower. Then she dropped down on Atlas' chest, and began to spasm on top of him.

She looked at his peaceful face and smiled. "Oh, Atlas," she breathed.

Kallipso could no longer sustain her own weight, and with her last ounce of strength she wrapped her arms around him and closed her eyes.

Tellus blew past the curious bystanders through the streets of Argos on his speeding horse. He urged his stallion to go fast. The horse obliged in fearful obedience and didn't stop until they had reached the palace. Tellus leapt off the horse in a hurry and then threw the reins over to a nearby attendant. The servant's eyes widened when he saw a small bundle that Tellus was carrying.

Andromeda sat in the courtyard, unaware of the servants around her. She soaked up the sun and tried to enjoy the tranquillity in this lazy afternoon. Then the sound of several attendants came rushing in, breaking the mood.

One of the handmaidens saw Andromeda and pointed to the others. "Here she is!" She exclaimed.

Andromeda looked over and she was surprised by the girl's behaviour. The maiden slowed her pace and then bowed respectfully to her lady.

"My Queen, you must come quickly. Arsenios has glorious news." She said smilingly, while Andromeda exchanged a confused look. "The gods smile on Argos once again."

Andromeda took off like a bat out of Hades, bursting through every door she passed. She never let up not even for a second as she picked up her stride. Her maidens and servants tried to keep up with her. They were all puffing for air, but it didn't make the smiles on their faces vanish.

The Queen stopped in the middle of the great hall to see Arsenios, Tellus, and other palace guards waiting together on the court.

"Arsenios, is this true?" She frantically asked him. "Where is he?!"

Arsenios turned from the group, smiling. He held the bundle Tellus carried when he entered the palace. Arsenios lifted up the blanket to reveal little Perses' face.

Andromeda screamed out in joy, startling everyone. She grabbed her long-lost son from Arsenios and showered him with affection.

"Perses! I thought I had lost you forever." She said, tears were flowing down her face. "Thank the gods you are safe!" Everyone else in the court admired the touching reunion. Andromeda looked at Arsenios and asked, "Where did you find him?"

Arsenios stepped back and motioned to Tellus. "Tellus did, actually."

Tellus approached Andromeda to tell his tale. "While on my search for the monsters who so…cruelly murdered…our King, I came across a band of vagrants, traveling with an infant. Our Prince, no less."

"Did you find the nursemaid?" Andromeda fretfully asked.

"One of the wretched creatures, my Lady." He answered with disgust. "Upon pressing her further, she finally confessed to the crime but would not reveal a motive."

Andromeda looked at her child's saviour in puzzlement. "How strange…"

"No doubt they were hired by someone in Corinth." Deduced Arsenios. "I'll send for Charon."

Andromeda suspiciously stared at Arsenios. "And what became of these nomads?"

Tellus hesitantly replied, "Forgive me, but their fate is not appropriate to share with a lady. They were made an example of."

Andromeda attempted to hide her revulsion of his barbarity by turning once again to Perses, who was cooing happily in her bosom. Arsenios nodded approvingly to Tellus.

Polydectes' palace was a large structure, built from slabs of quarried stone near the wooded jungle, outside the city. Perseus had always wondered at the size of it. The captain of the guards led him along the dark and ominous path, and past the heavy metal door. They walked a small distance to the palace itself, where a guard unlocked the great barrier that held fast the door in which allowed them access to pass through. Perseus felt the sweat on the back of his neck grow cold as they left the sunny day and entered the damp, cool air inside the great hall.

They moved to the back of the corridor and took the stairs that led down to the throne room. A pair of heavily armoured guards guarded the entrance. In spite of the torches flanking the dim hallway, it took a moment for Perseus' eyes to adjust to the gloom. The captain led Perseus past the guards, toward the royal court.

Perseus stumbled into the massive and ornate throne room of King Polydectes. The King of Argos tried to fight off the guards who were escorting them, but it caught the ruler of Seriphus' attention. Polydectes shifted his fat body on his marble seat and glared furtively about, as if in a quest for a lurking enemy. He quickly dismissed his advisor once he saw Perseus, and then got off his marble throne.

"Perseus?!" He said, sounding both surprised and aversion. He waved to his guards, who were roughly handling his former friend. "Let him go."

The guards released their prisoner, but doing so caused Perseus to trip forward. A dozen more guards emerged from the gloom and stood in rows flanking the entranceway to the throne room. They carried weapons that were sharp and well-polished. With military precision, they surrounded Perseus, making their intent crystal clear. He regained his balance and walked toward Polydectes.

"Where is he?!" Perseus loudly exclaimed, wondering if the gods on Olympus would be able to hear it.

Polydectes was utterly confused by Perseus' outburst. "Where is who?" He asked Perseus, who was about to foam at the mouth. "Have you been shipwrecked? Are your men missing?"

Perseus laughed psychotically, sending a shiver down Polydectes' spine. The guards started to pull their swords, but Polydectes shook his head over to them. The guards sheathed their swords—for now—but kept their eye on Perseus. They didn't like the craziness in his eyes or that huge vein in his forehead that was about to erupt, like Mt. Vesuvius.

"Your naiveté fools no one, my old friend." Perseus irrationally said to him. Then he looked over the court on a demented exploration. "Now, where is he?!"

"You are mad!" Shouted Polydectes. "I know not who you speak of—"

"Perses!" Perseus screamed, silencing the fat lazy king. "My son! Take me to him!"

Polydectes stared at his old comrade. Perseus was no longer the confident heroic warrior. He was now a restless, beaten, and defeated version of his former self.

"I am truly sorry that you believed he was here." Polydectes addressed to him with sympathy in his voice. "I do not have your son."

"That is a lie!" Perseus cried. Then he dove toward Polydectes, while the guards drew their swords. Suddenly the Son of Zeus was surround by iron.

"I left Corinth only knowing Queen Andromeda was with child." Explained Polydectes, backing away. "I was not aware you had a son, nor that he was taken from you." Perseus violently shook his head in disbelief. "I suppose it is only natural for you to suspect me. My son died under your care, and you arrogantly blamed my absence as the cause. It is believable that I would want to exact revenge. But I did not. I am sorry for any disappointment this brings you."

He turned away, but Perseus broke through the guards and pursued Polydectes. "You are sorry?" He said perplexed and feeling insulted. "I did not come here for apologizes, Polydectes. I came here for my son."

Polydectes whipped around, he was glowering. He stood up with such violence that his chair legs scraped back with a furious squeal. The scowl on his face was so charged with dangerous fury that most of his men recoiled.

"I do not have him! Search my entire kingdom, if you like! But I promise that you will not find your son. Though my dislike for you runs deep, I would not put you through that pain and guilt." The sneer came unbidden but unstoppable to Polydectes' mouth. He took a moment to compose himself, and then faced Perseus with compassionate eyes. "Surely there are others you could suspect."

"There are none." Perseus replied with a grimace. "Only you."

He had reached his limit with this nonsense.

"You are smarter than that. Let us reason, then, why I would benefit from your son's disappearance." The two started to work together. The guards followed them closely, watching Perseus' every move. "Personal satisfaction? Despite what you may think, I am not completely heartless. What joy would I receive in harming a defenceless child? That is beneath men of honour. And besides, what would I do with your son? Bring him all the way back to Seriphus?"

"Well—" Perseus started to answer, but Polydectes sharply cut him off abruptly.

"Which leads me to another thought you may have…that I would wish you absent from your throne, so that I may attack Argos when she is weak." Perseus' expression suddenly turned to terror, but Polydectes gave him an assured look. "As much as any king loves to expand his empire, I am a reasonable man. Argos is thousands of miles away. How could I possible reign over your city from here?"

"You—"

"I couldn't." Polydectes honestly replied. "Nor would I want to spread my army so thin as to try."

Perseus quickly understood where he was getting at, but he was still utterly confused. "But the Granae, Diona of Jobba—they all led me to you. Why would they do that?"

"Perhaps they were also tricked." Inferred Polydectes. "Perhaps that is what the real villain hoped to accomplish. Send you all in the wrong direction, so that he may succeed in his plan. Tell me, what charges did these women bring against me?"

"Diona did confess to stealing my son on behalf of another." Perseus informed Polydectes. "When I asked her who, she uttered the same words you did, at the camp in Corinth."

"What words were those?"

Perseus remembered the haunting speech quite well. It was forever burned in his memory and nightmares. "'There is no honour in death' and your hope that 'no ill fortune befalls the son of King Perseus.'"

Polydectes reflected on this for a moment. "There was another with us, was there not?" He asked, piecing together the time and place. "One who might have more to gain by your absence from Argos?"

Perseus thought all the way back to Polydectes' tent at the Corinthian campaign. The ruler of Seriphus was pacing back and forth. Perseus suddenly remembered Arsenios was in the tent with him—he was lurking about in the shadows, eavesdropping on their conversation.

Perseus shook his head in disbelief. "No…Arsenios is my second in command. Why would he—"

"Oftentimes we are betrayed by those closest to us." Polydectes said to Perseus, who still couldn't accept the fact.

"He wouldn't…he has no reason."

"Only because you refuse to see it."

When Perseus remembered when he arrived home at Argos to meet his new born son, he briefly saw a menacingly leer from Arsenios.

And then when Perseus was done meeting with an imprisoned Alexion, he noticed Arsenios was panting very heavily. He also discovered his horse was drenched in sweat as if it galloped at top speed.

As soon as Perses was pronounced missing, Arsenios entered the bedroom to speak with Perseus and stared at a heartbroken Andromeda in a lecherous matter.

"I must admire his cunning." Said Polydectes, breaking Perseus' epiphany. "Send you on the trail of your enemy, while he usurps the throne. And your lovely Queen."

Perseus was mortified. "I have been so foolish."

"No, he has." Polydectes told him. "For he has awakened the wrath of a titan." Polydectes took Perseus' sword from one of the guards and handed it back to his friend. "Go seek your revenge, Perseus." Perseus nodded idly. "My guards shall accompany you to the mainland. Do you need transportation from here?"

"No." Perseus replied, as a bewildered look stretched across his face.

He couldn't stand it anymore. Tears were filling his eyes and he shook his head in disbelief. All of a sudden, his worst fears and suspicions were coming true right before his eyes.

His hands curled into fists, his shoulders tensed. He was angry at himself, and that anger wrapped around him like a sheet of cold air.

He wanted to scream. He did not. Instead he stood there and wept.

For his beautiful fair-haired son, who Perseus feared he may never see again.

For his wife and queen—Andromeda.

For opportunities lost forever.

And most of all: for himself.

He had to return to Argos immediately. For now he had found the perfect sheath for his sword.

Perseus had never faced this kind of evil before in his life. There was nothing he had done to deserve such a cruel injustice, but the evil never ceased coming into his life. He had been a model son, a model husband and model ruler. For his own part on inflicting grief on no one, yet it always managed to find him.

First, he suffered the loss of his mother, and then a much different loss in Perses. Now Perseus was being forced to kill and it would have led to nothing he had done.

His right hand gripped the sword so tightly that the skin above his knuckles paled to the colour of the bone beneath. He hardly realized that he was still holding it, that he had clutched it tightly through the long fitful day. He was knotted with the need for revenge, for his son, for Euripides, and for himself. But there would never by any retribution for him. Perhaps for Perses and Euripides, if Arsenios died quickly. It was their sake that he would consider it.

CHAPTER TWENTY-THREE

As the guards escorted Perseus back down the mountain, and they came across Atlas' lifeless body. Perseus closed his eyes in sorrow when he saw Kallipso draped over his fallen friend. Then he discovered the blood-soaked dagger at Kallipso's side and looked at the fatal wound on her neck. Quickly he perceived what had happened.

The guards looked at the grisly scene with horror.

"What in the gods' name—" One of them gasped.

"Help me care for them." Perseus ordered the guards, as he walked toward the bodies while two guards gingerly followed.

"They were friends of yours?" Asked one of them.

Perseus silently nodded, gently lifting Kallipso off of Atlas.

The two guards dragged Atlas into an alcove behind some rocks. Perseus carried Kallipso and laid her next to him. Then he turned to one of the guards.

"Give me your cloak." He commanded.

The soldier looked at him in confusion. "What?"

The other guard nudged his friend to do as Perseus ordered. Perseus took the cloak and used to cover his fallen friends.

"Father, I have disgraced your name," He said under his breath, "but if you still hear my prayers, watch over my friends in the afterlife."

Then Perseus turned over to face the guards to take him to their small boat was berthed and rowed him back from whence Perseus came. Pegasus and Atlas' horse were still there, waiting for their riders. The guards were astounded by the beauty and grace of the two horses.

"Thank you for escorting me." Perseus said to the group of guards.

"I hope you find your son, King Perseus." Stated the captain.

Perseus nodded in appreciation and advanced to the horses. He greeted Pegasus and then turned to face the one that belonged to Atlas.

"Your master is not returning." He said sombrely. "Find the wood nymphs; they will look after you." The horse seemed to understand what Perseus was saying, and started to go off into the woods. "Come, Pegasus, we must make haste to Argos."

Perseus leapt on the back of Pegasus, and they were off in a flash. Pegasus sense the urgency in Perseus' tone and galloped at alarming speed.

Andromeda stood on the balcony, staring out at the early evening. The surrounding lights from the torches of the city's buildings blocked her view. It had a calming effect on her, as did the fact that she finally had some time alone with her son. She savoured the sight of the city. She absolutely loved her kingdom on nights like these. The moon was already showing with its heavenly glow. It was thin and was in a perfect crescent. The wind was brisk and cool.

Argos was almost quiet until thunder rumbled over the city, as dark clouds blocked out the last rays of the sun. The sky grew darker above her, shades of grey turning into swaths of deep purple and black. A strong wind ripped through people's houses and shops, and the harbour. Andromeda shuddered, closing the balcony's curtains. She breathed the air in deeply and made her way back inside. Then she turned to smile at Perses who was asleep in his crib.

Suddenly the doors were thrown open, as Arsenios, Tellus, Charon, and a small squad of palace guards poured into the room like an angry flash flood. Andromeda stepped back in shock.

"Arsenios, what is the meaning of this?"

"We come for a conference with our Queen." He coolly replied.

"It is not granted." She bitterly retorted. "**Leave**." But no one moved. Andromeda assertively marched up to Arsenios and his minions. "I have given you an order. It is treason if you do not obey."

Arsenios smirked. "And who would you have to arrest us?"

Andromeda looked around to witness all of her palace guards were staring very coldly at her.

She shifted her gaze back at Arsenios, who was waiting patiently. "What is it you wish to speak with me about then?"

"My reward." Arsenios said greedily.

"For what?" Snorted Andromeda, thinking he had lost his mind.

"Bringing our Prince home."

"You had nothing to do with that." Andromeda said, aghast. "Tellus found him."

"Under *my* direction." Arsenios quickly responded.

"Your position is your reward." Andromeda resolutely confirmed for him. "Your duty is to serve your King and Queen."

"Yet our King has passed to Elysium."

Andromeda sneered at him. "But your Queen has not.

Arsenios approached her in an intimidating demeanour. "If she is not careful, she will." He whispered to her.

He could see her eyes narrowed. "Do not come in here to threaten me, Arsenios."

"How brave our Queen is, how defiant in the face of adversary." He nastily mocked. Then he walked around her like a wolf stalking a lamb before it mauls it in front of its herd. Andromeda never took her eyes off him. "So back to the matter of rewards, my *Queen*. What would you give for us saving a life so dear to you?"

"What are you asking?" She said, sounding very defensive.

Arsenios stared at her body perversely. "There are things you can share with me, Andromeda." He said, coarsely tugging at the helm of her skirt.

Andromeda heard one of the guards snicker and she glared coldly at him.

She wanted to wring the smirk out of Arsenios' smarmy voice with her bare hands, but settled for giving him a warning—for now.

But she quickly reconsidered her decision.

She slapped Arsenios across the face. The sound reverberated throughout the whole room. Arsenios reached up to his cheek to foster the stinging. Andromeda couldn't notice to see a large ornate blue ring on his finger.

The same blue ring Princess Diona of Jobba noticed on her employer's finger before she was torn to shreds by a pack of ravenous wolves, and left alone to die in the woods like an animal.

"I would rather die than let you dishonour me." She boldly rebuffed his treacherous advances.

"And leave your child an orphan?" Taunted Arsenios. "After we've worked so hard to find him?" Andromeda clenched her jaw in rage. "Very well." Arsenios said, discerning her furious expression. "If you will not share your love with me, I can only think of one other option…your city."

"You are mad."

"Perhaps." He nonchalantly replied. "So, which is it?"

"I am not foolish enough to believe that if I give you one, you will be satisfied. You will simply take the other."

Arsenios nodded in agreement. "You are right, but by cooperating, it shall be less painful for you. Take me as your husband and new king, and I shall see that your son is protected. If I am to take your city by force, he shall become a slave like his mother, and I will rule Argos independently." Andromeda looked to the palace guards who betrayed her. Tellus smirked at her, as did most of the guards. Only Charon seemed to be uncomfortable by this proposed arrangement. "Andromeda, you are wasting time. Which do you choose to keep? Your honour or your city?"

Andromeda lowered her eyes. Grief gave way to all-consuming rage, and she looked about avidly for a weapon. She wouldn't dare give him the satisfaction of eye contact.

"My city." She softly answered.

Arsenios smiled devilishly. "I knew you would see reason in giving yourself to me."

He reached out for her, but before he could full her forward to kiss her Andromeda grabbed a sword from one of the palace guards near her.

"And my honour." She declared, turning back to stab Arsenios, but he was too quick. She only managed to slash him across the face before he wrestled the weapon away from her.

Blood was trickling down his face. He backhanded Andromeda so hard she spun in the air before landing hard on the marble floor.

"You snake!" He spat at her, holding his cheek in pain. "I cannot be killed as easily as Phineus can!" Andromeda scrambled to get up, but Arsenios picked her up and threw her against the wall. Then he began to strangle her. "I offered you mercy because I thought I could love you. And this is how you repay me?"

Andromeda struggled in vain to break free. Before she closed her eyes, she could see Tellus running to her aid and pulled Arsenios' hand away.

"Remember, you cannot kill her, Arsenios!" Shouted Tellus. Andromeda gasped to catch her breath. "Neither her nor her child."

Arsenios shook off his rage, as Andromeda reached for her throat. "Fine, but I never wish to see her again." He said in sheer hatred. "Lock them up in the prison. I shall inform our citizens that their Queen had fallen ill and has entrusted her kingdom. They will not question it."

He took one last look at Andromeda before he stormed out of her chambers. Tellus and Charon followed him, as Charon caught a glance of his fallen queen. The palace guards seized her and Perses who was now bawling, and sent them to the dungeon.

CHAPTER TWENTY-FOUR

Candlelight provided the only illumination in the private baths in the palace of Olympus. Gods and goddesses alike each lounged lazily in the pools or near them. Water flowed everywhere within the baths, rising and falling magically behind the walls and ceilings.

Poseidon liked that. The ever-present water conveyed an aura of cleanliness, of purity, that insulated him.

It was a very tranquil atmosphere until Zeus stormed through the doors, with Hermes in tow. The all-father's stocky, brushy figure scraped angrily at his family. He strode up the familiar steps to the baths, frowning as he went.

Thunder receded behind him as he entered the chamber. Mist that was composed not of water, but of the fog of eternity, drifted through the room. It obscured distance as this very place obscured time.

The rest of the gods who flanked him seemed motionless. They were not. It was just that they moved through an existence withiest the boundaries or restrictions. As such, they were contemptuous of time.

Zeus scanned the crowd while all of his children and servants looked toward him very nervously. Finally, he found the one he was looking for, and she was the only one who was continuing a steady conversation and ignored Zeus' presence.

Zeus stalked through the baths until he reached Hera. "All of this for your son, Hera?!" He boomed.

Hera looked up annoyed, but then changed her expression when she saw the intensity of his anger. "Husband—"

"Answer me." He viciously retorted. "All of this for your son?"

Hera looked at him like a spoiled child. "Why should Arsenios not receive the glory that Perseus has?"

"Because he is not the man Perseus is."

"You punish the outcome of my one indiscretion, yet you display all of yours for the world to see." She berated him. "Can you not see how this humiliates me?"

"And how humiliated does a king feel, who has been tricked by his own queen?" The gods kept silent and couldn't turn away from the drama. "You went in secrecy to others for assistance in your revenge. As an immortal, I supposed you to be above the trivialities of man. I was wrong in my assumption."

Aphrodite and Thetis both looked down in shame. Zeus noted their behaviour. Hera pulled herself out of the pool and grabbed her rich silk robes.

"Husband, let us talk about this matter in private."

"Why, when you have already made it public?" He motioned over to all the gods and goddesses who quickly looked away from the spectacle. "As my queen, I held you in great esteem and set you apart from all others…unfortunately that was not enough for you." Hera's eyes welled up with tears, realizing her desire for revenge had gone too far. "Just as Arsenios has banished Andromeda to darkness, I banish you from my palace." He turned and walked away.

Hera ran after him. She was no longer the strong conniving goddess, but she was reduced to a weak and apologetic woman.

"No, Zeus—" She pleaded.

Zeus whipped around, looking as if he was going to strike her. "Your son's name will be disgraced for all time."

Thunder rumbled through the chamber and down the slopes of Olympus. The fog twisted uneasily at the violence.

Zeus may have been the most imposing figure in the room, but the most elegant and confident now angered by his wife's betrayal and to all those who were involved in this vile conspiracy.

As he turned his back on Hera, he gazed down at Aphrodite and Thetis who were both cowering.

"I will have words with the both of you later." He grimly stated.

The stern expression he gave them resembled a gargoyle. Thetis remembered the look all too well. She hadn't seen her king so enraged since he cursed her son Calibos. But now Zeus' rage was aimed directly at her. She was frozen in fear and held onto her sister Aphrodite very tightly. Her grip was so tight it blemished the goddess of love's clear flawless skin. Suddenly Aphrodite could feel her hair turning white and her blood running cold.

Zeus stared heatedly at Thetis. He fumed and fought hard to control his temper. Thetis could see small crackles of electricity dancing violently in his eyes.

"Thetis," he finally said, "even for you this was a deliberate and malicious act. Have you learned nothing since the last time you went behind my back?"

"You-you are accusing *me*?" She stuttered, feeling her heart beating rapidly.

"And not wrongly." He glared a moment longer at Thetis to choke on her own fear. "You have been warned, Thetis. If you weren't my brother's wife, I swear your punishment would be most severe."

Then he looked over to Aphrodite, who was about to get out of the water. She was hoping while Father Zeus was busy reprimanding Thetis she would slip away unnoticed. Aphrodite manically grabbed her robe, but she was stopped dead in her tracks when she locked eyes with Zeus.

There was no escape now.

"You have brought great shame to me, Daughter." He said with rancorous disappointment. "I expected this kind of duplicity from your mother and Thetis." He quickly looked back to his sister-in-law, who was still frightened by the very sight of him. She was afraid to move and speak. Then he met with Aphrodite once again and saw her heaving anxiously. "But I did not imagine you would deign yourself into this loathsome behaviour."

The mistress of affection's eyes swelled and then burned with hot stinging tears. She buried her face in her hands and sobbed loudly.

"Father, I'm—"

"Don't you dare speak to me!" Zeus roared, sending her back, nearing crashing into the petrified Thetis. Then he turned his head to the side. "I just cannot look at you right now."

Zeus stormed out of the baths, while Hermes took off after him. The aggravated ruler of Olympus bundled his robes around him and then proceeded to brood on the solitary throne which crowned the very crest of the mountain. There he would commune silently with his friends the winds and perhaps cast earthward the occasional angry thunderbolt.

Hera looked around to see all of the gods staring at her with pity and shaking their heads. That was the last thing she ever wanted.

Perseus and Pegasus raced across the countryside. Pegasus knew he was getting tired but he continued on in steady speed. As they reached the canyon, Pegasus' wings expanded and leapt to the air as he took flight.

Perseus gently kicked his heels in the horse feathers of Pegasus. The beast's wings flapped hard through a sky as blue as a peacock's breast.

Angry at being emasculated in front of his men, Arsenios had his followers confine Andromeda and her child to the dungeon. An unnecessary shove sent her almost stumbling into the cell. She grunted in pain as her body partially hit the wall, while she shielded Perses from the impact.

"We had better have no more trouble from you," a guard warned her. "Believe it or not, there are worse cells in the bowls of the palace—even places you have absolutely no knowledge of—*Your Highness.* Just be grateful."

Andromeda viewed this place with distaste. She figured Arsenios was on the verge to make some allowances for her. His temper would soon cool and then forgive Andromeda for her foolish and violent outburst. No doubt her emotions had been overwhelmed by all the hardships she had recently endured.

Andromeda cradled Perses in her arms, and began to hum him a soft lullaby. They sat in almost complete darkness in the dungeon just beneath the palace.

Water dripped into several puddles on the dirt floor. The prison was filled with the squeaks from various nocturnal animals, where one can only imagine the rancid smell. Andromeda stopped singing when she heard an awful rumbling above her, but then resumed when it was over.

Suddenly a door at the other side of the dungeon opened. Andromeda stood up and peered between the bars to see a prison guard carrying a lantern. He walked over to her cell and handed her a metal plate filled with unidentifiable gruel. But Andromeda was more fixated on his guest—Charon. He couldn't look her in the eye.

"Tell me, Charon, is this how you imagined your queen to live out the rest of her life?" She sneered at him. "You served under Perseus. You swore an oath to protect Argos from all enemies. Have you forgotten?" Charon didn't answer her, and couldn't find the nerve to look her in the eye. "Yet you stood like a coward, as you watched your Queen being dishonoured." Still Charon had no response. "Look at me." She demanded, rattling the cell bars. "Look at me, Charon!" The disgraced soldier finally looked up at Andromeda. "May you receive everything Arsenios promised you."

Charon immediately looked away, and said to the jailer, "Thank you. This will do."

The prison guard guided him with the use of his lantern, and walked back down the darkened hallway. When the door had shut, Andromeda was once again engulfed in darkness and solitude.

The gates slowly opened for Perseus, as he walked Pegasus through the border. The palace guards they were all waiting for him at the other side. Each and every one of the soldiers had their weapons drawn out in front of the bewildered king. Perseus quickly dismounted from his house and raised his arms in surrender as the soldiers quickly surrounded him and took his sword. One of them even knocked Perseus to the ground, while another grabbed Pegasus' reins and jerked the horse forward. Pegasus whinnied in protest, and Perseus looked to him sadly.

The leader grabbed one of his subordinates, who had relieved Perseus of his weapon. "Run ahead and tell Arsenios Perseus has finally arrived." He ordered, as the soldier jumped on his horse and took off through the streets. The captain of the guards gazed at Perseus who was in forlorn. "He's been expecting you. Welcome home, Perseus." He derided, putting his dethroned King in shackles and then forced him to walk all the way to the palace.

CHAPTER TWENTY-FIVE

Curious citizens had emerged from their homes to see what the disturbance was going on the city streets. They all caught a glimpse of their once majestic king and gasped in shock. The palace guards monitored the streets and quickly forced everyone back inside their homes. The last thing they all wanted was the people to incite a riot. The once peaceful city has become a tyrannical compound. Perseus was on the verge of tears when he witnessed what his kingdom had become.

Arsenios relaxed on the throne, while he listened to the citizens recount their woes.

"You assured us this matter would be fixed." Said one of the delegates.

Arsenios ignored the old man, and saw Tellus entering the room with a border guard in tow. Tellus whispered in Arsenios' ear, making the tyrant's face light up with joy.

"And you're sure it's him?" He asked the guard before him. The soldier nodded in response. "This is the moment I have been waiting for." Arsenios said to Tellus, his smile never waned. "Come, let us not keep him waiting." He jumped up and left the hall, ignoring the confused citizens.

Arsenios appeared out of the palace, just as the guards arrived with Perseus. The two men eyed other—Arsenios with a boyish grin, while Perseus remained expressionless. A group of palace guards encircled the both of them. They were all eager to protect their new king, should Perseus would try anything. The guards forced Perseus to knee before Arsenios.

"The great Perseus, on his knees before me! What an honour!" Ridiculed Arsenios. "As you can see things are a little different than when you left—"

"Perses…" Perseus growled, staring at his former friend and now traitor of the realm with hatred.

"Oh, right." It suddenly dawned on Arsenios. "You were looking for your son. Tell me, did you find him?"

"Where is he?" Demanded Perseus. His mouth was set in a hard, grim line.

Arsenios seemed very despondent. "Did Polydectes help you realize that I had taken him? He always was very wise."

"Where is he?" Perseus strongly repeated.

There was a sneer on Arsenios' lips. "Oh, don't worry. He is here, with his mother."

Perseus grew much angrier. "Andromeda."

"You remember her?" Arsenios asked him spitefully. "Good. I don't believe she has forgotten about you either. In fact, why don't we bring her out? Have a little reunion before we kill you?"

He signalled for Tellus to run back into the palace to fetch the woman who had spurned his advances. Arsenios looked around, trying to avoid the awkward silence between him and Perseus. Moments later, Tellus returned with Andromeda, who was now pale and fragile. She slowly led Perses outside. Both of them squint because they were unaccustomed to the light due to being incarcerated in very dark and dismal surroundings. Even bruised and frail, Andromeda still possessed an air of grace and beauty. When Perseus saw her in this condition, he began to break down.

Andromeda squinted to see Perseus, and she shifted into a state of disbelief. "Perseus?" She asked, and then her eyes adjusted to the light to see her husband alive and well. "Perseus!" She cried out, with tears of joy running down her sullen cheeks.

She tried to go to him, but Tellus held her back. She broke into loud agonizing sobs when she saw the condition of her husband.

"Unbelievable that she still recognizes you after such a long absence." Arsenios said to Perseus.

"What have you done to her?" He snarled at the betrayer.

"You have a very honourable wife, Perseus." Arsenios replied, sounding somewhat impressed. "She was punished because of such morals." Then he looked over to Andromeda who spat at his direction. "I'm sorry, Andromeda, that though your husband is in fact still alive, he will not be for much longer." Then he shifted his attention over to the guards. "Where is his sword?"

One of the soldiers rushed to Arsenios with it. He examined the sword for a moment, captivated by its magnificence.

"The 'Sword of Zeus?' It is only fitting you should be killed with this."

Perseus said nothing, but took one last look at Andromeda before lowering his head. As he walked toward Perseus with the sword in his hand, Arsenios addressed everyone around him.

"There once was a king who had everything. A beautiful wife who loved him—a powerful army that respected him—and all who knew him, called him 'Mighty.' Oh, yes, he was blessed. But even heroes must fall, Perseus. Only the gods can have everything."

Arsenios raised the sword over Perseus. Andromeda screamed out, wrestling with Tellus.

"I'm not a hero…" Perseus said under his breath, "…only a man."

As Arsenios lowered the sword down, Perseus caught the blade in his chains.

He stood up and twisted the blade away from Arsenios.

Then the rightful king used it to cut his chains, while Arsenios scrambled for his own sword.

The palace guards moved in, but Arsenios held up his hand. Then he gave Perseus a smile. "I've dreamt of this day. The chance to fight you…"

Arsenios drew his sword and eyed Perseus. They circled for a moment, sizing each other up. Arsenios finally nodded, and beckoned Perseus forward.

Perseus darted in, thrusting low, and began the intense duel with the throne of Argos as the grand prize.

Arsenios took advantage of the fact that Perseus was tired and injured. He moved on the offensive, as Perseus was forced to retreat.

Perseus deflected all of Arsenios' blows but he was not able to return any volleys. Arsenios was quick, and what he lacked in skill, he totally made it up in speed. He expertly dodged Perseus' thrusts. Whereas Perseus was growing tired and his moves were slow and a bit clumsy.

The remaining palace guards congregated near the closed gate outside of Argos. They were talking excitedly about the siege they established over the city. Before they could break out the wine, they heard the sound of a hundred lightning bolts thundering up in the heavens. Then the entire gate shook, as if it was being forced open.

One guard climbed up to the lookout tower, as the gates shook yet again. The man peered out into the horizon and his face became as white as a sheet.

"By the gods—" Before he could finish that sentence, an arrow pierced through his chest. He fell to the ground before the rest of the guards.

They looked to each other in confusion until the gates were busted open to reveal Charon, who was on horseback, leading the Argos army into the city.

There was chaos of combat, screams and smoke and the ringing crash of metal against metal. The battle was going to spill from the gates and onto Argos. Charon fought fiercely alongside his comrades, their scattered allies rallying to their cause, but the fighting was brutal and the kingdom's defenders they faced were formidable. All of them rose up to Ares' call and viciously raged on against the uprising of Perseus' supporters.

Charon caught brief glimpses of the fight, death and grace in equal measure. The images were gone in a blink of an eye as he was caught in the fury. Right now, he was fighting for redemption and honour.

One of Arsenios' lieutenants tore a rebel from his horse. A bearded man fell to his knees, clutching the spear that impaled him. A blood-soaked warrior screamed in savagery, hacking several enemies away. Charon buried his sword in a snarling man's chest, and then whipped it out again to slash another attacker's throat. He almost believed he could take on the army single-handedly. His bitter rage was an eternal wellspring of strength. He felt partially responsible for all this. As well as they fought; too many had already died in this coup. He knew this wouldn't make up for what he did to his Queen, but it was going to be a start. He wouldn't mind spending several decades in Tartarus to atone for his crimes. He would have just said he was following orders, but that was no excuse. He had to own up to his transgressions.

Charon took out a few more palace guards, as he raced through the streets. The massive amount of heavily armed men behind him gladly finished off the remaining traitors, and then headed for the palace.

Arsenios and Perseus paused when they heard the commotion in the streets. Everyone turned to see the mass making its way through the city, but they couldn't make out what it was.

Arsenios turned to Tellus, looking so scared as if he had seen Hades himself. "See what's going on!"

Tellus roughly handed Andromeda over to another guard, as he mounted his horse and rode toward the commotion. Perseus squinted and discovered it was his men. He smiled to himself.

Arsenios capitalized this moment to attack and sliced at Perseus' chest and side. It opened up the wound from the Minotaur. With all that blood pouring out surprised even Arsenios. Perseus cried out in pain and stumbled back, falling down the steps. He tussled to get up when he saw Arsenios charged at him like an angry bull.

Andromeda cried out in fear. Perseus locked eyes with her and saw the hopelessness in her face. He quickly looked up just in time to see Arsenios take swing down at him. Perseus rolled away as Arsenios' sword set out a ray of sparks, as if it hit the stone steps.

Perseus got up and charged back at Arsenios with renewed strength. This time Perseus was on the offense, forcing Arsenios back up the stairs. With a quick strike, Perseus stabbed Arsenios in the shoulder. He grimaced and took it with stride.

Then Perseus brought his blade out and up for a cut at Arsenios' groin. The traitor parried the blade in a circle, as the steel went skirling. Perseus drew his sword back as they passed, and then whirled and stopped, knowing his blade would hit flat. Arsenios had expected that, but still turned and avoided most of the blow. Nevertheless, the blade caught him over the ear, knocking him back and sent him off stumbling.

Charon had prayed for forgiveness and a victorious outcome for the raging battle as the heart of the battle rose around him in blood stinking gusts, but his prayers were not answered. He prayed for victory, knowing that it was only himself and his fellow rebels on which he could rely for a favourable answer. He prayed for strength and was at least hoping. But if not, he would draw on his own reserve anyway, without the assistance of the gods. Charon had developed a much firmer belief in the power of his sword and in his own skills than in the willingness of the gods to condescend and aid him in his trials. He worshipped them for having created him, but he knew better than to rely on them in his time of need.

He drew strength from the battle. His consciousness was retreating into the numb single-mindless necessary in order to fight—and win. He had ceased to be aware of the blooming ache between his shoulder blades. His armour was heavy, but he could scarcely feel its weight upon his shoulders. He was only half conscious of the screams and groans of the rest of the warriors. Charon also heard the snapping of their bones and the pounding of their falling bodies as they hit the solid ground. He ceased to be aware of his own voice crying out in victory each time another adversary was slain by his own weapon.

But he was very aware of his former friend Tellus nearby. Charon could even listen to his own heart beating, and how it seemed to throb in tandem with every thrust of his sword. Its steady murmur insisting that he could not hesitate for even one beat.

Tellus, poised and lethal, swung his sword with both hands. The blade slammed into one combatant and then another, and then he was ready to turn and strike at one more as he came up behind him.

Charon's sword met Tellus' steel.

My enemy. Tellus.

How Charon hated him. For a brief time, he had thought better of Tellus. He even thought of him that he was capable of contrition, but not anymore. He would kill him, or die in the attempt.

Charon was his subordinate. When he first arrived in the army, Tellus took him under his wing and trained him at every step of the way. Charon respected the man very much, but what his mentor had done to him and Argos was the most unspeakable wrong that man could ever commit.

Even when Charon saw him just moments ago from the crest of the hill on his warhorse, he bared witnessed to the slaughter that both Tellus and Arsenios had created. As he now stood before his disgraced commanding officer, he could see Tellus' dark smile and the blood that tarnished his sword. Charon gripped his own sword ever tighter. The hilt was all sweaty in his clenched hand.

As he neared, Tellus growled loudly. His eyes were shining with sadistic pleasure.

"I had very high hopes for you, Charon." Tellus scowled in a deep and resonant voice. "You were one of my best soldiers and now you are nothing but a traitor to your people."

That Tellus would taunt him about his treachery caused Charon to lose control of his senses and to blindly charge right at him with his rage as his only guide. But Charon kept his wits.

"The only traitors are you and Arsenios," spat Charon, watching Tellus' grin vanishing in an instant. He raised his sword and charged.

Their blades came together hard enough that Charon felt his entire body vibrate with the blow, but he did not give way.

"Who are you to preach?" Sneered Tellus, reining back to seek another strike. "As I recall, you were the one who stood idly by and didn't do a damned thing."

"That may be so," Charon admitted before taking a swipe at Tellus. "But I have something you don't."

"And what is that?"

"I have Brave and Noble Perseus at my side, and his father Zeus is with him."

The look of contempt Tellus gave him was matched by the fury of his next blow, and the next, and the next. Charon's shield absorbed the worst of the assault, but he had to struggle to hold his ground.

Tellus' voice was a roar. It was as relentless as his heavy sword.

"You may be the best soldier…" then he struck again, and Charon felt his power. It was like a wave of raw energy, and understood that he might very well be outmatched. "…But I am the general!"

Perseus' sword came up in an overhand blow. Arsenios blocked it, but staggered back two steps. He thrust, hoping to drive Perseus back, but Perseus beat the blade aside and lunged again. Arsenios began to retreat, whereas a line on his armour revealed how close Perseus had come to opening an artery.

Arsenios drew back, becoming less arrogant in his stance. Perseus knew better than to mistake that as a retreat. He waited, knowing the man who had betrayed him and was now running his once beautiful city to the ground. And now he was trying to prove himself to be the superior warrior. Arsenios obligingly drove forward, a stamp feint raising dust, and then lunged. As Perseus went to parrying, Arsenios brought his blade up and over. That thrust missed and Arsenios settled past, giving Perseus an easy shot at his back.

Perseus hesitated for a heartbeat. As Arsenios whirled, the blade passed through where Perseus would have been. The blow would have cut him from hip to spine.

Then began the battle in good earnest, each man felt that he had met a worthy foe. The blows fell thick and fast, so that time and again that both Tellus and Charon each caught their breath and left them thinking that one of them must surely fall. But every stroke was strategically met and parried.

At last, and a din of yelling jeers and groans, Charon crashed a heavy blow on Tellus' broad chest. But as the blow fell so did Tellus bringing his sword down on

Charon's skull with a resending whack that was heard by all the throng. Another shout went up and then all fell silent.

Before Tellus could strike another blow Charon had gotten over the stupor caused by the stroke. He ducked, and then ran back while Tellus' sword crunched on the ground with a loud thud. The sword was the best forged in the city and it held sound.

In a fury of madness, Charon put forth all his strength and skill, and for a few minutes the air was filled with crackling blows that none but a tower of strength like Tellus could have withstood for a moment. But he stood there on guard, calm and crafty, just waiting for an opening for a final blow. He knew from such careless, angry fighting one of them would fall sooner or later.

In a sword fight a loss of temper was fatal.

Both fighters knew that a cool, watchful guard was the only way to victory. Tellus bided his time so coolly but emerged him the more. For some minutes his fearful, crashing blows fell what a break or pause. Many times Tellus escaped an ugly stroke that would have laid him low. But he steadily deflected and feinted until at last his time had come.

The sound of blades singing echoed through the battlefield. Tellus and Charon fought in the open air, their swords provided an unnerving, taunting music to those around them.

Tellus smiled to himself and delivered another strike, one that Charon very nearly failed to block.

Charon was good—one of the very best Tellus had trained—but his mentor was *better*, and he knew it. Charon felt it in every muscle, every reflex. He was younger and his body had never been subjected to the ravages of battle and time, of wounds that even to any veteran's knowledge and skill could not heal. He was also faster, and as he parried a thrust of Tellus' broadsword, followed through with a lightning-quick back-slash with his own steel. Charon knew—even before Tellus dropped his sword—that triumph was his.

Tellus retrieved his sword and fell back into a crouch. His eyes were snapping fire. Then he circled left, his grip on the hilt was loose and ready in his hands.

Charon adjusted his position, breathing easily. The sun beat steadily down. Then he saw a flash of something dark in Tellus' beady eyes and grinned wider. He was like a snake that cornered its prey. He locked eyes with Charon—almost mesmerizing him—and tried to fake him with several sudden movements. While Charon was being trained under Tellus, he would sometimes be frightened by his former instructor's poise and silence, and of course his intensity. He had grown up watching Tellus fight—and won—and had always admired the steady, casual quips the well-seasoned warrior at his opponents. Now that he was Tellus' equal in battle, he couldn't help wanting to knock that smile off his face.

Tellus was suddenly in flight, leaping straight at Charon. Startled, Charon blocked clumsily, falling back a step. Charon didn't try to recover his stance, instead throwing himself into the wobble, tucking his chin and pushing the sword to the side, using its weight to control a tight shoulder roll. Charon came up fast, bringing his leg up with the momentum, feeling the side of his sandal as it collided with Tellus' closed fist.

Tellus dodged Charon's thrust, but it sent him flying, and Charon quickly lunged forward. Tellus was ready for him, going into a spin. Charon ducked just in time, but Tellus drew up his blade. Charon lifted his own sword for a block just as Tellus set his got down heavily on the cold steel, forcing it from Charon's hands.

"You're dead," Tellus said with a wicked, lopsided grin.

Charon tried to back away, but thinking fast, he raced around Tellus' shoulder until his fingers closed over the tail of Tellus' dark hair. He jerked his mentor's head back with one hand and snatched is wrist with the other.

As Arsenios came around, Perseus parried his slashing blow low, and then whipped his left fist around, punching the traitor in the face. Arsenios spun away, floundering to catch his balance. He swayed drunkenly and then spat blood from a split lip.

"Damn you, Perseus!" Arsenios' face twisted in a demonical snarl. "You have interfered for far too long. It is time for you to die."

Their swords licked out like serpents' tongues. The blades rang together, as Perseus pushed forward, poking low with the long sword, and then withdrew the blade before Arsenios could parry. He blocked Perseus' return cuts with ease.

Weary, yet still fighting, Tellus' face was red and covered in sweat. As the fight went on, his blood grew hotter and flowed to his face. It darkened the colour to a deep purple. His long raven locks were clotted and damp with secretion. At each furious lunge, he swore dreadful oaths because he could not budge his young opponent.

Never before in all his life did Charon fight so desperately. Never before he was so near death—and he knew it. Early in the fight a terrible faintness fell upon him, but he grimly set his teeth, and new strength came. His strokes, though they dealt no wounds, began to tell upon Tellus, robed as he was in a hot skin. For all his wickedness, Tellus was a bold warrior, as many had found their cause, and he was too proud to ask for a moment's time to rest.

Charon watched him every second, fighting carefully for fear of some false, dishonourable blow, for he knew that he had to do with a man who had absolutely no scruples on killing him by such foul means.

Swords collided and sparks flew. Tellus was grunting and screaming with every thrust. He was so damned determined to either win the battle or die trying, even though it was looking more and more like the later would be his ultimate fate.

"Tellus," shouted Charon, "surrender at once! Have you not brought enough death and misery upon our people?"

The rebuke served only to strengthen Tellus' resolve as the two men engaged, their swords crashing together. Tellus threw back Charon's blows with equal force and measure.

Charon fought with formidable strength and fury. His sword struck at Tellus' throat, and Tellus tumbled out of the way, sprawling to the ground and then leaping to his feet once more, sword at the ready.

Charon struck out once again with his blade. Tellus blocked the blow with his own sword. Then Charon whirled about with his own sword, and it clashed against Tellus' breastplate, which cursed his ears to ring and his teeth to ache.

Charon struck again, but this time, Tellus wasn't quick enough to block it.

Charon's sword plunged between the plates of armour that protected Tellus' chest and back.

Tellus gasped with thc sudden explosion of pain. He grasped the sword hilt where it extended from his side. He attempted to wrench the blade from his body. Bul Tellus only managed to inch it out only a small fraction of the way before the intense pain prevented him to speak. He cried out in pain and began to gasp and pant in sheer agony.

Charon had stopped moving. He was simply watching Tellus now.

Just watching him die.

Tellus sank to his knees as his mind began to drift. The pain fell away, as if it were outside his body. His body became a warm fog, and his thoughts were overtaken by an eerie sense of calm. As he drew his final breath, his whole world faded into painless black.

He had just enough time to see Charon's sword flying at his head.

Tellus' head was separated from his shoulders.

It tumbled through the air and came to rest on a short distance away from his body.

Thick droplets of blood flung from Charon's sword, patterned to the earth.

The sword was hot and heavy in his hands. His arms still vibrated from the slaughter of his former superior officer and that power swept right through him. His stomach knotted and flushed his veins as he stood over the remains of his enemy.

Arsenios' frustration grew.

Perseus swung his sword, loosening his wrist as Arsenios looked for an opening. Perseus saw no part in letting his take the offensive. With a cry, Perseus feinted left, then charged right, bringing his sword down.

Arsenios blocked the blow with a tremendous clash of metal. Perseus did not give him a chance to recover, and went for Arsenios' head. Arsenios ducked and fell back.

Before Perseus could recover his balance, Arsenios brought his sword around; a slow, powerful blow that Perseus had time to block. Again, the crash of metal rang through the battlefield. The wayward Son of Zeus swung his own sword around to counterattack, but Arsenios was fast. The traitor easily deflected the stroke that sent Perseus back.

Arsenios had a long reach but often left his midsection open when he was coming in for an attack.

There!

Perseus thrust and Arsenios leapt backward, almost falling. Perseus followed with a second thrust, not wanting Arsenios to have time to regain his footing, but the vile despot stepped aside just in time.

Perseus overextended and he was coming in too low. It was exactly the right position for Arsenios to drive his knee into Perseus' face.

Hard.

The pain was staggering, and Perseus felt his sword slip from his fingers as he fell flat on his back. Reflexively, he brought the blade up to his chest—a wise choice—as Arsenios brought his sword straight down.

The impact seemed to barely dull the defence by Perseus' own sword. It was all he could do not to gasp for air, but he did not let this blind him to the opportunity of Arsenios' open upper right. Perseus swung his left leg out and up, connecting solidly with the side of Arsenios' face.

Arsenios fell away and Perseus jumped to his feet, lunging after him. Perseus bashed his opponent's face in with a devastating head-butt that drove Arsenios off balance. Perseus could see Arsenios' rage as he came up in the way he held his sword. In also the way he hunched his shoulders and the maddening rasp of his breath.

Perseus felt a rush of confidence. *An angry opponent does not think. He'll come in at a charge, I'll sidestep him and—*

Arsenios stepped forward and kicked Perseus' legs out from under him. Perseus lost his grip on his weapon and hit the dirt, thus resulting on the hard lesson he just learned on to never to think so much as Arsenios swung his sword back to finish the duel. Perseus rolled away from it as Arsenios brought his sword down. Perseus rolled again, grabbed his sword and then came to his feet.

The usurper advanced quickly, stabbing low and coming high. He thrust at Perseus and the rightful ruler deflected the blade with his own. Perseus returned the attack, driving Arsenios back, but then came right back at him like a madman on fire swinging wildly in the wind.

Perseus retreated before him, working his way back for some more legroom. They'd come all the way around, Arsenios quickening his pace as Perseus stepped. The traitor lunged, but Perseus leaned left.

But Perseus was relentless and he struck again. Arsenios tried to deflect it but ended up losing his sword.

Now he stood unarmed against Perseus, who pointed his sword to the villain's chest.

Just then, Charon galloped up the palace steps with his men trailing behind him. Arsenios and his henchmen stared in shock. Perseus turned his attention to Charon but still kept his sword to Arsenios' chest. Charon held up the head of Tellus, and threw it at the feet of the palace guards.

He leapt off his horse and stabbed the guard holding Andromeda. As he fell to the ground, Charon bowed before Andromeda.

"My Queen, forgive me." He kneeled before her, lowering his eyes. He did not deserve to look at her. "I only serve you and my true King, but I needed time to gather the army."

She nodded to him, and they both turned to Perseus. Moved, as he watched his men disarmed the traitorous palace guards.

Perseus turned to see Arsenios, who was snivelling. "Perseus, have mercy, please."

Perseus lowered his sword, and Arsenios gave a sigh of relief. The Son of Zeus glanced over to Charon and Andromeda, who were held spellbound by this act. He turned back to Arsenios who gave him a jeeringly grin.

"'Only a man…'" Remembering Atlas' words, he stabbed Arsenios in the heart.

The traitor's eyes bulged in shock, as the blade entered the body. His hands fumbled round the blade, locking eyes with Perseus.

Emotionless, Perseus kicked Arsenios off his sword and watch as he writhed on the ground during his final moments.

Perseus turned back around only to see Andromeda almost to him. He swooped her up in his arms and kissed her passionately.

"The fighting ends now." He promised her. "I am done."

She embraced him. Perseus ran to his son and held up high in the air. Tears clouded his eyes, as he drew his son into his arms. When Perseus opened his eyes, Charon and all of his men were on their knees before him.

"Hail Perseus, King of Argos!" Charon led the men in cheer.

In an instant, the Argos army raised their swords and began to cheer. They ran toward Perseus with excitement and congratulations.

Exhausted and hurting, Perseus lifted his bloody sword and shouted in triumph.

EPILOGUE

It took forever for Perseus to cleanse himself from all the blood and dirt that covered him from the battlefield. He lightly towelled off his hair as his long flowing locks flipped over to both sides of his temples. He opened his eyes to see Andromeda giggling at him.

"What is so funny, darling?" He asked, draping the damp towel around his shoulders.

"You look like a wet dog." She laughed.

"Oh?" Perseus replied, shaking his head like an animal that just emerged from the lake. Drops of water sprayed all over Andromeda. She raised her hands right in front of her and laughed hysterically.

"Perseus!" She laughed, as Perseus joined in. "Stop!"

"With this ordeal behind us, Andromeda it feels good to laugh again." He said, as he swiftly took the towel and lassoed it around Andromeda's waist and pulled her forward to give her a kiss.

She lifted her eyes to meet Perseus, who was looking more like his normal self. "Are you ready for bed?"

Perseus' smile grew even wider. After all those months of being at war and then going to hell and back on finding his lost son, he had forgotten the simple luxury of sleeping on a real bed and nestling with his wife.

Then something caught his eye over at the balcony. He reacted defensively on impulse but then he felt the presence of the interloper. It wasn't threatening, but soothing. It was as if there were some familiarity between him and Perseus.

Andromeda smile rapidly disappeared. "Perseus, what's wrong?"

Perseus stared out to the balcony and saw a dark figure that was wrapped inside a flowing cloak. He stood there behind the filmy curtains with no vile agenda.

"Nothing is wrong, my love." Perseus assured her. "I will join you soon. I am going to look out the balcony for a moment."

Andromeda released him from her embrace and kissed him on the cheek. "Don't be long." She cooed, as headed for the hallway for one last inspection.

Perseus advanced to the terrace so he could discover the true identity of this mystery visitor, but he knew exactly who it was.

"How long have you been standing there, Father?" Asked Perseus.

The cloaked figure pulled down his hood to reveal the face of the all-powerful Zeus. He wasn't clad in his usual golden glowing robes or any form of chain mail, but he was dressed as a common man. He looked more than a pauper than he did a king in those trappings.

"On the balcony, or idly by in the halls of my palace on Olympus?" Zeus replied.

A silence had fallen between them. Perseus had not forgotten the things he said about his father in vain, nor did Zeus. The King of the Gods figured his favourite son had every right to be angry with him. He would understand that Perseus wouldn't want to speak to him again.

"It was a test, was it not?" Said Perseus, finally. "I was depending more on your guidance and you wanted to teach me a lesson on humility and wanted me to fend for myself. Is that it?"

"Perseus," Zeus softly spoke. His voice didn't boom like the sound of thunder or its pace wasn't as quick as a bolt of lightning. "I have never been so proud of you. You were a victim of tragedy ever since you were an infant and you have never given in to despair or hate. You stood for what was right, and I know how easy it is to go down a dark path and find yourself lost in the abyss. But you got yourself out of it all by yourself."

Perseus looked at him for a moment. "You never answered my question."

Zeus sighed and stared Perseus squarely in the eye. "There were parties involved." He confessed. "Parties that will be dealt with severely by me—and me alone—and there was nothing I could do to prevent it. I was bounded by an agreement that I shouldn't interfere and let you solve your son's abduction by yourself. I tried to extradite myself there was nothing more I can do."

"So, I went through all this torment because you wanted to prove a point?"

"The disappearance of your son was not intended." Answered Zeus.

"But you let it happened!"

"Yes," Zeus said, his voice was hollow. "Yes, I did." He lowered his head in shame. "You are a man, Perseus. You are entitled to your own choices and to your own destiny. *You* chose to act. *You* chose to track down your enemies. And *you* chose to abandon me and take matters into your own hands, and you succeeded. Isn't that enough for you?"

"I lost in combat." Perseus confessed softly. Zeus noticed a trace of ignominy in his son's voice. Perseus wasn't even sure that he could even look him in the eye to explain his first ever loss. But he suddenly found the courage to confront his father with the humiliating experience. "When I fought the Minotaur for the first time. I thought I was indomitable but he defeated me."

"What are you implying?" Zeus asked, feeling agitated.

"In all the battles and the wars I've been in and I always emerged victorious, but that fight was the only one I ever lost."

"You cannot expect to win every battle, Perseus. You are only human."

"Yes, Father, I know that. But what I meant to say is how long have you been helping me with all those campaigns. The last five years have been a lie. I didn't win all those battles—*you* did!"

Zeus' nostrils flared up. "You dare accuse me of such an action? The nerve on you, boy."

"That's the only way to explain how I keep facing all these challenges and I keep living."

"I let you fight your own battles for quite some time now."

"You lie!"

"Listen to me, Perseus." Zeus' raised his voice. Even though it didn't summon thunder and lightning, Zeus' abrasive tone daunted Perseus. "You are my son and I love you very much. I love you more than all my children on Olympus. If I kept on aiding you all your life than you will have no will of your own. All the victories and merits were all done by your own esteem. I know by letting off on your own will leave you a vulnerability to fail. But I let you fail so you can learn from your own errors and be a better warrior and king. If I intervened on every aspect of your life than I would fail as a father. Someday you will have to do the same to Perses."

Taken back by this revelation, Perseus rested on the railing of the balcony.

"Do you at least hear my prayers?"

Zeus gave a small smile. "Every night."

Then something caught Perseus' eye up in the darkened sky. There seemed to be three new constellations that spread across the heavens.

"Father," Perseus squinted his eyes to make out the formations, "what are those in the sky?"

Zeus walked casually near the ledge and gazed up into the stars with his son.

"Those are the new souls that are going to Elysium. They truly earned their place there."

As Perseus' eyes adjusted, he could slowly make out the outlines of the constellations, and then he smiled. One of them resembled a beautiful woman with gorgeous wings that unfolded throughout the night. Right by her were two formations that were grouped together. It was in the shape of a man who stood strong with a smaller pattern that seemed like a child.

"Rest well, my friends." Perseus said softly to the silhouettes of Kallipso, Atlas and his son. "You have earned your peace."

The sound of Perses crying turned both of Perseus and Zeus head back. Perseus looked over to Zeus, who laughed heartily.

"Would you like to come in and meet your grandson?"

"I appreciate the offer, son, but I see him all the time." He patted Perseus on the shoulder, and lifted up his hood. "I must be getting back to Olympus. There is much to look over."

"Are you going to look over Perses as well?" Perseus asked.

"Oh, I have already appointed someone for that position." Zeus replied, as he began to fade away from sight. "Compliments of Hephaestus."

Perseus smiled at Zeus as he disappeared into the night, but then was surprised by the sound of rhythmic chimes and chirping, and Perses' crying had stopped.

"Is Perses all right?" Andromeda asked Perseus, when she came running into the bedroom. "I've heard him crying and..." Then she came to an abrupt halt and saw something perched on the railing of Perses' crib.

It was large and round, and its head was spinning. Perseus came forward to investigate and smiled when the light hit the creature.

It was Bubo!

He was now fully rebuilt and better than ever before. No longer he was made entirely out of bronze, but there were parts of gold and silver as well. The most impressing feature was his eyes. They were larger and brighter than ever. They were so immense that he can see everything.

"It is good to see you, old friend." Perseus said to the newly constructed owl.

Bubo chirped happily and blinked his eyes. He even performed a merry jig and twirled around the rail. Andromeda laughed, as she and Perseus looked down on their son who was sleeping peacefully—probably the best slumber he had in his infantile life.

Both Andromeda and Perseus would sleep serenely tonight. For they knew their son was under the best of care because Bubo, the guardian of the night, was never going to let the young prince out of his sight.

THE END.

ALSO AVAILABLE FROM MARKOSIA

SINBAD: ROGUE OF MARS

A prophecy foretells of a stranger from distant lands who will vanquish the false king. Eight years after the assassination of King Dadgar, his vile nephew, Adhkar, has usurped his throne and enslaved the Azurian people, igniting a violent civil war.Having sailed the seven seas, exploring unknown lands, fighting countless monsters and battling evil wizards, could Sinbad be the stranger of the prophecy, or will he merely be a pawn in Adhkar's bloody game?

ISBN: 978-1-911243-92-2

www.ingramcontent.com/pod-product-compliance
Lightning Source LLC
Chambersburg PA
CBHW070028260626
47159CB00005B/1988

* 9 7 8 1 9 1 3 3 5 9 1 2 6 *